Cobwebs

Cobwebs

a suspense novel

MARY COLEY

Cobwebs: A Suspense Novel

Published by Wheatmark®
1760 East River Road, Suite 145, Tucson, Arizona 85718 U.S.A.
www.wheatmark.com

ISBN: 978-1-62787-019-1 (paperback)
ISBN: 978-1-62787-026-9 (ebook)
LCCN: 2013942739

rev201801

I dedicate this book to my parents, John and Catherine McIntyre, who encouraged my lifelong love of reading, beginning at a very early age. My father's extensive home library fed my early love of mystery and history.

His books introduced me to authors from Mary Renault to Agatha Christie, Edgar Allen Poe to Jack Higgins. Their stories continue to feed my imagination.

I also dedicate this book to my children, Heather and Brian, who learned early in their lives that their mother was a writer, and have always supported that passion in me.

Finally, I dedicate this book to my husband, Daryl, for constant support and encouragement of his writer wife.

Acknowledgments

Many, many thanks go to many, many people who have helped me along the way as I developed as a writer. Perhaps the first person was my second grade teacher at Taft Elementary School in Enid, Oklahoma, Miss Lansdon, who loved my first story, "Chippy the Squirrel," and told me I was a good writer. Dorothy Cozart, my creative writing teacher at Enid High school years ago, also encouraged my early fiction.

As an adult I've had many writing friends, so many that I fear I may leave some of them out of this list. I hope they will forgive my oversight if I do not mention them by name.

I first attended the Oklahoma Writers Federation, Inc.'s annual conference in the early '80s. There, I began to learn what writing, plotting, character, and theme are really all about. After a hiatus of nearly two decades, as I raised my children as a single parent, I returned to the conference in 2002 and have found valuable knowledge and support from fellow writers in the years since.

My home chapter of OWFI is the Tulsa Nightwriters, and I am thankful for the support of other Nightwriters throughout the last decade, in particular, Peggy Fielding, Jackie King, Chuck Sasser, Joan Rhine, Dale Whisman, Bob Avey, and so many other successful writers from my area.

I've attended many workshops over the past decade as well, and have learned from the expertise of experienced writers, including: Gail Provost Stockwell, Anna Myers, Jody Thomas, Teresa Miller, and Bill Bernhart.

I have also learned much from critique partners in Tulsa and elsewhere. Big thanks to my Tulsa critique group, including Mark Darrah, Casey Morgan, Paula Alfred, Jill Hoilien, and Jackie King for struggling with me through that earliest version of *Cobwebs*. Thank you to members of Jody's Pioneers, including Jan Morrill, Linda Joyce, Patti Stith, and others, for their support and encouragement.

Thank you to the Around the Block Writers Collaborative, led by Sara Kay Rupnik, Tracy Robert, and Liz Abrams-Morley. I have travelled with my family of ABW writers to Bemis Point, New York; Treasure Beach, Jamaica; and Dublin, Ireland where we have enjoyed wonderful opportunities to learn, write, and relax.

Thank you to my fellow writers and critique partners who are members of the Tulsa Chapter of the Society of Children's Book Writers and Illustrators.

Finally, a special thanks to Kathryn Grace Draper for providing valuable insight and a great copyedit of this latest *Cobwebs* manuscript.

I would be remiss as a writer if I didn't offer thanks to all of those agents and publishing houses who considered *Cobwebs* in earlier forms. I received valuable feedback and all of it helped to make *Cobwebs* a better book. Particular thanks to Pamela Ahearn, Doris Booth, the staff of Hawk Publishing, the staff of Poison Pen Press, the staff of Avalon Books, and the staff at University of Oklahoma Press for taking time to offer specific critique as well as encouragement.

Research is crucial when completing a historical mystery, and I'd like to thank the volunteer staff at the Osage County Museum in Pawhuska, as well as volunteers and staff of the Immaculate Conception Church, all of whom spent many hours answering questions over the years. For some time, I worked for The Nature Conservancy of Oklahoma, and spent much time training volunteers at the Tallgrass Prairie Preserve north of Pawhuska. Through that experience, I first learned about the unique and troubled Osage history, and became intrigued with both the people and the landscape.

Osage writer John Joseph Mathews provided inspiration through his writing, especially for the character of Sam Mazie and Osage legends. Many sources were used as I researched the Osage Reign of Terror, as well as the general history of Osage County, which remains the headquarters of the thriving Osage Nation in Oklahoma.

And last, but not least, I want to offer my thanks to my great-great-great-grandmother, for 3 percent of the Native American blood that runs through my veins. I'm still searching for the ancestor who provided the other 3 percent. She's out there somewhere!

Prologue

"I'm going to tell her what I think … what I know," Elizabeth Graham moaned.

"Dearest, we've been over this. Don't talk nonsense," the familiar voice cooed to Elizabeth from the foot of her bed.

She heard the words, and they sounded molasses-thick, all soft and sweetened up. She'd been a damn fool all these years. But it wasn't over yet; she still had hope. Jamie was coming.

Her old eyes shifted to the bedroom window. Outside, gray storm clouds piled up.

"Finish your soup, dearest. She'll be here any minute."

"No more." Elizabeth jerked as pain gripped her. The spoon clattered in the bowl and chicken broth splashed out onto the silver-plated tray.

Fingers smoothed her thin white hair and then swabbed a damp cloth across her forehead. "There, now. Better?"

"No." Elizabeth cleared the phlegm from her throat and repeated, louder, "No!"

"My, we're in a temper today." The tray was lifted away. "Calm down." The figure faced her from the shadows. "And just what are you going to tell her?"

"The truth."

The chuckle was soft and long. "After all these years? She'll think you're senile. My dear Elizabeth, you're not thinking straight. Telling her now, in your condition, would be a big mistake."

Chapter 1

April 1, 2000—Noon

"Come now, Jamie. You must come before it's too late."

Great-Aunt Elizabeth's voice had been shaking during her call to me last night at midnight. I'd never heard her sound so frail or so frightened.

Sweat popped out on my forehead. I held down the car's electric window switch and then peered over the grimy window as the glass lowered and the fresh, moist air rushed into the car. The distant rumbling of thunder reverberated, clear through my bones.

I had a bad feeling about this sudden trip to my great-aunt's home in Oklahoma. And the weather was not giving me any reason to change my expectations. Instead, my imagination went into high gear.

Bits of my dark memory rushed back from where I had buried them: blackness; the scent of earth and damp and mildew; the feel of coarse string as I touched ... something. The memory produced a shiver that moved through the nerves of my body from my toes to my ears in two seconds flat.

The stoplight thirty feet away turned red, and with a delayed reaction, I jerked and slammed on the brake. Empty sidewalks stretched down the street, and everything looked old, like I had stepped back in time to the early twentieth century. I halfway expected that when I turned the next corner, Osage Indians, wrapped in blankets, would be sitting on the sidewalks and alongside the buildings, as I'd seen them in pictures from long ago.

I tightened my grip on the steering wheel and accelerated up the hill. From the look of the clouds, the storm would be here in less than an hour. By that time, I hoped to be settled into the room I had shared with my sister, Ellen, so many years ago. And I hoped Aunt Elizabeth felt reassured by my presence.

Old trees and overgrown shrubs hid several of the older houses in this neighborhood. My car thumped into a hole where the asphalt street had dissolved down to the original bricks, inches below. Then I saw it. Aunt Elizabeth's place could have been featured in an advertisement for the *Most Haunted* television series.

My wet palms slipped on the steering wheel.

The black-cloud backdrop framed the old two-story stone-and-wood house. Faded and chipped brown and cream paint showed bare wood. Missing spindles on the veranda railing left gaps, like teeth missing from a grin. I glanced up at the center window, Elizabeth's bedroom. I half-expected to see the proverbial shadow move behind the lacy sheer curtain, and there did seem to be a shape—something—there.

It had to be Elizabeth, watching for me. Now, she'd hurry down the front stairs and be at the door in no time, arms open wide. It had been nearly two years since we'd last seen one another—in Santa Fe, just before Ben's terminal diagnosis.

Pain shot up my back as I opened the car door, shifted my legs, and pulled them out from under the steering wheel for the first time since my last stop, about five hours ago. The cold wind gusted and the sky darkened. It seemed almost cliché— the coming storm, the spooky house in the derelict old town, and my aunt's frightened plea twelve hours ago to come immediately.

I had no explanation for the knot of fear low in my stomach.

I couldn't seem to stop shivering, even though the damp air wasn't cold.

As a child, I'd spent four or five summers here with my siblings, Randy and Ellen—fun and games, racing through the house, playing hide-and-seek among the scents of cinnamon and vanilla and fresh-baked bread. Initially, the memories made me happy, but then, as I tried to remember more details, my gut tensed, and all the muscle groups tightened in my core.

When I got out of the car, I struggled against the gusty west wind. It whipped my hair out of the ponytail holder and across my eyes. I made my way up the crumbling sidewalk, my long skirt plastered around my legs. After clomping up the rickety steps in my favorite cowboy boots, I crossed the veranda to the old walnut door.

No doorbell, no knocker. My knuckles hammered against the wood, and I expected the door to swing open instantly. It didn't budge. With a push of my thumb on the brass latch, the door screeched inward. Rays of dim daylight arced into the shadowy entry and revealed an empty front hall.

"Elizabeth?" I pushed the door shut behind me and then turned in a half circle, looking first to the right—the study—and then to the left—the parlor. The heavy wool drapes I remembered were all closed. Fingers of light poked into the front hall from the windows beside and above the massive front door.

Wide stairs rose up to the second level; beside them, the adjacent dark hallway stretched back to the kitchen and the backstairs.

A man stepped through the door from the kitchen. "Jamie?" Long black hair reached to his shoulders, and deep-set brown eyes stared into my green ones.

Something stirred inside me, something almost like recognition, like I knew him. But that wasn't possible. I knew no one in this town but Aunt Elizabeth; I hadn't been here in thirty years. "Yes. And you are…?"

"Your aunt's attorney. Sam Mazie. When I learned you were

coming, I came over to wait with her. I'll go now." He crossed the hallway, brushing past me on his way to the door. The air stirred around him, lifting up the scent of his aftershave, reminding me of grass and something both musky and sweet.

"Don't leave on my account," I said. "How is she? Last night she sounded so desperate."

He shook his head. "Her mind comes and goes. She is tired. It is good you came."

A quivering voice floated down from the second floor. "Jamie? Is that ... you?"

"I'm here. I'll come up." My hands shook as I smoothed my hair and tucked the windblown strands behind my ears. I smiled at Sam, suddenly feeling the exhaustion of the long drive and the emotional weight of my aunt's condition, as well as all the *should-have-dones* that pounded down as I realized once again I was losing someone I loved. It had been true with Ben, and now it was true of my great-aunt.

I was in the house but still had no real memories of that last summer, just a dark, fear-filled sensation and whispery voices swirling together and fluttering like moths at a twilight window. I'd never talked about it. All of us—my mother, my aunt, and I—had buried it, like my family seemed to bury every negative thing any of us ever experienced. It hadn't happened if we never talked about it. Only now, after forty-one years, had I learned other, healthier ways to deal with unpleasant events.

But on the drive here, I'd continually been struck by the thought that thirty years was a long time to not remember... and a long time to stay away from this town. I had answered Aunt Elizabeth's call not only because of her desperation but also because I needed to know what had gone so terribly wrong that last summer. These shadows had haunted my dreams for far too long.

I hitched up my skirt and charged up the front stairs. When I slowed on the top step, another shiver slithered down my back, this one brought on by a whiff of disinfectant. A dreadful image flashed in my head: Ben, in bed at home on his last day on this earth. His hair was gone, his cheeks sunken, his eyes burning with pain. I'd stroked his head, remembering his thick, curly dark hair, and then traced my finger down his cheeks, hoping to fill in those pale hollows with my touch and make them ruddy red, the way they often were when we came home after a long hike in the Sangre de Cristo foothills on a winter day.

My heartbeat drummed in my temples. The ache slashed at my heart.

Five more quick steps, and I stood in the doorway to Elizabeth's room.

The handmade quilts and the white chenille bedspread folded at the foot of the bed looked as if someone had just smoothed them. A half-filled water glass sat near a vase of daffodils on the nightstand. A book lay open across a small pillow on the upholstered straight-backed chair, as if someone had just been reading.

And Aunt Elizabeth lay on the bed, her thin white hair falling in short wavy layers all around her creased face. Her dark brown eyes, sharp and inquisitive, focused on me and pulled me across the room. I grabbed those bony hands and squeezed them. *My God, how she has aged.* She looked every bit of her ninety years.

"Jamie," Aunt Elizabeth breathed. She pressed her lips together, raised her thin eyebrows, and began to hum off-key.

It was *Name That Tune*, and it only took three notes before I was singing along. "Take me out to the ballgame; take me out to the crowd. Buy me some peanuts and Cracker Jack, I don't care—"

Aunt Elizabeth stopped humming and closed her eyes. Her wrinkles deepened as she grimaced. She looked skeletal, far worse than I had expected.

I stroked her hand and felt my heart thud to the bottom of my chest.

Chapter 2

April 1, 2000—Afternoon

The song Aunt Elizabeth hummed brought back memories of those summers spent with her in Oklahoma. I could picture a baseball team, made up of my brother and sister and other kids Elizabeth had gathered up to play baseball with the three of us. Their faces were shrouded by my mental cobwebs.

"Thank goodness you're here," Elizabeth sighed. "You look so much like Sarah." A smile stretched Aunt Elizabeth's thin lips, and her eyes sparkled. I smiled back, knowing it was true. I favored my grandmother, Elizabeth's only sister, Sarah.

The picture still stood on the dresser—two slender young women wearing the drop-waist clothing style of the thirties. I glanced into the dresser mirror and back at the photograph. The resemblance was there: a heart-shaped face with high cheekbones, wide eyes, and a strong nose.

"But I'm going gray." I smoothed a wiry gray strand back into the thick mass of hair I'd pulled into a low ponytail.

"You still look young!" Aunt Elizabeth's eyes clouded. "Then there's me, shriveled up like an old prune, lying here in this pitiful bed."

One of Aunt Elizabeth's bony hands reached up and searched the folds of nightgown at her throat. For a second, the battered round locket glinted in the light of the table lamp, and then her hand closed around it.

I eased down onto the edge of the mattress. *Just lying here?*

I noticed a folded metal walker tucked between the open door and the wall. How could she manage the stairs? Apparently, she didn't.

Great-Aunt Elizabeth cleared her throat. "My dear, are you all right?"

"I'm all right." I stuffed my trembling hands deep into the folds of my skirt and hoped she hadn't noticed.

"I can see grief in your eyes." Aunt Elizabeth's voice was raspy but soft.

At her words, my throat closed up, and tears burned in my eyes. "Will it ever get easier?" I tried to swallow the imaginary obstruction in my throat. Ben had died thirteen months ago last week.

"Lord knows, you just go on. Ben will always be in your heart. Just like Dodie and our two babies, gone for so many years. And Robert and Herbert. They're still here in my heart." Aunt Elizabeth reached to pat my leg and then coughed. Her fingers moved back to clutch the old gold locket again.

I reached for the chain looping my own neck and let it slip through my fingers until I felt the cold gold of Ben's wedding band. Grief still stung like fresh sunburn all over my body.

"Have you eaten lunch?" I asked. I couldn't see any signs that lunch had been served in this room.

"I had a late breakfast. There should be lunchmeat in the icebox or soup in the cupboard. Get something for yourself, honey, and then we'll talk." Aunt Elizabeth's eyes shut firmly, and her hand released the locket and dropped onto the bed.

"Oh, I met Sam. Downstairs," I told her, though Elizabeth's eyes stayed closed. "Your attorney?"

"Yes. Dear Sam. I'd forgotten he was here. What would I do without him?"

I patted her hand. "I'll be back up in a jiffy. Have a quick rest."

The steep backstairs creaked as I moved down, gripping the worn banister. Thunder rumbled outside. I stepped off the bottom step and moved quickly through the doorway and into the kitchen. Black and white linoleum squares crackled as I stepped on them, and a draft of cold air touched my cheek.

Uncluttered counters. Empty sink. There was no evidence anyone had been cooking. Maybe she hadn't eaten; maybe her mind only imagined she had. But then, maybe Sam had cleaned up.

"Sam? You still here?"

Silence filled the house. I wished he hadn't left. My mind was full of questions about Aunt Elizabeth's condition.

Fresh cold-cuts packages filled the meat drawer in the refrigerator. Soup cans lined the lower shelf of an adjacent cabinet. I opened first one drawer and then another until I found a hand-held can opener. The muscles of my arms quivered as I opened the can. I needed caffeine. While the soup warmed in a small saucepan on the gas stove, I sat down at the old plastic and aluminum table, rested my head on one arm, and closed my eyes.

"Do you know the muffin man, the muffin man, the muffin man?" The children's tune ran through my head. Years ago, Aunt Elizabeth had hidden cookies in the flour bin in the pantry. When a treat was waiting, she would sing "The Muffin Man" to all of us. My mouth watered. Molasses cookies, sugar cookies, and chocolate chip. It had been years, with one long diet after another, since I'd allowed myself to snack on cookies in the afternoon.

I looked across the room; the pantry door was ajar.

A sugar pick-me-up would taste so good. Might even get rid of these shakes. Was it too much to hope the flour bin would be full of Snickerdoodles or molasses treats? The imaginary aroma swirled around me.

Inside the pantry, the flour bin was empty. But provisions lined the shelves—boxes of cereal, rice, and canned goods were proof someone was coming in to prepare meals for Elizabeth. Nothing fancy, but she had never been one to eat rich foods.

The simpler the better, it had always seemed. Between her and my grandmother, she was by far the more relaxed and easily pleased personality. It was something the two of us shared.

Five minutes later, I carried my bowl of soup on a wicker tray up the rear stairs. Outside, the wind lashed at the house. The bedroom window rattled. I listened for the wail of a tornado siren but heard only the wind.

Elizabeth opened her eyes as I entered her room.

"You sure you're not hungry?"

"No." Her head moved almost imperceptibly.

I set the tray on the dresser and then picked up the embroidered pillow from the hardback chair beside the bed. My fingers ran over the stitches. It was crewel embroidery, multicolored flowers, loop-stitched with French-knot centers. I'd made it myself, one of those long-ago summers. Touching the fine threads, I could almost feel the hot summer breeze on my face and taste the tart lemonade Elizabeth would bring out to the gazebo, where we would sit in the late afternoon.

I laid the pillow at the foot of Elizabeth's bed, sat down in the chair, and reached over to bring the tray onto my lap.

"Jamie, we must talk." Aunt Elizabeth's voice now sounded thin and strained. Her eyes were closed again. Phlegm rattled in her throat.

"I'll stay for as long as you need me. I want to be here for you." I'd started to say, *like you were there for me with Ben,* but I stopped. She wasn't going to die, and I didn't want to imply I thought she was. She was just sick. With some tender loving care, she would snap back and soon be the energetic, caring aunt I remembered.

I blew on a spoonful of soup. "I see the walker there. You must not be getting around so well. Will your helper be back this afternoon?"

Aunt Elizabeth plucked at the chenille puffs on the bed-spread. Suddenly, she raised one hand and banged the bed with her fist. Her face crumpled. "It's nearly too late, and there's so much you don't know."

Her shrill voice sent a chill of alarm through me. I stood up and set the wicker tray on the dresser again. Then I bent over Elizabeth, stroking her smooth white hair. "We'll have plenty of time to talk in the next week or two." Cold air fingered my cheek, and suddenly, all the breathable oxygen seemed to have been sucked out of the room.

Tears squeezed between Aunt Elizabeth's closed eyelids and zigzagged down the life lines of her face. Her head jerked back and forth on the pillow. "My whole life has been a sham."

"Don't talk like that." I continued to stroke her hair, but my back stiffened. The lawyer had warned me. He had said, "Her mind comes and goes." Confusion. Dementia?

Aunt Elizabeth's wide eyes looked around the room. "Then how should I talk? Somebody should have stood up to them. We accepted their lie as truth. Especially me ... I should have questioned." One bony hand gripped the locket. Her look darted to the door again.

"You're tired," I said. "How about a nap, and then we'll talk."

"Time is running out." Aunt Elizabeth's voice cracked.

"I'm not going anywhere." I pressed my palm against her forehead and then touched her cool cheeks with the backs of my fingers. Aunt Elizabeth's skin felt as thin as onion paper.

Something—a tree limb?—banged against the front bedroom window. The house groaned and creaked.

Another chilly air current swept around me and then across the back of my neck. "Let's talk about something else." My throat tightened, and I searched for something to revive pleasant memories. "We had such great summers here!" Even as I said the words, I knew I didn't totally believe them. "Mom got after you for filling my head with the Osage creation stories and tales about Coyote and the animal legends. She thought the stories were too scary for us."

Aunt Elizabeth nodded. "Not any scarier than real life, my dear." Her words lingered in the silence, and then a crack of thunder emphasized her point. I rubbed the hairs that prickled on the back of my neck. Her gaze locked on something behind me.

Glancing over my shoulder at the empty doorway, I was sure someone *had* been there. I turned back to my aunt and forced a little laugh. "You taught me all the prairie plant and animal names. And I've always felt like everything on the planet was connected to everything else. I've taught the same lesson to kids for nearly twenty years, Elizabeth." That was the positive side of things. But my shaking hands told the darker side of the story.

"You needed to know those things. People never take the time to learn what matters most." Aunt Elizabeth's sad eyes roamed over my face. Suddenly, she thrashed on the bed and then pushed herself partially up on her arms and looked straight at me. "You need to free me," she said.

My breath caught, and I squeezed my eyes shut as the hairs on the back of my neck stiffened again. *Free me. Oh, God.* The nightmare I had lived through with Ben had returned, in a new form.

I peered into my aunt's eyes and recognized the look Ben had in his last months. I swallowed again. *This isn't right. She isn't going to die. And even if she is ... Don't jump to conclusions. Aunt Elizabeth hasn't asked for anything—yet.*

Elizabeth eased back down onto the bed and closed her eyes. "You must do it, Jamie. You can. The others won't." She spoke in that familiar firm tone, against which no one had ever been able to argue. Then she began to hum another children's song, "Here We Go 'Round the Mulberry Bush."

I shivered and rubbed at the gooseflesh on my arms. I chose not to believe Aunt Elizabeth was talking about assisted suicide. Not like Ben.

More tears leaked out of Aunt Elizabeth's closed eyes.

I stepped back from the bed. My throat constricted and my ears rang. Where was the afternoon caregiver? I glanced at the dresser, looking for bottles of medication. If she was taking meds, it must be time for a dose. But where were the bottles?

Over the knocking of the tree limbs against the window and the groaning of the house as it struggled to stand against the wind, I heard pounding downstairs. The storm was here, and someone was at the front door. The caregiver?

When I turned toward the door, Aunt Elizabeth gasped and sat up. "Stay here!" she demanded, her eyes begging. "Stay!"

The pounding continued, louder and more insistent.

"It's okay, Elizabeth." I hurried to the doorway and looked down the front staircase. A shape darkened one of the frosted side-panel windows. "There's a terrible storm starting, and someone's on the porch. I'll be right back." I smiled at her.

Aunt Elizabeth's eyes were open and huge. Her white hand clenched the locket at her throat. "Jamie, if you go—" Aunt Elizabeth's voice stopped as she fell back onto the bed.

"I'll be right back."

The air in the room had become stifling. Clutching the ring on the chain around my neck, I hurried down the stairs to the front door and pulled it open. I leaned out the doorway and called into the roar of the rain-laden wind. "Hello? Sam? Hello?"

The porch was empty.

The gusty wind spat rain onto the veranda. Empty side-walks stretched down the block. I pulled back and then hurried down the hall and into the kitchen to check the back door, thinking whoever it was had probably dashed around the house. No one waited on the enclosed back porch.

Inside, a hoarse whisper of unintelligible words swirled with the dust motes in the dim light of the kitchen. It sounded as if someone was speaking somewhere in the house, but the wail of the wind and the pound of heavy rain drowned out the voice. Still no tornado siren.

I swabbed my wet face and hair with a dish towel. Then I filled a kettle with water and put it on the stove to boil as I searched the cabinets for tea bags. Minutes later, when the water was hot and the tea brewed, I climbed the narrow back-stairs with two steaming mugs of tea.

Aunt Elizabeth's eyes were closed, and she lay still, her hands now underneath the quilt. The embroidered pillow had fallen to the floor. I set the two mugs on the nightstand, tossed the pillow back onto the chair, and turned to the lunch tray on the old oak dresser. I scooped up a spoonful of the soup I'd warmed earlier. Ice cold. I glanced at Elizabeth. She lay so still, sleeping so soundly. I carried the tray down to the kitchen.

Minutes later, when I returned to the bedroom, Aunt Elizabeth still hadn't moved. I watched her. She was too still. Was she even breathing?

"Aunt Elizabeth?" I touched her right shoulder. Elizabeth's head rolled to one side. When I placed two fingers on her left carotid artery, I barely felt a pulse.

I threw the covers off and shifted my head close to Elizabeth's mouth to listen for a breath. Slow, shallow, but breathing.

I ran downstairs to dial the Pawhuska 911 on the hall phone, Elizabeth's only phone.

The wind pounded. Clicks on the receiver told me a phone line was down somewhere, I didn't have a connection. I grabbed my purse from the hall bench and turned on my cell phone. No signal.

I dashed back up the stairs and once again listened to her breathing and felt her slow pulse. She might have only minutes—seconds—to live, but there was nothing I could do except hold onto her hand and rub her thin, bluish flesh. I gnawed at the knuckle of my right hand. A sob froze in my throat.

Elizabeth, don't go! What did you want to tell me? Why didn't I listen when you wanted to talk?

A dark red clump of something clung to a broken fingernail on Aunt Elizabeth's right hand. A knot of red threads. I looked at the pillow in the chair, where I had tossed it minutes ago when I'd come back upstairs with my soup. Even from here, I could tell from the stretched fabric that some threads had been pulled too tight and some were missing. The embroidery work had not been damaged earlier. What had happened to the pillow in the few minutes I'd been downstairs?

Elizabeth hadn't done this, but someone had.

With shivers running up my arms and in an adrenaline rush, I dashed into the bathroom and jerked back the shower curtain from the claw-foot tub. I ran back to the armoire and pulled the doors open. Elizabeth's dresses hung in a neat row across the width of the tall maple piece. I thrust my hand inside until my fingertips rammed the smooth surface of the back wall.

Something metallic scraped somewhere in the house. Outside, the wind howled. Somewhere on the gables, something knocked against the wood siding.

Was there someone else in the house? Had they tried to smother Elizabeth with that pillow?

Chapter 3

April 1, 2000—Afternoon

In desperation, I dashed out to the yard with my cell phone, searching for a signal. Two bars appeared on the power indicator. I made the call to 911.

Now, minutes ticked by as I sat stroking Elizabeth's hand, waiting. My wet hair dripped on my blouse, and my damp skirt clung to my legs.

Finally, I heard sirens. The emergency vehicles screeched up in front of the house. I rushed down the front stairs to let them in.

Torrents of rain fell as three men got out of the ambulance and ran for the house. Only five minutes had passed from the time my call went through to the Pawhuska dispatcher. Now, the EMTs stood on the entry hall rug, dripping water from their rain ponchos.

"She's upstairs, at the top. Her room is straight ahead."

They pushed past, carrying a collapsed gurney. Outside the house, another siren wailed up the street and more car doors slammed. Two more men raced through the rain toward the front door.

The one in the uniform held out a badge. "Chief Toby Green, ma'am." The chief was short and muscular with curly reddish-gray hair and freckle-spattered cheeks. His small smile seemed kind and oddly familiar. His eyes moved quickly over my face. "Kindly" was a far cry from the way the police had treated me back home during the past year.

"Lieutenant Alvarez," the other policeman, clad in a blue golf shirt, said.

"I'm Jamie Aldrich, Elizabeth Graham's great-niece." I let them into the house, but blocked the stairs when they started to follow the EMTs. "Is it customary for the police to come when someone is taken to the hospital? Shouldn't you be out chasing criminals or something?"

"She's still alive?" A look passed between the lieutenant and the chief.

"Barely, but she is. She might have had a stroke." The men tried to move past me. "You didn't answer my question. Why are you here?"

Green pushed around me and up the stairs, but the other man stopped. "We had a call ma'am. Anonymous. The tip was that your aunt had just been murdered."

Outside, the storm raged. I stared at the butterscotch oak flooring and rubbed at my temples with my fingertips. The motion didn't help the headache throbbing across the top of my head. I sank down on the bench in the hallway.

A mixed scent of old wood and lemon oil hung in the air, but over it, like mist, hung the smell of mildew and illness.

I hugged the little crewel embroidery pillow from Elizabeth's bedroom, not remembering why I had picked it up or why I had carried it downstairs. That last summer, sitting on the bench in the shady gazebo with my legs tucked beneath me, I'd been so careful sewing each stitch, each knot.

Now, I studied the pillow under the light from the hall floor lamp. One of the daisies in the flower field was missing its red French-knot center. And the knot was now under Elizabeth's fingernail. An image flashed into my mind of someone holding the pillow over Elizabeth's face while she clawed at it, frantically. A chill ran across my scalp and down my neck.

"Spell your name for me, please," the lieutenant requested.

After I spelled it slowly, he sidled into the study. Seconds later, I heard him speaking, into a cell phone.

"A-L-D-R-I-C-H. Las Vegas, New Mexico."

Upstairs on the landing, something thumped and wheels rolled. The men pushed the gurney to the stairs, and then, one on each end, maneuvered the gurney and Elizabeth down to the front hall.

I stood, wanting to see her face, to be sure that blood still pulsed through her body, keeping her face more pink than gray. "I'm going with you to the hospital."

The police chief followed the gurney down. "I'll take you, Mrs. Aldrich. I have a few more questions."

I was sure he did. Since the policemen were sure to follow up by calling my hometown, I was certain both men would soon have more information about me than I wanted anyone anywhere to have.

In one phone call to Las Vegas, they would find out about Ben. They would know I was charged in his death, and although charges were dropped and I was never brought to trial, the implication was there. Now, if they determined someone had tried to kill my aunt, I would top the list of suspects. And back home in Las Vegas, the police chief wouldn't pass up the chance to reopen the investigation into Ben's death.

I grabbed my purse and followed the procession out the door and onto the veranda. The rain had slowed to drips, but gray clouds raced and tumbled overhead. The men lifted the gurney into the back of the ambulance and closed the red-and-white doors. Chief Green motioned toward his police cruiser.

My eyes itched and burned with fatigue; I blinked to focus my vision. The wide old street rose up the hillside past big neighboring houses surrounded by towering elms and oaks.

A black Cadillac pulled up to the front of the house and parked behind the police cruiser. The tall man who climbed out wore a three-piece gray silk suit. His thick silver-white hair was perfectly combed, unaffected by the wind and rain. Ignoring the chief, he focused his gleaming blue eyes on me.

"So very sorry to hear my dear friend Elizabeth has passed. As mayor, it is the least I can do to come immediately and pay my respects when something like this happens. Is there anything I can do?"

"She's not dead," I said. "A stroke, I think. They're taking her to the hospital."

The man stood taller still and looked at Green for confirmation.

Green nodded. "Elizabeth is still alive. We're taking her to the hospital. May have to transport her to Tulsa. Time will tell."

"Not dead. Now that is good news." The older man clasped his hands in front of him. His smooth, clipped nails had been buffed to a polish. One of Ben's favorite scents, musky and masculine, lingered in the air, making my heart ache.

The ambulance chugged away from the curb and down the street.

"Please, Chief Green," I said. "We need to follow." I looked at the silver-haired mayor, feeling instant dislike. What man in Pawhuska wore a thousand-dollar suit and had his nails and hair done? This was cowboy-and-Indian country.

His eyes glittered. With no indication of hurry, he pulled out an octagonal, antique, gold pocket watch and checked the time. As he returned the watch to his vest pocket, he corrected the drape of the rectangular chain links. "My family is quite close to Elizabeth. I'm sure they would all join me in wishing her a speedy recovery from this episode."

Elizabeth had rarely mentioned anyone from home during her visits to New Mexico, but at the same time, I knew she wasn't a recluse. It wouldn't take long for the chains of communication in Pawhuska to get the word out about what had happened. Apparently, it had already begun, but the information was incorrect.

"Elizabeth was lovely. You have the same dark green eyes, olive skin, and lustrous, thick hair." The mayor sighed. "Quite a fortunate family resemblance." He winked his left eye.

Every tired muscle in my body clenched. I turned to Chief Green. "Can we go now, please? I want to be with her when she wakes up."

"And I'd like to follow along, if you don't mind," the mayor said.

I slid into the backseat, behind the lieutenant. As uncomfortable as it was to be riding in the police car, I would get to the hospital faster this way. And there was no use putting off the inevitable questions Green was bound to ask.

I knew those questions too well. I reminded myself that this time was much different from last year in Las Vegas. Aunt Elizabeth was still alive. I hoped there was still enough time for her to tell me whatever it was she had needed to say. *"My life has been a scam,"* and *"Free me."* What did she mean?

The chief coughed. "Mrs. Aldrich? My question."

"Sorry. I was thinking about Aunt Elizabeth. We hardly had a chance to say hello before this happened."

At that moment, I would have given anything not to have made last night's crazy dash from New Mexico. If I hadn't come, I would have been in my familiar science classroom, surrounded by high school students. Today's lesson plan listed a pH experiment. Acids and bases. Easy enough for a substitute to handle—that is, unless there was another student who decided to mix a base with an acid and create a dangerous gas, like Trey Woodard had done last year.

"So tell me about that. Was she coherent when you got there? Was she alone?"

I pulled back to the present. "She was coherent. And her attorney, Sam something, was in the house when I arrived. He left when I went upstairs."

"What did you talk to your aunt about?" He watched me in the rearview mirror.

"Hardly anything." I pulled up the memory of the short conversation we'd had before I fixed my lunch. "She was glad to see me. I was glad to see her. It had been two years."

The police chief glanced from the street ahead to me in his rearview mirror. "When did you arrive, and why did you come?"

"She called late last night and asked me to come." I rubbed my forehead with my fingertips. "I left home at midnight. It was shortly after noon when I got here."

When his eyes returned to the street, I studied his face in the mirror. Tiny wrinkles creased his lower lids and fanned out onto his cheeks at the corners of his greenish-blue eyes. He looked older than I'd first thought—maybe mid-forties; maybe my age.

Dizziness twirled me around. I closed my eyes and took a deep breath. I was tired, and I hadn't eaten. And I wasn't in the mood to be interrogated. "Before the storm." I remembered the odd yellow light and the miles of highway just before I got to town. At one point, a coyote had darted across the asphalt road. The animal had stopped and looked back before melting into the shadowed landscape beneath the gray-black, boiling cloud banks. His ragged coat was a mottled patchwork of gray, orange, and brown.

"Why the rush?" the police chief prodded.

"Aunt Elizabeth sounded upset. I hated the thought of her being alone, especially if she was … in pain."

"Why would you think she was alone?"

"We're all in New Mexico. She has no family here."

"No family." His statement hung in the air. "When was the last time you were here, in Pawhuska?"

"Thirty years ago." I sought a memory, something to share to prove I had indeed been here the summer before I turned twelve. Nothing but wisps. The next summer, when my family started discussing the yearly visit, I'd used the excuse that I was too old for a family vacation. Instead, I'd gone to church camp for a week by myself while the rest of the family came here.

The police chief's eyes sought some other answer in mine, but there was no other answer to find. "So Sam was with her when you got here?"

"Yes. We talked briefly, but when she called to me from upstairs, I believe he left. When I came downstairs to get something to eat a few minutes later, he was gone."

"And then later. What happened right before you called the ambulance?"

My heart pounded. I didn't like the way this was going. All I knew was the truth, but I also knew how other people could twist and turn my words for their own ends. I had no way of knowing if this man was friend or foe.

"I was talking with her. She said she had something to tell me, but the storm was raging outside. Someone knocked on the front door. I assumed it was her caregiver, but when I got to the door, no one was there. I checked the back porch, made tea, and then returned upstairs. That's when I realized something had happened. She was unconscious."

"And so she was alert when you went downstairs to answer the door, but when you came back up, she was unconscious," Green repeated my story. "Took you a while to realize it—a good while."

Numbness crept into my bones. I knew about death and not just from teaching biology dissections. But it had never occurred to me that Elizabeth might be near death—even though she was unconscious.

"Have you ever been in the room with a dead person, Mrs. Aldrich? Had any experience with death?"

My heart thumped. He knew. There was no other reason to ask the question.

"Yes," I finally admitted.

He waited for something more.

"My husband. A year ago." I rubbed my forehead and shut my eyes. "Cancer."

"Sorry for your loss." He turned on the blinker and pulled into the hospital's emergency driveway.

I climbed out of the car and started toward the automatic door. The ambulance that had carried Elizabeth was parked not far from the ramp leading inside.

"Here's my card. I hope Elizabeth recovers quickly," Police Chief Green said. "You'll be staying at the house?"

I nodded and waited for him to tell me not to leave town. The words never came.

Inside the hospital, I went through the admissions process for Aunt Elizabeth. I tried to fill out the form, but there was a lot I didn't know. Who was her doctor? Who was her emergency contact?

The admissions clerk seemed impatient with me. I didn't blame her. I was a stupid relative who claimed to be the next of kin, and I'd not been to Pawhuska for a very long time.

An hour later, Aunt Elizabeth was settled into her room. It was a small hospital, and my biggest question was whether she should be moved to one of several large hospitals in Tulsa, less than a two-hour drive away. As I pondered this question, another stranger paused in the doorway.

With steel-gray eyes, he surveyed the room, his gaze lingering on my aunt and then moving to me for only an instant before he hurried in. The gray-haired man frowned, wiped his hands on his slacks, and then thrust them into his pants pockets. Deep creases marked his forehead and bracketed his eyes.

"Elizabeth?" he asked. His voice was deep and melodious and stirred inside me. I shivered. Either I was reminded of someone else's voice, or I had heard this man speak before.

I stood up. "I'm Jamie Aldrich, Elizabeth's great-niece.

His eyes widened. "And I'm her doctor. What happened?"

"She was upstairs in her bed. I went up to talk with her, and—"

"What happened to Elizabeth?" he asked sharply.

After I repeated the events, he moved to the opposite side of the bed and began to check the monitors. Then he listened to her heart and lungs with his stethoscope. He peered at her face and checked her neck, her hands, and her wrists and ankles. Then he stuffed his hands into his pockets again and rocked back on his heels, his eyes still focused on Elizabeth. "Did you think she needed to be put out of her misery?"

"Wha-at?"

"Chief Green?" the doctor said loudly.

The chief stepped into the room.

"Slight bruising around her mouth, possibly indicating something was held against her mouth with heavy pressure; a torn fingernail, possibly indicating a defensive wound. Was there evidence of a struggle in her bedroom?"

"None the EMTs reported. However, we're going back to the house now, with this." He handed me a search warrant. Green had been hard at work since he dropped me off. His eyes met mine. "I think you might as well come with us."

I nodded. "I think I'd like to have my aunt's attorney present. Do you know how to get in touch with him?"

Green nodded and then stepped out into the hall, pulling out his cell phone.

I turned to the doctor. "I love my aunt. There's no way I would come here to hurt her." The hardness in my voice surprised me.

The doctor shrugged. "Illness and pain in those we love can make us do things we otherwise wouldn't."

"Mrs. Aldrich? Let's go. Sam will meet us there."

"Wait. I might as well take her personal items back to the house. She has no need for them here."

The doctor turned to the closet and handed me a plastic bag. A quick look inside revealed her clothes.

"And her jewelry? She was wearing her wedding band and a locket." I pulled out the clothes, and then turned the bag upside down. Her wedding ring fell out on the floor. "There was a locket. A round gold locket."

The doctor frowned. "No. There must have been just the ring. If there'd been anything else, it would be here."

"But it's not. Aunt Elizabeth grasped the locket several times as we talked." But then my mind flashed to those moments when I searched for her pulse. The locket hadn't been around her neck then. And now, it was nowhere to be found.

Chief Green studied my face. "Maybe it's in her bedroom."

Somehow, I knew it wasn't.

Chapter 4

April 1, 2000—Afternoon

Another uniformed policeman—someone I hadn't seen before—was waiting on the porch when we arrived at my aunt's home. A red Jeep Cherokee hugged the curb behind the police cruiser. As we pulled into the driveway, Sam Mazie got out of the Jeep.

The officer on the porch opened the front door as we approached. He immediately headed up the front stairs with a black briefcase.

"Wait down here, please, Mrs. Aldrich. Sam will be right in." Green said before he took the front stairs two at a time.

I tried to breathe slowly and settle my thoughts. Someone tried to smother the life out of Elizabeth. If I had stayed in the room with her and not gone downstairs, it never would have happened. As it was, somehow the would-be murderer had not completed the job. Where had he—or she—gone? And why had I not seen anyone?

Sam stepped into the front hall and closed the door behind him. He took one look at my face and motioned toward the kitchen. "You need some tea, I think."

He was right. I'd been keyed up for the past eighteen hours. I was sure I wasn't thinking clearly, and that wasn't like me. It also wasn't like me to feel a fluttery stomach around a man I had met only a few hours ago. But there was something about this handsome, silent man that unsettled my heart.

He stepped into the pantry to retrieve the tea bags and

then filled the teakettle and put it on the stove. He pulled out a chair at the little table, saying, "Sit, Jamie."

I was comforted by his voice. Weird, because I wasn't ordinarily fond of take-charge men. I had always been the take-charge person, with the single exception of my husband, Ben. Today, I felt especially glad to have someone walk in and take charge. I had no idea what to do next.

"I've told Green what I know about your arrival. I told him you didn't seem to be intent on doing Elizabeth harm. Unfortunately, I didn't stay around to see how you reacted to her physical and mental condition. I should have." He retrieved the sugar bowl and set it on the table between us. "What was your reaction?"

I folded my hands on the table. "She was so weak. And I saw the walker in the corner. Obviously, she's declined in health since I last saw her two years ago."

"She visited your home?"

I nodded. "She loved to travel. She'd come through every couple of years, sometimes on her way to someplace else. Sometimes just to see us."

"Us?"

"My family—two children, grown now, and my husband, Ben." I paused and pulled in a deep breath. "He died a year ago. The last time Elizabeth visited was right after we received his diagnosis. There were treatments, the waiting, and then the funeral. Haven't seen Elizabeth since he died."

"I'm sorry. Of course there had been no time." The kettle whistled, and Sam got up to brew two cups of strong black tea. He pulled milk from the refrigerator and retrieved the sugar bowl from near the stove. "Seeing her physical condition must have been a shock. How did she seem mentally?"

I thought back a few hours, remembering how I had felt when she began to talk with me and how quickly her words had turned frantic and almost angry. "I was surprised she was angry at herself. She called her life a 'sham.' I'd never heard her talk that way. She's always been such a positive person. I couldn't imagine what she meant."

"Did she say anything to you about her illness?"

"No. She was tired. The storm started. And someone came to the door."

"Who?"

"I don't know. Elizabeth begged me not to leave her. Whoever it was had disappeared by the time I went down to answer. That must have been when someone came in and tried to kill her."

Sam stared down at his teacup. "And you didn't see or hear anybody in her room or anywhere in the house?"

"There *was* something. Almost like someone was talking upstairs while I was down in the kitchen, making tea."

I watched his handsome face. Sam had been in the house. I didn't know when he actually left, only that he had not responded to my call when I came down to heat some soup. He could have been in the house the entire time, hiding somewhere. He was certainly familiar with the place. Should I trust him? I really had no idea what his relationship was with my aunt or what his motives might be.

The phone trilled in the entry hall. I hurried to answer, thinking the call had to be from my mother in Albuquerque. As old as I was, she still expected me to call to let her know I had arrived safely. I had not yet made that call.

"Elizabeth Graham's residence."

"This is Father Bertrand of the Immaculate Conception Catholic Church. To whom am I speaking?" The soft voice was hard to hear.

"This is Jamie Aldrich. Elizabeth Graham is my great aunt."

"Ah, your great-aunt is my parishioner. I've just learned she's in the hospital. You're unfamiliar with our community. How can I help?"

I reflected on his words for a few seconds but didn't immediately come up with anything he could do. Could he clue me in on my aunt's life for the past thirty years and who her friends and enemies were? Would he know who might want Elizabeth dead—and why?

"Thank you for calling, Father. She's in the hospital, and I'm hoping she'll be conscious soon. Sam Mazie is here, as well as Chief Green. They are both being very helpful. I'll let you know if I think of anything you can do."

"Ah, Sam's there. You're in good hands. He will see that you have what you need, I'm sure. God bless you, my child."

I hung up the receiver. News traveled like wildfire here. Everyone probably knew Elizabeth was in the hospital and that I was in town.

What if, instead of slipping into unconsciousness, Aunt Elizabeth had died?

I didn't want to think about it, but it was still a possibility. She might never wake up. I would be in charge of planning the service and burial. Where did she keep the papers detailing her wishes for funeral plans, legal arrangements already made, existing wills, or bank accounts? An obituary would need to be written. What should it say?

A huge ache grew behind my eyes as my mind spun with questions. I sank down onto the padded bench in the front hall. If there was a funeral, who would come from New Mexico? Mother was physically unable to travel. My sister, Ellen, still had my youngest nephew, Jacob, living at home and going to school. My brother, Randy, hadn't been outside the veterans hospital in six years. Aunt Martha no longer went anywhere, and her children, my first cousins, wouldn't take the time off for this. My own children were occupied with their young lives.

Most likely, the attendees would be Elizabeth's friends here in Pawhuska, whoever they were.

I leaned back against the walnut paneling. Planning Ben's funeral had been grueling, even with the support of Matt and Allison, Mom, and other family and friends. Here, I was alone.

I shook my head. What was I thinking? Aunt Elizabeth was

not dead, and she wasn't going to die now. She was going to recover from this. I'd stay for a week or so until she regained her strength, and then she and I would talk about her living situation. Obviously, assisted living, either here or near me back in Las Vegas, was a good idea. Then, once the plans were finalized, I'd be on my way home again. Maybe I would get there in time to give semester finals.

Probably thanks to the tea, my mental fog cleared a little. I straightened my slumped shoulders. Someone had just tried to kill my aunt. How could I let her stay here in Pawhuska if someone was trying to kill her? I had to keep her safe. And I had to find out why anyone would want my sweet aunt dead.

Even if it had been an attempt at assisted suicide, I wanted to know who tried to help her. Cold chills raced through my body. I'd just spent the last year of my life trying to convince the legal system in Las Vegas that I hadn't "killed" my husband. What if the whole scenario repeated itself here in Pawhuska with my great-aunt?

"Jamie? You okay?" Sam stepped into the hallway from the kitchen.

I walked past him to retrieve my teacup and then moved over to the window overlooking the greening back lawn. Shadows crept across the expanse toward the one-car garage standing off the alley at the rear of the lot.

One day, I'd cut my hand on a razor blade while playing with the boys in that garage. I'd made a trip to the local hospital emergency room for a stitch, and Mom had lectured the boys.

But now, a second structure stood at the back of the lot, near the alley. With frilly white curtains and baby-blue paint, the cottage looked like a playhouse. I didn't remember it.

Voices and a noise in the hallway signaled the return of the policemen.

"We've collected some evidence, including some prints. And there's a pillow I'm taking for processing. No signs of a struggle. And no sign of a necklace." Green looked at us. "The two of you both admit you were here. You both sure no one else was in the house?"

"I saw no one else," Sam said.

"Me either."

"You'll be staying here, Mrs. Aldrich?"

"Yes. I hope Elizabeth will regain consciousness soon. I think it will help her to have me here."

I followed the men to the front door.

Green locked eyes with me. "Can you think of anything else that might indicate someone else besides Sam was in the house when you arrived?"

I maintained eye contact as my mind sped through the moments after I arrived. "You know ... I would swear I saw the upstairs curtains move after I drove up. But I don't think Elizabeth had been out of bed. And Sam was downstairs in the kitchen."

"Did she mention anyone else having visited today?"

"No." I paused and then added, "But she wanted to tell me something. And she didn't want to be left alone. She seemed frightened."

Chief Green frowned. He pulled a white business card from one pocket and tucked it between the mirror and the wood frame of the hallstand. "I'll have someone ask around the neighborhood. Perhaps someone noticed another car or someone going in or out of the house," he said. "I'll be in touch." His eyes passed quickly over my face before he motioned for Sam to go past him out onto the porch, and then he pulled the door closed.

The backs of my legs found the hall bench, and I slumped onto it.

The chief would call New Mexico again and talk to the detectives who had investigated Ben's death. Should I call Nathan Taylor back home in Las Vegas? He'd brought me through the fiasco over Ben's so-called "assisted suicide." But I wasn't sure he could do the same thing here.

Sam and I had been the last people to see my aunt before she became unconscious. Thing was, if I used Sam as my attorney, wasn't it like one suspect being trusted to defend the other?

Chapter 5

Monday, April 1—Evening

"Mom? We need to talk." My voice sounded stronger than I felt; I actually sounded as if I was in control. I explained what had happened after I got to Pawhuska, speaking in a low, calm voice, like the one I used when I lectured a class of hormone-crazed high school kids about cell reproduction. Then I waited for the expected rush of words.

"My God. Elizabeth. She's in a coma?" Mom's voice quivered. Then, with her voice an octave above normal pitch, she said, "I'll get the next plane."

"No, Mom." I rubbed my forehead. "You're not up for the trip. And there's no need to come here. I can take care of things." My voice caught, but I cleared my throat and went on. "I've been in touch with her doctor and her lawyer, and I've spoken with Father Bertrand, the priest at her church. We all hope she'll wake up. If not, I'll arrange for a long-term care facility here or back home. I expect to have a better idea of which way it's going later this week. Right now, I need some information."

"I wish she hadn't demanded you come," Mom sputtered. "You're still not over Ben's death. I told you the situation might be upsetting, and now look what's happened." Her voice broke. "What were you two talking about before she fell into the coma? Did you say something to upset her?" Mother sniffed.

She was right; this was upsetting for me but not just

because Elizabeth was in a coma. It was her request: *Free me.* And it was the pillow and the missing stitch. And it was the anonymous person who had tried to suffocate her, but didn't finish the job. I couldn't tell Mother any of that; it would send her into a fit of anxiety.

"Mom, one thing I can do is pull together some history for the obituary. If it's not needed now—and I really hope it isn't— we will need it at some point. Might as well have those details close at hand. Can you get the family genealogy file?"

I heard a clunk as Mother set down the phone. When she picked it up again and began to read from the family notes and charts, I pulled a scratch pad and pencil from the center drawer of the writing desk and scribbled down the facts.

Elizabeth had been born in 1909 to Clara and James O'Day in Carthage, Missouri. She had one sister, Sarah (deceased), two nieces, and five great-nieces and great-nephews. Moved to Bigheart as a baby, attended school there. Married Robert "Dodie" Darcey in 1928. Two children of this marriage died at birth. Darcey died in 1956. Married Robert Rourke in 1960. No children. Rourke died in 1967. Married Herbert Graham in 1970. Graham died in 1990.

"Do you know if she had any club memberships or did any local charity work?"

"Oh, dear. I don't know." Mother's voice had a funny sound to it. And she spoke too softly.

"Who in Pawhuska can I ask?" I drummed my fingers on the scratch pad and sighed into the phone. "Mom? There has to be someone else who has more information."

I could hear her breathing. Several seconds passed.

"Well, she had no education past eighth grade. I know she moved with Darcey to Pawhuska sometime in the '40s. I didn't know her friends."

I laid down the pencil. An entire life, more than ninety years. None of this really said anything about Elizabeth. She was a loving and kind woman, especially to two generations of nieces and nephews. And she had loved living here, refusing to leave northern Oklahoma's wild, rolling hills, even though her remaining family lived elsewhere.

"Give Allison and Matt a call. Let them know what's up, would you? Tell them I'll call in a few days. I'll call again, Mom." I hung up.

Elizabeth's own family hardly knew her.

I trudged up the front stairs to Elizabeth's room. At the second floor landing, I stopped.

Someone had been hiding up here, waiting for me to leave her room, waiting for a chance to be alone with her. I grabbed onto the wooden ball on the end baluster and looked around. Three bedroom doors, one bathroom door, and an alcove leading to the backstairs and the doorway up to the attic. Where had he—or she—been hiding?

Elizabeth had wanted to tell me something; she called herself a fraud. It could be that someone had wanted to shut her up before she shared the truth.

Would she still have a chance to tell me, or would that someone make sure she never woke up again?

Chapter 6

Monday, April 1—Night

The cozy bedroom felt like a return to the 1960s—pink-and-white gingham coverlet with white eyelet trim, *Alice in Wonderland* characters printed, then outlined by stitches. Aunt Elizabeth had kept the room just as it had been when we'd come for summer visits.

I still had to put one knee up first and then climb onto the tall four-poster bed. My feet dangled over the sides as I kicked off my shoes. I lay back on the bedspread and stared up at the painted ceiling planks. Even now, exhausted, my brain reverted back thirty years and started constructing a maze from the center light fixture along the seams of the planks to one corner, just as I had done on so many summer nights, all those years ago. My mind wouldn't shut off. Outside, the wind began to wail again, and the house began to creak. I pulled back the spread and scooted in between the cool sheets.

The locket.

I rolled off the bed, stuffed my feet back into my slings, and shuffled into Elizabeth's bedroom, flicking on the lamp as I entered. The police had not remade the bed after they had rifled through it. The bed frame hunkered over a multicolored oval braided rug. I dropped to my hands and knees and crawled over the rag rug, looked under the bed, and then reached out and ran my hand over it. No locket. I checked the nightstand, shifted the lamp and the clock radio to one side, and looked under the doily. I opened the drawer, dug through old greeting cards and pens and pencils. No locket.

Whoever had been here with Aunt Elizabeth had taken the necklace.

I closed my eyes to recall our last conversation. Her voice had sounded urgent. I wished for the umpteenth time I had let her speak and had not gone downstairs to answer the door. If I had done what Aunt Elizabeth wanted—if I had stayed with her and listened—she would be in this bed now, sleeping.

I glanced around the room again, at the lamp in the corner, the wrapped walker, the crocheted doilies, and the photographs. If she was bedridden, how had she been able to make it downstairs last night to call me in New Mexico? Why had she stayed in bed today, when I arrived?

I turned off the lamp and went back to my room to climb into bed. I set my glasses on the bedside table and pulled the covers up, cocooning under the thick quilt. The wind wailed around the house, and tree branches tapped at the window.

A loud bang reverberated up the stairs. *Not* just the wind.

I fumbled for my robe.

Was someone downstairs? Did they think the house was empty? I didn't want to risk revealing my presence by turning on the lights. My emergency flashlight was still stowed in my suitcase in the armoire. I dug it out, and then crept toward the stairway. I turned it on as I descended the front stairs.

Black night hung outside the front windows.

I played the flashlight beam around the hallway and then into the study. Cracks spider-webbed across the glass of one large beveled front window. The glass was still intact, although for how long was anyone's guess.

It had to have been the wind, throwing some bit of debris into the window. The only other alternative, that someone had thrown something at it, seemed unlikely but was possible. Whoever had done this might still be out there. Might be watching right now through the cracked window. I flicked off the flashlight and stood in the dark. My heartbeat thundered in my ears.

If something else struck the window, the glass would pelt in on me. It could even happen right now, as close as I was standing to the glass.

I backed out of the study and into the shadowy entry hall. Then I checked the front door lock. It was secure.

I waited, listening, then moved down the hallway to the kitchen to check the back door and the door to the basement.

Back in the front hall, I stopped to listen again.

The strong wind rattled the house.

The window was probably broken by a branch, not by vandalism. Daylight would tell. I hoped that duct tape would hold it together until a new window could be ordered and a repairman could get over to put it in.

I climbed the front stairs and got into bed again but this time with my robe still on; I couldn't stop shivering. On the ceiling, shadows of branches outside the window fought with each other. My mind chased my thoughts around and around in circles.

Did someone break the window on purpose? Did someone know I was here alone? My thoughts fuzzed, crawling around like caterpillars.

I couldn't fall asleep.

Across the street, deep in the shadows, a hand reaches down to smooth the wind-whipped black slicker. The slightest glimmer of teeth, smiling, catches the glow from the corner street light. Inside the house, the beam of a flashlight flickers on the study window and then blinks off. A few minutes later, when the house darkens again, the figure turns and melts away into the night.

Chapter 7

Tuesday, April 2—Morning

From the entry hall, I stared at the morning light beaming through the webbed window in the study. If I placed a big duct-tape X across the glass, it might hold together until I could get it replaced. My head felt heavy and my thoughts were thick as potato soup. Where would Elizabeth keep duct tape?

In the kitchen, I rifled through drawers and then the upper cabinets, but all I found was a roll of masking tape. I checked below the sink. Nothing. Through the window, I caught a glimpse of the side lawn and Elizabeth's gazebo. Gray wood peeked through peeling, white paint. Bare ivy tendrils swayed in the breeze, hanging down from the peaked roof.

"Casey would dance with the strawberry blonde, and the band played on. ..." Aunt Elizabeth often sang her favorite waltz as she taught us all how to dance—me and the other kids. Randy and one other boy—what was his name?—would practice the waltz. More neighborhood boys stood by, hands stuffed into the pockets of their shorts. The music was clear in my memory; the faces were blurred.

A crow swooped past the gazebo to land in the far corner of the yard on the now-dilapidated greenhouse. In my memory, the glass and steel building was whole—a green, sweet-smelling oasis. Now, weed skeletons poked from the debris, and I could even see a small tree growing through the broken glass roof.

I strolled back through the house and stepped onto the veranda for an outside look at the ruined window. The trim paint on the porch was peeling off in strips. Years ago, Elizabeth had been so proud of this house. After her last husband's death, she had no one to help take care of it. Guilt rose up in my throat, tasting as bad as stomach bile. I wished I could spread the blame out on my brother and sister and even my mother and my aunt, but I knew in my heart that I had always been her favorite. I should have been the one to make sure she had what she needed and that her home was safe and well kept.

From the porch, I saw the extent of the window damage. Masking tape wouldn't do the trick. I'd have to search harder for thicker tape, or go to the hardware store to buy some. Below the window, a softball-sized object lay on the porch, wrapped in a worn chamois skin, like Ben had used to dry the car after a wash. Cotton string held the covering snug around the object.

I picked it up and carried it into the kitchen to the old chrome and plastic table, found a pair of scissors in a drawer, and snipped the string. The soft leather fell away to reveal a large rock.

Get out, or I'll finish the job. The black words were scrawled on the chamois.

Back home, high school students were always vandalizing something at the school, sometimes even a car or some teacher's yard or home. It wasn't personal; it was high school. This was different. Someone had thrown this rock to break the window.

I retrieved the chief's business card from the hall mirror and punched in his private office number; his answering machine picked up. The hands on the mantle clock in the study read 7:45 AM. I left a message. I really hoped this police chief would be helpful, not just another guy in authority on a power trip.

I folded the chamois and laid it on the laminate counter by

the sink. Outside, two robins raced across the yard, stopped, and plucked worms from the grass. I walked out on the back porch and stared up at the sky, hoping the dazzling blue would erase the image of those words on the chamois.

A light breeze touched my cheek. Rose-pink azalea buds had already opened in the south-facing flower beds. Daffodils nodded their yellow and white heads. A purple carpet of phlox spread around the base of one of the oak trees.

I rolled my shoulders and shook out my arms. I reached high and then folded to touch the ground. I stood again and breathed in the flowery moist scent of rich brown earth. Elizabeth's garden—rows of corn, beans, squash, and lettuce—had been in the grassy space between that small cottage and the one-car garage on the back side of the wide lot.

For an instant, I could almost see Elizabeth wearing a sunbonnet and a faded checked apron as she chopped weeds with a hoe between two rows of green corn stalks.

Across the yard, the weathered siding of the garage looked rotten. I stepped onto the cracked cement drive leading from the back alleyway to the garage. Flecks of gray paint speckled the soil like bits of bland confetti.

The cottage stood thirty feet from the garage; freshly painted blue siding and white trim told me this house had been cared for. Frilly curtains hung in the windows. Clumps of iris hugged the foundation, and showy red tulips accented rows of evergreen yew. A bird feeder swung from a shepherd's hook by the front stoop.

I stepped up to the door and knocked. Sheer curtains covered the window in the front door. Inside, I could make out furniture shapes, but nothing moved.

Voices erupted next door. A lanky, dark-haired boy chased a girl with auburn hair toward Elizabeth's backyard.

"I'll beat you!" the boy shouted. But the slender girl outran him and was nearly to Elizabeth's side driveway before she stopped, laughing.

"Beat you! Again!"

The boy growled as he hunkered down to tackle her but straightened when a man emerged from the back of the house, calling their names.

"Daniel! Rory! Breakfast's nearly ready. Come back in."

"Oh, I'll eat mine out here," the girl shouted as she twirled away from her brother onto Aunt Elizabeth's driveway. She saw me, smiled, and waved. "Hi!"

I waved back. I'd heard these children playing yesterday, too.

The girl took a step closer, and I moved toward them. So these were Elizabeth's neighbors. I hoped they could tell me who had been helping Elizabeth. They might even have seen another person leaving the house yesterday.

"I'm Rory," the girl introduced herself. "She went to the hospital, didn't she? Are you going to live there now? Do you have any kids?"

A gray-haired man frowned as he hurried toward the girl, wiping his hands on a navy apron slung around his neck and cinched at the waist. I peered at him; I'd seen him before. At the hospital. The doctor.

"Don't bother her with so many questions!" He gently shook Rory's shoulder.

"Oh, it's okay. I'm Jamie Aldrich, Elizabeth Graham's great-niece," I explained. "My kids are all grown up. And I'm only here for a little while." The girl smiled shyly at me, revealing a gap in her teeth where her front teeth should have been. I turned to the man. "Didn't we meet yesterday? At the hospital?"

The man stepped across the driveway and shook my extended hand, and then thrust his hands into the apron's deep pockets. "Drake Goodwin." Steel-gray eyes squinted at me. "My sister—their mother—lives there." He nodded at the house next door, pulled his shoulders back, and lifted his chin. "Come on, kids."

The girl fidgeted as her uncle slid his arm around her shoulders again and turned her toward the house.

"How long you going to be here?" Daniel called from the edge of the neighboring lawn.

His uncle frowned at him.

"Only until my aunt's feeling better. And there are a few things I need to take care of in the house."

"You're not going to live here?" Rory said wistfully, looking back over her shoulder as she and the man stepped off the driveway.

"Don't think so. But you might ask me again in a week."

The girl gave me a hopeful look.

A week? Surely I wouldn't still be here in another week. Allison needed my help with wedding plans, and I hadn't finished composing the test questions for the Biology II final.

Drake Goodwin draped his other arm across Daniel's shoulders. He flapped one hand in my direction and steered the children toward the house next door.

I turned back to the garage.

A padlock secured the main door, but the side door was unlocked. I pushed inward, but the door moved only a few inches before it thudded against something.

The crack between the door and the frame was just big enough that I could squeeze in. The earthy smell of mold, dust, and age floated on the stale air, along with memories of dice games and poker. Ellen and I had only been observers on the few occasions when Randy and the other boys had let us inside their hangout. After the razor blade incident, the boys weren't allowed to play here. Instead, they'd built a tree house somewhere. No girls allowed.

I extended my hands in front of me and stepped inside as my eyes adjusted to the darkness. A large tarp-covered object filled the small garage. Old paint cans, bottles, and boxes crowded the shelves lining the walls. A small dusty window on the wall opposite the door let in natural light.

Next to me on the countertop loomed a stack of old drawer boxes covered by a clear plastic drop cloth. Across the garage below the north window sat a rectangular red toolbox. Most likely, it was full of tools, duct tape—fix-it supplies.

I tried to slip sideways between the front of the tarp-covered object and the cabinet. My right elbow bumped the drawers; they shifted. The shelves crashed down.

Chapter 8

Tuesday, April 2—Midmorning

I coughed from where I lay on the floor of the garage. Dust coated my tongue, my throat, my eyes, and my skin.

"Are you all right?" I thought the voice belonged to the little girl.

Shadowy shapes lingered in the doorway. Dust motes floated in light beams. Someone bent over me. A man. Drake Goodwin.

"Just another minute, and I'll have these off you," Goodwin said. He stacked each drawer on the counter and then helped me to a sitting position. Holding my head steady between his hands, he peered into my eyes and then touched the top of my head. "Nasty gash. Needs a stitch at the ER."

"I don't need to go to the hospital—except to see Aunt Elizabeth."

"You must take care of this," Goodwin said. "You could have a concussion."

Rory took my hand and pulled me out of the building and across the lawn toward a late-model Toyota. "We almost didn't hear the crash," the girl said. "I stopped to show Uncle Drake the tulips I planted last fall. Otherwise, we'd have been in the house. And if it wasn't a parent conference day, I wouldn't have even been home. You'd still be lying there, knocked out. Maybe you'd have died."

"It's just a bruise," I insisted, digging my heels into the yard and resisting the little girl's tug on my hand.

When Goodwin glanced at me, his smile didn't reach his eyes.

"You're bleeding!" Rory tugged at my hand.

I swiped at the blood trickling down my forehead and into my brows. My eyes lost focus for a second. I let the girl lead me to the car.

Rory kept up a running conversation, mostly with herself, as Goodwin drove. Her constant chatter made the pain in my head worse. Once, she leaned close and peered into my eyes, mimicking her uncle.

At the triage desk in the ER, I waited alone; Goodwin and the kids rambled off in search of a candy machine. I leaned my head against the wall. The heady antiseptic smell made me nauseated, a reminder of all the hours I'd spent in the hospital with Ben.

Before Goodwin and the kids could return, a nurse led me to a bright, sterile exam room. Seconds later, the door opened and a man with a white lab coat came in; it was Drake Goodwin, hands tucked into his pockets. He stepped up to examine the cut on my forehead.

"We can close that cut with a butterfly bandage. You okay with that?" He swabbed on antiseptic.

I nodded. The nurse applied the butterfly and then taped a gauze pad to my forehead.

"Ow," I winced as Goodwin pressed his fingers into the flesh of my right upper arm.

"You bruised your right shoulder and upper arm," he said. He turned to the nurse, saying, "Let's put on a sling," and then told me, "Keep it immobilized for several days. No lifting." Drake stepped back and let the nurse wrap a stiff fabric sling around my arm.

Mechanically, he washed his hands in a little sink.

"I'll check on you next time I'm at Susan's, if I don't run into you here." He shuffled toward the doorway, rubbing his hands on a paper towel that he then pitched into a waste can near the door.

As the room began another slow spin, I lay back on the exam table. "Wait," I called.

Goodwin stepped close enough that I could see the checkerboard pattern made by the fine lines on his forehead and cheeks. His lips pressed together, making a short straight slash.

"Thanks for your help," I said. "Good thing you were next door."

Goodwin's eyes brightened. He returned my quick smile, but then his wrinkles dropped back into place. "It sounded like the whole garage was coming down. Promise me you won't try to deal with the mess until your arm is better."

The nurse helped me to sit up and swing my legs over to the edge of the exam table as Goodwin left the room.

"Still woozy?" the nurse asked. A petite woman with delicate features and short hair, the nurse seemed out of place. She was graceful even in thick-soled white nurse shoes; she would look great in a designer dress, dining on Broadway.

"I think I'll be okay."

"When was your last tetanus shot? Any allergies?" The nurse dropped the bandage packaging into a lidded trash receptacle.

"Penicillin. And I probably do need a tetanus shot."

The nurse scribbled on the patient chart. "We'll take care of this, and then I'll have a volunteer take you home."

"Give me ten minutes. I want to check on my aunt—she's a patient here—and then I'll come to the front entry," I told the nurse after she'd given me the two inoculations.

I padded down the hall, went up the elevator, and stuck my head into Elizabeth's room. The machines were beeping a rhythm that meant, for now, nothing had changed. I took the elevator back down and checked in at the volunteer station for someone to drive me home.

A few minutes later, at the drive-in burger joint, I sat in the elderly volunteer's car, savoring a breakfast burrito. Stopping here had been the old man's idea, and although at first I'd wanted to get right home—my right shoulder ached—I was glad I'd agreed to let him stop. I hadn't eaten before the accident, and I was starving. I had no set schedule this morning, other than dealing with the window.

"Sorry to hear about your accident this morning," the white-haired man said softly. "Hope it doesn't ruin your stay." He leaned away from me and against the driver's side door as I wolfed down the food. He brushed some lint from his red volunteer coat and then cleaned the lenses of his trifocals with a pocket handkerchief. Deep wrinkles across his forehead and around the corners of his eyes and cheeks indicated he must be in his eighties, if not even older.

"Where are you from?" he asked.

He was making polite conversation, so I answered, and then he asked another question. "And why did you come to Pawhuska?"

After I told him that Elizabeth Graham was my great-aunt, he shook his head. His thick white hair fell across his forehead.

"She is a wonderful woman." His shoulders slumped, and his head drooped. "She was so lovely," he whispered.

I leaned toward him in case he had more to say, but he lifted his eyes and stared out the windshield.

I finished the last bite of my burrito, wadded up the metallic wrapper, and put it into the paper sack. He set the sack onto the plastic ledge beneath the menu board.

"You have children?" he asked as he started the car and threw the gears into reverse.

"A daughter, Allison, and a son, Matthew."

As he turned onto the street, the car bumped the curb on

the right side of the street and then crossed the center stripe when he overcorrected.

"Are you all right?" I asked.

His head jerked. "I'm all right." He squinted at the road.

Luckily, traffic was light and the other cars kept to the far side of the street. As he turned the final corner, one wheel crashed over the curb and onto a lawn. When the wheel thudded back down onto the pavement, the old man gasped. His eyes watered.

I grabbed the edge of my seat and held on until he finally stopped in front of Elizabeth's house.

"Thanks for the ride." I got out of the car and rushed up the sidewalk.

At the porch, I glanced back. The car was still there. He waved.

The old fellow probably shouldn't be driving. I thought about calling the hospital and letting them know about my experience. Then it occurred to me—he'd driven straight to Elizabeth's house without asking the address. But it was a small town. Everyone knew everything about everybody.

And they all knew more about Elizabeth than I did.

Chapter 9

Tuesday, April 2—Late Morning

I took it slow up the steps and onto the porch; my whole body ached.

The cracked study window was holding together for now. I glanced up at the second-story windows. No shadows, no movement.

A car engine roared up behind me and then stopped at the curb. Chief Green climbed out of his cruiser and looked up at the house.

"You called. Said you had something to show me. The window, I'm guessing. When did that happen?"

"Last night, about ten. And that's not what I need to show you." He followed me into the house and to the kitchen. "This was wrapped around the rock that cracked the window," I said as he fingered the soft chamois. "I found it on the porch this morning. What's going on?"

"I was hoping you'd be able to tell me." Toby Green handed the skin back to me.

"What do you mean?"

"This is a nasty bit of advice. Did you write it?"

"Of course not." I straightened to all of my five foot five inches and glared at him. "And there's something else. Her locket *is* missing."

"And when did you last see it?"

"I already told you. Around her neck, yesterday afternoon."

"Before she fell into a coma but not after?"

"The hospital doesn't have it, and it's not in her room. Whoever tried to kill her took it."

"What was in the locket?"

"She never opened it, at least not in front of me."

He sighed. "Never opened it," he drawled. "It wasn't with the items we collected from her room. We'll check the pawn shops."

"Whoever took it knew her and took it for a keepsake."

"Who would do that?" He honestly seemed to ignore what I'd just said. "Where did she get the locket?"

I shrugged. "She's always worn it. Maybe it had a photo of one of her husbands in it."

"Not likely someone would take a locket that held a picture of another woman's dead husband."

I let out an exasperated sigh. "If I could tell you why someone took the locket, I could probably tell you who attacked her. She was wearing it and then she wasn't. If I was the only person in the house, it should be with the things you took to the police station, at the hospital, or on the floor in her bedroom."

Green studied my face. "You know much about Pawhuska?"

What did that have to do with any of this? "Only what I remember from visits here as a child. The Osage tribe and ranching history, mostly. Maybe a little about the oil fields. Animals, flowers, plants of the area—things Elizabeth taught me." Where was he going with this sudden chit-chat? My head throbbed. My arm hurt. I wanted to lie down.

"Remember anything else? Any of Elizabeth's friends and their families?"

"That was thirty years ago. Those people are dead or moved away. Look, Chief Green, if there isn't anything else, I'd like to lie down. And take another pain pill." I gestured toward the sling on my arm, and he seemed to notice it for the first time.

"What happened?"

Quickly, I detailed what had happened in the garage and at the ER with Dr. Goodwin and the kids.

"Nice of Goodwin to take you to the hospital," the chief said. "Lucky he was close by." His eyes narrowed. He didn't seem to like Drake Goodwin. Maybe Goodwin was as cold and impersonal with everyone else as he had been with me.

Toby Green walked back into the entry hall and stopped in the doorway to the study. "Really ought to tape up that window. You got someone in mind for the repair?"

"I was looking for tape when the accident happened. And as far as the repair, is there someone you could suggest?"

"I've got some duct tape out in the car; I'll get it. And for the repair, Pawhuska's not a very big town. They'll probably have to get the plate glass from Tulsa. Check the phone book for Rocky's Glass." He stepped out of the house, leaving the front door ajar.

I went over to the phone desk and found the narrow Pawhuska area phone book in a drawer. Rocky's was listed in the Yellow Pages under "glass." I punched in the number.

A few minutes later, when I stepped out onto the porch, Chief Green had already placed several long pieces of tape over the cracks in the study window.

"You get a hold of Rocky?"

"It'll be Thursday before they can send someone to measure. Can't be that much business in Pawhuska." I rubbed at my throbbing shoulder. The pill samples Goodwin had given me were in my pocket.

"We had a storm yesterday, remember? And with all these old homes around here, plenty of windows are replaced every year." The chief stepped to the veranda rail and assessed his work.

"Other jobs are probably more important than mine." I couldn't keep the sarcasm out of my voice.

"Don't take it personal. Things happen in due time. No

need to get crazy over it." Green stepped off the porch and down the sidewalk.

I hadn't been "getting crazy" over it, and yes, I knew some things were the same, whether in Oklahoma or in New Mexico. For one, in the rural areas, nothing happened in a rush. Most people lived in the moment and enjoyed small talk, family, and nature. Elizabeth had insisted my family live by those rules during their summer visits. It had bothered my mother most of all.

I watched as Green's black-and-white disappeared down the street, and then I pushed the front door closed.

Chapter 10

Tuesday, April 2—Afternoon

Just inside the front door, I stopped. An old memory tape played. Young versions of me and Ellen racing down the stairs, screaming as our brother, Randy, caught us. We turned, laughed, and played the jumping sing-song game on the bottom steps.

"Two up, one down, four up, three down, six up, five down," and on and on, always ending on the first step. Aunt Elizabeth stood in the parlor doorway, smiling. She clapped her hands as we played this strange game she had taught us. Thinking back on it, and remembering my own boisterous children, I knew we were lucky no one fell and broke an arm, a leg, or worse while jumping on the stairs. If any of the other grownups had seen the silly game, they'd have put an end to the horseplay. But Elizabeth had reserved the game for times when only she and we kids were at home.

I had yet to explore much of the house, but I had no desire to. At the same time, getting to the bottom of my unreasonable discomfort about Pawhuska and this house was overdue. If something had happened in this house, I needed to remember.

I stopped in the parlor doorway. The dark oak Eastlake furniture was still there, including an Eastlake pump organ.

As children, we'd been forbidden to play in this room. Now, I stepped in and crossed to the padded rocking chair Elizabeth favored as a reading retreat. A striped threadbare hand towel had been pinned across the back cushion. I folded myself into the chair, tucking my legs up under me, and began to rock.

Great-Aunt Elizabeth and I had gotten close during those early summers of my life, much closer than my brother and sister had done. She and I kept up the relationship, even though I didn't come back here. Elizabeth and I had spent hours talking on the phone, and she had often come to visit us in New Mexico. She was always ready to listen and offer reassurance, whatever crisis I imagined myself to be having. But now, thinking back, I realized that in all those conversations she had told me very little about herself, her life, her loves, her dreams and accomplishments.

Elizabeth had offered me the only unconditional love I'd ever felt, until Ben. So unlike the love I had experienced from my mother or my grandmother. I had learned at a young age that the only way to receive their affection was to be perfect. Make the best grades, have friends from the "best" families, and share only positive thoughts.

Tears welled in my eyes. I wasn't ready to lose Elizabeth, too. Loneliness pressed against me from all sides. *Crying won't do any good*, my mother's voice said inside my head. Mother had worked hard to be sure her philosophy was my conscience.

I'd never seen my mother cry. Not even when I was eight and she'd met me and seven-year-old Randy at the door after school to tell us our father wouldn't be coming home again. Inside, on the dining room floor, four-year-old Ellen had been playing jacks as if nothing had happened. I'd stood in the doorway in shocked silence, watching Randy's lower lip quiver as he blinked fast to keep back the tears.

"Accident. Nobody's fault," Mother had said matter-of-factly. "He went quickly. We should be grateful for that."

I could still hear my mother's voice as if she were standing in Elizabeth's parlor. I blinked to banish the image and pushed the rocker into motion with my foot.

Elizabeth had been my lifeline to emotion. And I'd clutched that line desperately. Those summers, spending a month or more with someone who laughed and played with the three of us, had been like heaven, like an oasis in the emotional desert of life at home.

Why had I stopped coming to Pawhuska? I was certain whatever had happened had affected me and had created phobias and doomed relationships.

I rocked the chair harder, faster. *Elizabeth, I don't want you to die; I miss you already.* Tears spilled down my face.

On the round table next to the rocker, a fingernail file and clippers rested in a glass coaster. Next to them lay a book with green binding—*The Osages* by John Joseph Mathews. The author, a Pawhuska Osage and educated Ivy Leaguer, returned to Pawhuska to write, back in the 1930s. I swiped away the wet trail down my cheek and flipped through the pages of the book. Elizabeth had lived much of this local history and probably absorbed the rest.

Elizabeth had tucked her bookmark at the beginning of the chapter on Osage myths. I thought of the coyote I'd seen just off the road as I neared Pawhuska. Coyote was the trickster of Osage legend. Elizabeth had loved to entertain us with stories of his exploits and the way he had altered the universe.

I wasn't superstitious; I was too grounded in the scientific method. But I'd been introduced to Coyote's world as a child, and now I was back in the land of the Osage, where the pits and falls of our lives might be due to Coyote's tricks.

I let my head fall back and closed my scratchy eyes. I quieted my breathing, taking one deep, slow breath at a time. Golden light glowed on the insides of my eyelids. I concentrated on breathing; the golden light blinked and became filtered narrow beams, as if shining through cracks. Even as relaxed as I was, it suddenly became hard to breathe, and the dank smell of earth and moisture and mold was overwhelming. The need to breathe faster, to suck in more thin air, was intense and unbearable.

I opened my eyes; something banged somewhere in the house. I waited, listening. The floor above me creaked.

I moved quietly toward the staircase in the front hall. At the bottom of the stairs, I stopped. Shadows filled the second floor hallway above.

"Hello? Anyone there?"

I looked around the hallway for a weapon to grab—fireplace tools back in the parlor, an old sword hanging above the mantle in the study—if indeed there was an intruder in the house.

Less than two feet from me, on the hallstand, the phone rang. The sound almost lifted me off the floor.

"Hello?" Silence, and then a click as the caller disconnected. The dial tone buzzed.

I eased down onto the hall bench. If someone was up in my aunt's room, that person would have to come out into the hallway. I would wait—at least until it began to get dark.

Chapter 11

Tuesday, April 2—Evening

My vigil in the hallway lasted nearly an hour. I heard no more sounds, other than the creaks and groans an old house makes in a boisterous wind. My mind drifted off into thoughts about Elizabeth, thoughts about all the times my great-aunt had been there for me.

Unlike the other women in my family, Elizabeth had not seemed to wonder why I married Rob, my first husband. He had been good-looking and fun to be with. But the flip side of the coin was he was always looking for more fun and for an easy way to make a buck. He tended to hook up with undesirables who were also looking for fun and quick money.

Our marriage had turned into a roller coaster of good and bad deals and uncertain finances. I had drawn the line at borrowing money from family members to finance the ventures, but Rob had not been above asking anyway, without my approval.

Elizabeth had offered me emotional support and a friendly voice on the phone line throughout the tumultuous marriage. Even though she was one of the ones Rob had fleeced, Elizabeth never held me responsible and had even refused to let me repay the debt.

The shadows were lengthening in the hallway, so I got up to turn on a small hallstand lamp. I glanced at the top of the stairs and then started up. The hair on the back of my neck bristled, but I shook it off and thought of the students in my biology class. The boys would all laugh if they could see me now, afraid to go upstairs and check out a simple creak. I reached the top of the stairs and turned toward Elizabeth's room.

I had wasted so many years by not coming back here to see Elizabeth. Had she been frightened, living here alone? She'd never said so.

She'd made countless phone calls and visited whenever something required celebration. Allison and Matt had grown up thinking of Elizabeth as their fairy godmother.

I had never wondered about the reality of Elizabeth's life here alone in Pawhuska, after her third husband died. The guilt I felt was becoming a growing, breathing entity.

I stepped toward my aunt's room. At the door, I peaked in. The wrecked bedclothes waited for someone to straighten them again. I rose to the challenge and struggled to make the bed with my one good arm. I managed to keep from looking over my shoulder every few seconds.

Another true test of Elizabeth's love had come during the hellish nightmare of my divorce from Rob. Divorce—for any reason—was never an option to my mother or my sister.

"You have done *what*?" I could still hear the icy tone of Mother's voice when I'd told her Rob and I had separated.

Five years later, when I'd married Ben, Aunt Elizabeth had been there to support me. Two years ago, when Ben was diagnosed with cancer, she'd been a rock of strength on the phone. He'd struggled with pain for months before he finally gave in. Elizabeth had wanted to come to New Mexico, but she didn't want to fly and could no longer drive. Her calm voice on the phone had been a lifeline.

I plumped the pillows and smoothed the quilt, wanting her bed to be welcoming when Elizabeth returned.

Ben had never seen this house. He had laughed hard, imagining me with my siblings during those summers in

Oklahoma. Then he had bawled me out for not taking him to visit Elizabeth. I'd never been able to explain to him exactly why I didn't want to come back; I couldn't explain what I didn't understand myself.

Yes, I loved my aunt. Yes, her house was like a step back in time. And yes, I'd had fun there. But no, I could not make myself go for a visit.

I wrapped my good left arm across my right arm and sat on the bed. I had wasted an hour sitting downstairs, imagining an intruder above me on the second floor. Maybe it had been only my imagination today, but I was very sure that yesterday, someone *had* shared the house with me and Elizabeth. How could I prove it?

An hour later, after finishing a soup supper, I settled into the rocker again. I picked up Mathews's book but found myself reading the same page over and over again. The sounds that the house made—groaning with the wind, popping and creaking—distracted me. Eventually, I put the book back on the small side table, turned on the television, and flipped through the few channels the non-cable set could receive. Nothing caught my interest. My eyes were heavy, but when I dozed, the sounds of the house and a strange claustrophobic dream startled me awake.

Strange dreams, dancing shadows, children's songs, shapes shifting and stretching like figures in a funhouse mirror, moved in and out of my mind. I finally left the chair and climbed the stairs to bed. Once under the quilts, footstep-like noises sounded downstairs. I tried to ignore them, but images of dead Ben and nearly dead Aunt Elizabeth materialized.

Outside, the wind swirled around the house and tree branches knocked on the walls.

Across the street, the figure in the black slicker watches.

How long will she stay in Elizabeth's house? Or in Pawhuska? Will terror take over so that she leaves it all behind? Will there be a chance to take the revenge that is so tempting?

The figure stands there late into the night, watching, waiting, dreaming.

Chapter 12

Wednesday, April 3—Afternoon

By mid-afternoon Wednesday, Elizabeth still lay quietly in a coma. I had spent hours by her side, reading aloud and talking. My hopes were dimming. At 3:00 PM, someone knocked on the doorframe to her hospital room. The woman was the first person in a procession of people who came to see their friend as the afternoon passed.

One by one, they shook my hand, handed me a card or some flowers, and then paused to look at Elizabeth. They patted the bed or her hand, said a few words to her, and then moved out.

"Your aunt is a fine woman. Not ready to lose her."

"Our prayers are with your family."

"Hoping for a speedy recovery."

A few people recalled my childhood visits, but none of their faces seemed familiar. They were the ones who offered to bring food over to the house for me. I invited them to stay to share it when they came.

Late in the afternoon, just as I was thinking about heading back to Aunt Elizabeth's house, a familiar figure appeared in the doorway.

"Any change, Jamie?" Sam Mazie stepped in to stand beside me. Sorrow filled his warm, wide brown eyes and hung on his handsome face. His black hair, wind-tossed and long, hung over his collar. His brown skin suggested Native American ancestry, and here in Pawhuska, I knew it was most likely Osage.

I remembered we had played with Osage children during our summer visits. They came over with their parents, and often, someone's mother or father or even Elizabeth would tell Osage creation legends and animal stories. Had Sam been one of those children?

He stepped close and enveloped my cold hands in his warm ones. "I am your aunt's attorney, but my family has long been friends with your aunt. I hope you'll think of me as a friend." His eyes held mine for a few seconds and then flickered over to my aunt.

"Some people are bringing supper over a little later. Will you come?"

His warm look eased any suspicion I might have harbored that he was the one who had tried to suffocate my aunt. My skin tingled when he said, "I'll be there."

He stood beside the bed for a few minutes, stroking Elizabeth's hands and watching her face. When he walked out, his eyes glowed with emotion. It became very important that he join me for supper.

An hour later, I wandered in a trance through the house, waiting for people to arrive. I found a dark green tablecloth in the linen closet and threw it over the walnut table. I lit the tall candles in the silver candelabra on the buffet, heated water for tea, and set out the silver tea service.

Clouds were hanging low in the late-afternoon sky when the doorbell finally rang. The opening door pulled in the scent of familiar cologne. Mayor Wells slipped one arm around me and pulled me into a quick hug. His other hand was enclosed in a large oven mitt and held a covered casserole dish.

"Hearty green bean casserole with bacon and almonds. My family wants to welcome you to Pawhuska. And to wish Elizabeth a speedy recovery." I stepped quickly away to the kitchen, and Wells followed.

"Is your family joining us tonight?" I motioned for him to set the dish on the kitchen table, where I had placed all the hot pads I could find, as well as potholders and folded towels.

"My wife is ill," he said. "She sends greetings."

The doorbell rang again. "Excuse me," I said and slipped out of the kitchen. I didn't trust the mayor. In the language of my teenage years, he was a creep.

When I opened the front door, a pair of women strode past carrying a large box. They walked straight to the kitchen and hung their coats on the wall hooks next to the pantry. Then they opened a drawer and pulled out serving spoons and ladles. I didn't remember either of them from the hospital, but somehow they had heard about tonight's impromptu dinner.

"I'm Jamie Aldrich, Elizabeth's great-niece. Could you tell me your names?" I leaned back against the kitchen sink.

"I'm Vera Peters."

She looked to be about my age, thin, with layered shoulder-length reddish-brown hair and skin that had seen too much sun for too many years. Dark eyes peered out of deep eye sockets on either side of a sharp nose.

"And I'm Trudy O'Day."

This middle-aged woman's blanched face had an unbalanced, unfinished look. Fine lines spider-webbed out from the corners of her eyes to meet straight chin-length salt-and-pepper hair. Splayed green eyes skimmed the world in nearly opposite directions. A sharp, high cheekbone on the right side was mated with a low, sunken cheek on the left, where a dent punctuated her jawbone.

Vera lifted a stack of plates out of the cupboard and set them on the counter, while Trudy pulled a pitcher from a shelf to the right of the sink.

They worked in silence, and I struggled to think of something to say. Being at a loss for words was unusual for me, but then, this situation wasn't usual. "My family came to see my great-aunt often when I was a child," I finally said into the silence. "Elizabeth and I have always been close."

Trudy pulled some glasses out of the cupboard, but Vera stopped and looked at me. "Close? When was your last visit?" The edge to her voice made me squirm.

"We talked nearly every week on the phone."

The look passing between them seemed to indicate they knew it had been thirty years since I was here last.

Another knock at the front door drew me out to the hall. When I opened the door, Sam Mazie smoothed his wind-whipped hair.

"Others are already here?" he asked quietly, holding two foil-covered pie plates stacked on top of each other. "I'd hoped we'd have a few moments to talk privately."

"There are a few people in the kitchen." I looked up into brown eyes, deep like Ben's. Something moved in the pit of my stomach. "I appreciate everyone bringing food." My throat clogged up, and I blinked to keep the tears at bay. "Hunger isn't my first priority, though; it's getting Elizabeth well again."

Sam was the only person I'd seen all day who looked as worried as I felt. I turned to lead the way into the kitchen.

He touched my arm with his fingertips. "I am so sorry. You weren't at all prepared for something like this to happen. All you wanted was a good visit."

"I haven't been to her home in a really long time."

Sam stepped closer, but when Mayor Wells's voice boomed from the kitchen doorway, Sam moved away.

"So, Sam, the noble brave, did you bring something to drink? I don't know if Mrs. Aldrich has anything to offer you. I hope not; he sure gets ugly when he's sauced!" Martin Wells's stage whisper could probably be heard by anyone in the front part of the house.

The muscles in Sam's jaw quivered. "You belittle yourself when you belittle others," he said.

"Aw. The philosopher!" Wells's eyes widened. "Another side to the ever-changing Sam Mazie, token Osage full-blood."

The two men glared at each other. The tension hung like heavy drapes. I tried to think of something to say but came up short. Clearly, this battle was not new to either of them.

"He reinvents himself every few years, dear," the mayor sneered.

Sam folded his hands together and smiled; the anger dropped off his face.

Another knock came at the door.

Police Chief Green and two elderly couples who had visited the hospital that afternoon filed into the house through the open door. The group carried their food—salads, vegetables, and a cake—into the kitchen, and I trailed behind them as far as the doorway. In the kitchen, people circulated through the buffet Vera and Trudy had set up and then moved on with full plates into the dining room and the parlor.

I answered the door again, letting a few more people—and food dishes—into the house. One of them, a middle-aged man with a cleric's collar, introduced himself as Father Bertrand. "This weather is certainly typical for early April," Father Bertrand said from the door to the dining room. "Uncertain."

I let him assume the role of host, and small talk carried the group through dinner.

I picked at the food. Even my taste buds were too tired to enjoy the home-cooked dishes. Voices buzzed in the background; I felt like heavy fog surrounded me. I got up and walked from the dining room into the parlor, where people stood eating or sat with plates in their laps.

These people had been Elizabeth's friends. Had she told them she wanted to die? Did any of them know the secret Elizabeth had wanted to share with me?

I looked up and caught Police Chief Green watching me. He

glanced away. Minutes later, I saw him studying Sam Mazie. Sam talked quietly to a few of the visitors but mostly kept to himself.

After the meal, Vera and Trudy took charge of the kitchen again. I stood in the hallway, accepting another round of well wishes for Elizabeth as her friends left. A few of them shared quick stories about Elizabeth or a summer memory of me or my family. When the last of them was gone, I went back to the kitchen.

Vera pulled on her coat. "Be careful," she whispered. "It's really not safe in this house."

I stared after her as she led Trudy out of the kitchen and down the front hall.

Chapter 13

Wednesday, April 3—Evening

Chief Green hung around until everyone else had gone. He didn't try to make conversation, and he didn't sit down. He paced or stared out the kitchen window into the backyard. Finally, when the elderly couple who lived across the street and two doors down had left, he glided through the front hallway to the front door, where I stood braced against the door frame. My body felt so heavy, I was ready for the day to end.

"I'll be in touch, Mrs. Aldrich," he said. Then he walked down the front steps to his patrol car.

I stepped out onto the porch.

Cold, damp air swirled around the yard. The police chief's taillights disappeared. Above, stars glittered like shimmering sequins thrown haphazardly onto a black velvet drape.

Sam Mazie's face and those dark sorrowful eyes filled my mind when I tried to empty it. He had been the only one who seemed to know how worried I was about Elizabeth. I had wanted to talk to him before he left, but the opportunity never came. He slipped out sometime before Vera and Trudy.

I had connected with Sam, and I felt certain I would see him again, especially if arrangements had to be made for Elizabeth's future care. Many things still had to happen before I could head home, including the conclusion of Chief Green's investigation. My throat constricted. What if Green tormented me like the Las Vegas police chief had when Ben died? The thought made me feel trapped, even here in the open yard.

A raspy, garbled whisper, like I had heard in the house when I'd left Aunt Elizabeth upstairs alone, cut through the quiet night. I whirled in a half circle, peering into deep shadows all around the house and under the trees. A light breeze ruffled my hair.

"Is anybody there?"

New leaves stroked each other, whispering.

Did Chief Green have someone watching the house?

I hurried up the front steps. With a snap, the old wood board of the second step split beneath my weight, and my right foot twisted and went through the crack. I grabbed the railing, struggling to keep my balance, and pulled my foot back through the broken board.

"Damn it! Damn, damn, damn!" I cried when I tried to climb another step. My ankle was sprained or at least certainly bruised. I limped the rest of the way into the house.

What else could happen?

"It's not safe," Vera had said.

Apparently not. The house was full of hidden hazards. Maybe tomorrow I would check out the local motels. Even better, maybe I'd go home. I'd tell Green he could reach me in New Mexico. They could find their own evidence. They had my side of the story. And Elizabeth could take her time recovering. I'd come back once she regained consciousness and was ready to either go home or move into assisted living.

I put away the dinner dishes Vera and Trudy had washed and dried, prepared an ice pack for my ankle, checked all the doors, and then hobbled up the backstairs to the bedroom.

Once under the quilt, the faces of the people who had come over for supper crowded my mind. I found myself imagining each of them holding the pillow over Elizabeth's mouth and nose.

Which one of them could have held the pillow snugly as

she struggled—held it tight, relaxing the hold just as her lungs were ready to make that last shuddering gasp for air?

Which one of them could have waited for the right opportunity and then slipped out of the house, unseen?

I reviewed what I knew about each person—name and face, small bits of information gleaned during the evening's conversations. Not much to go on. They all knew each other. I was the stranger. Over tonight's dinner, they had not talked about work or dredged up family history. I had let the words wash over me and let Father Bertrand guide the conversation into non-confrontational channels. I'd missed a great opportunity to find out more about these so-called friends of my aunt.

I tossed from side to side and got tangled in the sheets. Somewhere in the house, floorboards creaked and whispers rose and fell. I told myself it was just the wind, howling around the house, and the house was creaking in response.

The streetlights blinked out as a strong gust rattled the window. My contact lenses were in the case in the bathroom, and my glasses were on the nightstand; the room became a blurry darkness. I reached for the bedside lamp and turned the switch. The light bulb stayed dark. I huddled in bed—an ice pack on my ankle, blankets pulled up to my chin, and eyes clamped shut—trying unsuccessfully to fall sleep.

Scraping noises wafted up the front stair. Cabinet doors squeaked open and banged shut. Drawers scraped open and then screeched shut.

Wind didn't make those kinds of noises.

I groped for my glasses but didn't feel them. Were they on the dresser? I started to climb out of bed to retrieve them, but remembered the floorboards squeaked. If someone was downstairs, that person would know I was upstairs and awake. But then, the front staircase began to creak and groan as someone—or something—climbed the stairs.

I slid off the side of the tall four-poster bed to crouch

beside the bed on the rug. The creaks continued; "it" neared the second floor.

I huddled partially under the bed frame. The force of the gale outside rattled the window panes.

Then, silence spread from the landing into the bedroom.

An off-key humming began. It sounded like "Take Me Out to the Ballgame."

The humming faded away.

"*Whooah?* Anyone here?" a voice bellowed.

My right shoulder crashed into the bed frame. "Ouch!"

Feet clomped into the room. I struggled to stand and then leaped for my flashlight on the dresser. When I swung it at the blurry form crossing the room, the metal casing connected with bone. The shape staggered back. Several objects fell to the wooden floor and rolled.

The intruder groaned and leaned onto the bed's footboard.

I flicked on the flashlight and aimed it like a gun. Once again, I felt for my glasses on the nightstand. This time I found them. I thrust them onto my face, and the spotlighted figure came into focus.

Chin-length salt-and-pepper hair framed a white face. The woman I had met earlier, Trudy O'Day, rubbed her jaw and shifted her weight from leg to leg.

"*What are you doing here?*" I wailed.

She shrank toward the doorway, her look jerking from floor to ceiling. "It's me, Trudy. The lights are out. You don't know where nothin' is. You need the candles."

I swung the light down to the floor, and the wide beam illuminated candlesticks strewn across the floor.

"How the hell did you get in?"

"I clean for My Liz sometimes." Trudy's gaze darted down to the rag rug beneath her feet and stayed there. She rubbed at her jaw again. "Didn't mean to scare you." Trudy grinned crookedly. "I knocked."

"Why didn't you wait until I came down to answer the door?

Why didn't you call out as you came in? If you have a key, let me have it—now."

Trudy fished around in the pocket of her blue-and-white striped overalls and then handed me a shiny house key. "Just 'cause I can't sleep when the wind is growling around don't mean other people are up. I know that." She nodded and then turned away, her hands clasped.

My heart rate slowed. She was Aunt Elizabeth's friend. Maybe she'd seen something that day; maybe she'd been here herself. Maybe she was the one who had made Elizabeth's lunch and cleaned up the kitchen. "Wait!"

"Yeah?" Trudy jammed both hands down into the tool pockets of the bib overalls.

My mind raced. "You can go ahead and clean the house while I'm here. Elizabeth will be back."

Trudy looked directly at me with one eye and nodded. "Sure."

"Tomorrow morning? Nine o'clock? I'm sure Elizabeth appreciates everything you do for her."

Trudy's jaw clamped shut.

After the front door clicked shut behind her, I limped down the stairs and jammed the deadbolt into place. By the faint light of the moon, I pulled a chair from the dining room and hooked it under the doorknob. Then I repeated the process with the kitchen door. Outside, the cold spring wind whined to come in.

I crawled back into bed. My mind still churned.

Had Trudy listened to Elizabeth's ravings on Monday and then tried to help her die, taking the locket to remember her by?

From the shadows of the old elm tree across the street, the figure in the black slicker watches. The tree limbs lash back and forth, and the wind whips the slicker's hood.

The other one has left, and the house is black again. She has, no doubt, locked all the doors. Lot of good it will do to lock the doors in that old house.

Fingers rattle a ring of keys in the slicker's front pocket.
So lovely, for just a while longer. Then it will all have to end.
How will it play out? Will she figure it out before it is finished?
She will need to be kept preoccupied.
Drag it out.
A little longer.

Chapter 14

Thursday, April 4—Morning

I chose my path to the door carefully, stepping over a dozen candles scattered across the floor of the bedroom and the upstairs hall. My foot throbbed, and so did my shoulder and my arm.

Here was the evidence last night had not been a bad dream. The thing was, in the morning light, the electric outage didn't seem a good enough excuse for Trudy to have come into the house uninvited. But if that wasn't the reason, what was?

I shuffled down the stairs and into the dining room. Trudy had to know this house forwards and backwards. She had either brought the candles with her, or she knew where the candles were kept. But she'd been opening drawers and cabinets. What had she been searching for? Nothing seemed out of place, but how would I know if anything was missing?

The china cabinet, walnut table, eight chairs, and sideboard had been here when I'd visited as a child. The same grouping of small botanical prints hung on the papered walls, and the same old gilt-framed mirror graced the wall above the sideboard. The crystal chandelier shimmered as it had back then, with dozens of crystal pendants ready to tinkle in the slightest breeze. The scuffed dining room floor needed a good buffing and polish, but nothing seemed out of the ordinary.

Pockets of lacy spider webs caught the morning sunlight from the corners of the upper bay window. I could picture my family circled around the table for Thanksgiving dinner. Great-Aunt Elizabeth, dressed in rich colors and wearing a red shawl over her shoulders, lifted her glass and offered a toast. I had my first taste of red wine right here.

I limped back to the front hall, pulled the chair away from the door, and eased out onto the veranda into the moist, cool spring air. The jagged board left a wide hole in the second step. With all those people coming and going last night, why was I the one who had broken through the board?

A long white florist's box with a bright purple bow balanced on the veranda railing.

When I picked it up, something inside rustled and shifted. At the porch swing, I set it down in my lap, pulled the bow loose and worked the lid off with my left hand.

The box and its contents crashed to the floor as I screamed and leapt away. Black widow spiders—red hour-glasses shining from plump abdomens—and hundreds of baby spiders crawled over a dozen shriveled long-stemmed roses. A note with words written in thick black pen strokes fluttered out of the box and lay on the porch: *Black widows run in your family?*

Little spiders scurried out of the box and raced across the face of the note. I lunged toward the front door, my skin quivering as imaginary spiders crawled up my legs and arms.

Suddenly, Trudy was beside me. "What's wrong?"

I tried to contain my shivers. Spiders swarmed over the porch boards.

"Lord have mercy!" Trudy cried. She stomped on the spiders, arms flailing.

I inched toward the front door, hugging my injured arm close to my body.

"Where'd they come from?" Trudy's horror-tinged voice echoed my thoughts. She continued to stomp on the boards.

"The box—on the railing." I looked back at her from the relative safety of the front doorway.

Trudy peered down at the note that had tumbled out of the

box with the dead flowers. She stopped stomping. "Not again," she whispered. Abruptly, she pushed past me and into the house. "I'll get the broom."

Slowly, the sensation of spiders crawling up my legs eased.

Trudy hustled back out of the house with a broom in one hand. With one hard sweep, the box and dead roses sailed over the edge of the porch and into the front yard. She picked the note up by one corner, checked both sides, and held it out to me.

"You want it?"

I took hold of one corner. The note was written in the same bold black writing as was on the chamois. I limped into the house. The broom swished as Trudy swept the porch over and over again.

In the kitchen, I stashed the note behind the napkin holder on the kitchen counter. Damn spiders. I couldn't deny I had always had a real phobia about them. I knew better than to let my students get wind of it. I cringed, imagining the pranks I was in for if word got out. Lord help me if Trey Woodard, my "favorite" junior, ever knew. He was no doubt saving his worst tricks for his senior year.

A loud banging began out on the front porch. Trudy must have spotted another spider.

Not again, she'd whispered. How had she known about the other message, the one on the ragged chamois I'd tucked under the sink?

My hand shook as I poured a glass of water. Then I went into the dining room and eased down into a side chair at the table. Four days. In that short time, my aunt had nearly been murdered, the front window had been broken by a rock, I'd made an emergency trip to the hospital and sprained my ankle, and now someone had made a second nasty insinuation, delivered with an even nastier present. Even an idiot would pack her suitcase and get out of here. The motel was looking better all the time.

Footsteps stomped down the hall and then stopped in the dining room doorway behind me.

I looked over at Trudy. "Thanks for cleaning up that mess." I took a long sip of water as questions rolled around in my mind. "This sort of thing ever happen before?"

One of Trudy's turned-outward eyes roamed over my face. Her mouth dipped into a frown. "No," she whispered. "No spiders." Trudy bustled into the room, pulled a cloth napkin from one of the drawers in the buffet, and placed it between my glass and the walnut table top. "My Liz wouldn't like that," she scolded.

"Thanks," I mumbled. I sipped the water. *No spiders.* And *My Liz?* No one I knew had ever called Aunt Elizabeth by that name.

Trudy clasped her hands together and twiddled her thumbs 'round and 'round.

"When you were down here last night, what were you looking for?" I had others questions, too, but first things first.

Trudy sidled over to the china cabinet and began to open drawers and cabinets, one after the other. She hummed a few bars of "Take Me Out to the Ballgame."

My skin crawled.

"Jasper gave her this," Trudy said, as she pulled out a "bluebird of happiness" and stroked the smooth, deep-blue glass bird with one finger.

"Who's Jasper?"

"My daddy, Jasper." Trudy smiled crookedly as she fingered the bird. Her smile faded. "He's dead."

"I'm sorry." The words were a reflex and pointless in the face of grief. I'd heard them often enough myself.

Trudy's frown deepened. Her eyes swam with tears, and her lips trembled. She turned away and moved to the parlor doorway, head down. As much as I wanted to ask more about Jasper and about Trudy and about the spiders and the dead flowers, this didn't seem to be a good time.

I carried my empty glass and limped back to the kitchen, leaving Trudy alone. In a minute, she followed.

"Trudy, can you help me find some of Elizabeth's supplies? Otherwise, I'll need to pick up a few things to make some repairs."

"What're you lookin' for?" Trudy sniffed and then wiped her nose with the back of her hand.

"A hammer and some nails. Some cleanser and rags."

"Out on the mud porch, in the cabinets," Trudy said, nodding toward the old porch jutting out from the kitchen on the north side of the house.

The mudroom. Of course.

I followed Trudy down two steps and out into the small room. The familiar, comforting smells of leather, shoe polish, and lubricants lingered in the air.

Plastic sheeting, secured over the screen windows, snapped with the wind and rustled and popped. This plastic might explain the creepy night noises keeping me awake.

Rag rugs concealed the concrete floor at one end of the narrow room. A clutter of clay pots, jars, worn-out shoes, and old metal machine parts covered the tabletops and floor.

Steel cabinets and wood worktables lined the wall. Trudy opened the doors of the first cabinet. I peeked inside. A variety of household cleansers, detergents, and polishes sat neatly in rows.

In the second cabinet, Trudy pulled a red tool chest from the bottom shelf and waved her hand toward shelves covered by tools as well as painting and wallpapering supplies, including three rolls of gray duct tape.

"Elizabeth kept everything well stocked," I observed.

Trudy's face relaxed as she smiled. "Jasper did. Then I did after he died."

Jasper, her dad, must have been in charge of property maintenance. Judging from the outside of the house, he had been dead for a while. Trudy had kept up with the supply inventory, but the exterior fix-it labor had not been replaced.

"Thanks, Trudy." Everything I needed was here. With my

arm in a sling, though, most of the work would have to wait a few days. I stepped back up into the kitchen.

"I might as well get some work done while I'm here. Things always need dusting," Trudy muttered behind me as she gathered cleaning supplies and rags into a plastic bucket.

With a straw broom, I made a final one-armed sweep of the front porch siding and window sills. There was no sign of any black widow spiders, but I still felt as if they were crawling on me.

Black widow. Elizabeth had buried three husbands. Did the note writer also know my second husband had recently died? Who in this town would even care?

When I stepped back into the entry hall, I expected to hear the sound of Trudy's humming, scrubbing, or sweeping. Instead, the house was silent.

"Trudy?"

I climbed the front stairs and called again. No response. When I passed the alcove off the second-floor landing, I saw the door to the attic was ajar.

Air squeezed from my lungs as I stared up the narrow stairway to the cluttered attic. Spiders loved attics and dark places. I didn't. But enough, already. I gritted my teeth, dashed into the bedroom, grabbed the flashlight, and started up the creaky stairs.

From the attic doorway, I could hear someone whistling "Do You Know the Muffin Man?" at the far end of the attic. It had to be Trudy. And the fact she was whistling the tune here in this house probably meant Elizabeth had played the "goody game" in the pantry with her, too.

The attic ran the length of the house with round circular windows at each end. Cobwebs hung thick. Dust swirled in the stale air. I sneezed.

The whistling stopped.

Sunlight filtered down from the windows and threw

shadows. My trembling hand caused the flashlight beam to jerk as it moved over the rafters.

"Trudy?"

Piles of boxes, furniture, trunks, and cloth-covered shapes left room for only a narrow aisle on either side of the long room. As I crept down one side of the attic, I played the flashlight beam over the piles, across the walls, and along the rafters. The light caught a fat eight-legged body scurrying across a web that stretched from box to roof rafter. I cringed and froze, waiting for the web to stop swinging and the spider to disappear. A small creature scurried across the narrow aisle.

My stomach clenched into a knot. This was ridiculous. I was an adult and a biologist. This was just an attic. I was fifty times as big as anything living here.

I reached the far end of the attic and started back down the other side. Why had Trudy come up here?

Something scraped behind me, and I turned. A sunbeam passing through the circular window spotlighted Trudy peering into a large box.

"Trudy?" I stepped around an old birdcage. "What are you doing?"

Trudy was engrossed in the box. Photographs, bundles of letters, and photo albums lay scattered around her on the floor. She held a picture up to the light. As I came even with her, I saw it was a picture of a couple—a pretty dark-haired woman wearing an over-the-knee sleeveless dress, and a smiling man in a plaid jacket. They had posed in front of a shiny green 1950s Chevy.

"Someone you know?"

Trudy hugged the picture to her chest. "That's Nancy and Jasper, my mom and dad."

In the picture, the couple stood posed in front of Elizabeth's house. The man's face had a kind, childlike quality. The woman had a cute pixie face.

"My Liz kept this in the study on the mantel in a gold frame.

Last year, she took the frame off and brought the picture up here. We'd get this whole box out when the weather was too bad to leave the house. She'd tell stories and we'd laugh. Sometimes we'd cry."

I helped her return the clutter of memorabilia to the box. One scrapbook fell open to faded snapshots of people wearing the clothing, haircuts, and eyeglasses popular in the decade when I grew up. One photo caught children by a backstop, with baseball bat and mitts. I easily picked myself out wearing glasses and shorts. Ellen and Randy and six other children completed the team. I slid the photo out of the album.

"Trudy, do you know who all these kids were?" I flipped the picture over. Someone had written the date in ballpoint pen.

"Some of 'em." Trudy took the album from me, closed it, and stowed it back in the box. Still clutching the photograph of her parents, she hurried away.

"Trudy, wait." I moved quickly after her.

Downstairs, the phone was ringing.

By the time I could make my way back down to the bottom floor, the kitchen screen door had slammed, and Trudy was gone.

The phone stopped ringing.

Chapter 15

Thursday, April 4—Late Morning

Sitting at the kitchen table, I studied the picture. Nine kids, ranging in height and age, enough for a baseball team. My brother and sister, five other little boys, one other girl. Who were they? Trudy probably knew.

The phone rang again in the front hall.

"You didn't call me," my mother whined from four hundred miles away. "What's happened? When are you coming home?"

I described the visiting friends and the following supper but didn't tell her about the cracked window, the incident in the garage, the spiders in the roses, or the notes. Anxiety would set in. She couldn't do anything from New Mexico, and I didn't want her here.

"How are Allison and Matt?" I countered. "Everything okay?"

I felt a void in my stomach as my mother filled me in on my children's activities. I was disconnected from the two people I cared about most: my children. I wanted to be with my daughter, helping her make plans for the events to come in autumn. And I wanted Matt to fill me in on every single day at the new job.

I was missing out. My cell phone battery had died yesterday, before I'd had time to call the kids, and I kept forgetting to go out to the car to charge it. If I stayed here much longer, I would have to buy a home charging unit. I wasn't even sure a cell phone store existed in Pawhuska.

"Is Elizabeth's house falling down around your ears? Does the heater work? You can't possibly clean that big house all by yourself." My mother started in on a long list of possible difficulties I didn't even want to contemplate.

"The house isn't falling down," I snapped. Mother didn't know the worst of it, and I didn't need her negative attitude. I tried my hardest to keep the bite out of my voice. "So far the heater has been fine," I said in a much sweeter tone. "There is a woman, Trudy O'Day, who has offered to help with cleaning. She said her father was Elizabeth's handyman."

"O'Day? You said Trudy O'Day? Her father. What's his name?" Mother's voice sounded pinched and wary.

"Jasper. And his wife was Nancy."

"Jasper!" Mother gasped. "I haven't thought of him in years. And Trudy ... she's still there. I had no idea." Her voice had an almost hysterical edge.

"No idea of what, Mother?"

"That she was still ... You don't remember." Her heavy sigh sounded like an accusation.

"Remember what? Mom, who was Jasper and why should I remember him or Trudy?" Even I could hear the irritation in my voice, but I couldn't smooth it out. I didn't need more drama today; I needed whatever information Mom could give me.

"Your grandma's maiden name—and Elizabeth's maiden name—was O'Day."

I knew the name had sounded familiar. But no one had referred to my grandmother or my great-aunt as an O'Day in a long time.

"So Elizabeth and Jasper were related," I said. "Cousins?"

"Do you remember playing in the little cottage out back?"

I had looked out at the cottage earlier and felt no memories, no emotions. Now my mind flashed a confused, shadowy picture, and I could faintly remember the sound of muffled crying. "We were ... forbidden to play back there," I said slowly, unsure where this memory came from. I chewed on one finger. "What does this have to do with Trudy and her father?"

"That was their home. Elizabeth didn't want you kids to play with Trudy."

"Why?"

"She was a frail little thing. Let's not go into it. We've all let it go. It was just an accident."

An accident? This was my life history, and I needed to know. I didn't want to let it go. "What happened? And who was Jasper?"

"Jasper was your great-uncle, your grandmother's—and Elizabeth's—younger brother. You and Ben were on vacation or something when he died. I didn't see a need to bother you at the time. Wasn't sure you'd remember him anyway. Guess I was right about that."

My great-uncle. How could I not know Elizabeth had a brother? Where had he been all those summers? And why had he and his family never come to family gatherings in New Mexico? Apparently, I didn't know or remember a huge part of my past.

"Mom, you never told me anything about him."

"He was retarded, honey."

I sucked in a quick breath. Even now, Mother was ashamed. Had Elizabeth been ashamed too? Kept him away from all of us intentionally? Was Jasper part of the "truth" Elizabeth had wanted to tell me?

Then it struck me. If Jasper was Elizabeth's brother, Trudy was Elizabeth's niece and my mother's first cousin. Aunt Elizabeth had family living in Pawhuska after all.

I was emotionally wrung out by the time I hung up the phone. Emotions buffeted my brain—sorrow, guilt, regret, and even anger. And I wanted—needed—more than anything to talk to my children. I wanted their normalcy, their openness—

all the things I had never been able to find in conversations with my own mother.

I went out to my car with my phone, turned on the engine, and let the phone charge for fifteen minutes while I waited to place a three-way call.

Allison and then Matt answered their cell phones. I quickly filled them in on what was happening in Pawhuska and then asked about every little detail of what was going on in their lives. When they asked more questions about Elizabeth and what would happen next, I couldn't offer details. Matt's biggest concern was that I had forgotten to bring my cell phone charger. And there was no answering machine at Elizabeth's home. Those were the least of my worries.

When the conversations were finished and my throat dry and scratchy, I limped back into the house, stopping in the kitchen before venturing out to the front veranda, where I settled onto the porch swing with a glass of lemonade and the old picture of the baseball team.

My eyelids grew heavy in the warm noonday sun, and I stretched and relaxed like a cat on a comfy cushion. A puffy robin raced across the brown lawn, stopped, bobbed his head down to the grass, and jerked up a fat worm. I pushed against the veranda floor with my good foot and made the wooden porch swing move.

I couldn't go home until Elizabeth had a firm prognosis. And then, there were the questions about who had tried to kill her and who was leaving those nasty notes. But I felt most concerned about an entirely different subject: why had the family kept Jasper and his family secret?

Trudy was much, much more than my aunt's housekeeper. Elizabeth had relied on Trudy daily, and Trudy had relied on her. They had a mutually beneficial relationship. I wasn't sure what Trudy's mental capacity was. If Jasper had been—as Mother said—"retarded," was Trudy mentally challenged, too?

What would happen to her if Elizabeth moved to an assisted living center?

A black-and-white squad car pulled over to the curb and Police Chief Green climbed out. He strode up the sidewalk and onto the porch. "Someone slid this under my office door this morning. Look familiar?" Toby Green handed me a slip of paper.

Black widows run in your family?

I handed the note back to him. "Did it come with spiders?" A shiver inched up my spine.

"Any idea what it might mean?"

I shrugged. "Black widows? What does that phrase have to do with me or Aunt Elizabeth?" I met his gaze.

"Elizabeth was a widow."

"Elizabeth didn't kill her husbands."

"And does the implication mean anything specific to you?" he asked.

A heavy, cold anger filled my chest.

"You said your husband died at home," Green continued. "Was there an investigation?"

I had endured weeks of horrible, constant questions from Police Chief Clay in Las Vegas. Now it was starting again. And I suspected Green knew the answer to the question before he asked.

"My sources tell me there *was* an investigation." He watched me closely. I knew he was seeing my chest heave and the uncertainty in my eyes. "Your aunt received lots of notes like this one. It's been going on for years."

I felt my eyes widen.

"In fact," the chief continued, "somewhere in the house there's probably a whole box full of notes like this. Sometimes duplicates were sent to our office. Like anonymous tips. We didn't feel they warranted an investigation. However, it might be worth your time to find them and read them."

Green noticed the old baseball team photo beside me on the

porch swing. Then he stepped across the veranda and down the sidewalk to his black-and-white.

When he'd looked at the photo, something seemed familiar about the tilt of his head, his smile, and even his eyes. He didn't remind me of anyone in particular, yet there was something ...

I didn't sense the same antagonism of Chief Clay in Las Vegas. Yet this man wasn't being completely open with me. No one was.

Chapter 16

Thursday, April 4—Afternoon

The telephone rang inside the house.

"Mrs. Aldrich? This is Sherry at the law office. Would you be available at three o'clock for a meeting with Mr. Mazie?"

After I agreed to come, the secretary gave an address and hung up.

The discussion had to be about Aunt Elizabeth, the first of many conversations about her future care. It seemed premature, and I felt angry with Sam. Was he anticipating her death?

He had been in the house. I didn't like where my thoughts were going.

Elizabeth was in the hospital, still in a coma, but yesterday evening the nurses had reported some movement. A visit to her was on my morning agenda, and I was hopeful—very hopeful—that when I arrived, her eyes would be open and her mind functioning.

The man from the window repair shop was due any minute to provide an estimate. Finding someone to repair the front step was next. Then, I wondered about the heating and air systems. And even the roof.

I pulled out the Pawhuska phone book and searched the Yellow Pages for entries under "carpentry," "heat and air," and "roofing." There were a few vendors in Bartlesville, but none listed for Pawhuska.

After the window repairman arrived and took the needed measurements, I left for the hospital. I needed to see Elizabeth, to talk to her. If Sam and I were going to discuss how to handle her care and maybe even her death, I needed to reinforce my personal belief that she was not going to die now. In the future, sure, but not now. She and I still had much to talk about.

At the hospital, Elizabeth showed no change. As time passed without her regaining consciousness, it became less and less likely she would ever wake up. I held her hand and talked to her about anything I could think of—Ben, my daughter, my son, and finally, my grief.

Her expression didn't change. Her body didn't move.

The sign outside the building read only "Law Offices." When I entered, the receptionist gestured toward a door at the end of a short, carpeted hallway. Inside the oak-paneled conference room, Vera Peters sat in a cushioned armchair at a long table. I stepped into the quiet room and skirted the table to sit opposite Vera. We nodded at each other, but the wide table in the paneled room didn't encourage conversation. When the door opened again, Trudy walked in. Eyes downcast, she scooted around the table to sit beside Vera.

Sam Mazie slipped in next, dressed in a dark blue suit but without a tie. His sky-blue shirt was open at the throat, giving him an easygoing appearance that contrasted with his intense dark eyes. Our eyes met, and my stomach quivered as his eyes held mine.

"Thank you all for coming." Sam Mazie's look swept across to Vera and Trudy. "I asked you ladies here today because every one of you has a stake in Elizabeth's well-being. She prepared instructions about what to do if she ever fell into a coma or was unresponsive. I have a copy of her living will. And she has designated certain things that should happen, should she be unable to manage her affairs or make end-of-life decisions. After discussing her condition with her doctor, I saw no reason to delay sharing these documents with the three of you."

I sat up straighter, watching Sam as he slid into a seat at the end of the table and then laid a thin black binder on the polished table.

"Elizabeth specifically requested each of you be here today so you could personally hear her requests. This living will is signed and dated two years ago on December 14, properly executed as required by Oklahoma law, as is a DNR, durable power of attorney, and other documents specifying medical treatment to be provided under certain conditions.

"I, Elizabeth Graham, being of sound mind, do ..." Various statements of legalese followed, and then Sam got to the real purpose of the meeting. He continued reading. "Upon my death or incapacitation, I request that Vera Peters be sold, for the price of one dollar, my Edsel, in the garage on my property. To my dear Trudy O'Day, I request that the cottage, all the contents therein, and land twenty feet from the foundations of the cottage in all four cardinal directions, be sold to her for the cost of one dollar. She may continue to live in or dispose of the cottage as she sees fit. A trust to cover maintenance costs, taxes, and other expenses has been established in her name. To my great-niece Jamie Aldrich, I request that the house at 814 Oak Street and all the contents therein, the remaining acreage, and outbuildings be sold to her for the sum of one dollar. A trust account to cover maintenance costs, taxes, and other expenses has been established in her name."

Trudy sniffed. I sat stunned. Elizabeth planned to leave me the house? I couldn't live here. I had tried several times to tell her about my fear of the place, but I had never been able to actually do it. She had seemed to want me to keep away. She was happy to travel to me and to not carry on with "family" weeks at her place each summer. Never had I indicated any desire to leave New Mexico and live here.

"What follows is another caveat," Sam said. "'Should any of those so named elect not to purchase what I have bequeathed for one dollar, I direct my attorney, Sam Mazie, to sell said property. My only directive is that said buyer may not be either Simpson Haugland or Martin Wells, or any such friend or relative of either man.'"

So much for the statement Wells had made about family friendships.

"Finally, to Vera, Trudy, Jamie, and all my other nieces and nephews, Jamie's children, and the children of my other nieces and nephews, at this time I transfer my ownership by deed to the Bigheart property. Following my death, proceeds from the sale of the property are to be equally divided among them all. Sam Mazie shall serve as my personal representative during the sale.

"All the rest, residue and remainder, I trust to the care of my great-niece Jamie, trusting her to take care of all of my worldly goods. Let there be no misunderstanding that my intent is for Jamie Aldrich to manage my affairs and to speak for me in the event that I am unable to do so myself."

Sam closed the small binder with a snap. "This living will is legally binding. Mrs. Aldrich and I will meet with Elizabeth's physicians to determine the best care that can be provided for her, should she recover or should she remain in an unconscious state. You are welcome to let Jamie know your wishes, but the final decision will rest with her."

The responsibility worried me.

Vera and Trudy stood and hugged and then nodded across the table at me.

"My great-aunt loves both of you," I began. "I hope we can be friends."

Great-Aunt Elizabeth was not dead, but after reading the document, I felt as though she might as well be. Tears spilled out of my eyes. Vera came around the table to pat my left shoulder. Trudy followed slowly. When she reached me, she moved in close.

"I live in the cottage where my family has always lived, you know. Now it's mine, and the house is yours. We're neighbors."

I pulled a tissue from my purse and dabbed at my eyes. "Please come to the house as often as you like while I'm in town. I'll need your help, you know."

Trudy nodded. "I'll help you take care of the house." She frowned. "Will you let Sam sell it?"

"This is all so new to me, Trudy. You'll be the first to know my decision."

The wrinkle in Trudy's forehead didn't smooth out. The two women left Sam and me alone.

"I'm sure that was a surprise," Sam said. "I had hoped to give you a heads-up last night." His look moved across my face and stopped on my moist cheeks. He lifted one finger to touch my cheek and tucked my hair behind my ear. It was the most intimate touch I had felt since Ben became ill. Blood rushed to my face.

"There was no opportunity to tell me last night," I said. "One question. This Bigheart property you're supposed to sell. Where is it? And what was that bit about Haugland and Wells? No love lost there. I had a totally different impression from Mr. Wells."

"Wells will be angry when he gets the word she's already moving on distribution of her property. I'm sure he expected to be here alongside you today. Maybe a warning is in order. Be careful, Jamie," Sam said in a low voice as we walked out into the hallway.

"Tell me about the Bigheart property."

"It's the old homestead where James and Clara O'Day settled when they first married." Sam leaned against the wall. "They built a house on forty-five acres near the town of Bigheart, but nothing's there now."

"I'd like to see it."

"When I have a free afternoon, I'll run out there with you."

"I'm spending most afternoons with Elizabeth at the hospital, but if you can give me advance notice, I'll sit with her one morning instead."

He nodded. The discussion seemed to be over.

What I really wanted to do was sit down and go over all my questions about Elizabeth and the family history. Sam could tell me a lot.

Chapter 17

Thursday, April 4—Evening

A few minutes later, when I pulled my car into the driveway, I found Police Chief Green waiting in his patrol car in front of the house. As I parked, he strolled up to the veranda, hat in hand.

"You've been at Sam's," he said as I crossed the lawn to the steps.

Nothing escaped anybody in this town. I skirted the broken step and then unlocked the front door and moved into the study to switch on a lamp. "Elizabeth has a living will. She wanted property distributed before she died. She left me this house. Trudy has the cottage."

"What will you do with the house?" The chief stayed in the hallway.

My breath rushed out in a puff. "The house needs a lot of repairs. It hasn't gotten much attention since Jasper died." I stood, arms crossed, in the center of the study. I didn't really want to stay here to get the house ready to sell. But then, how long would it take Elizabeth to recover? If she recovered.

Green waited in the doorway. He rubbed his thumb back and forth over something furry and white in his palm. A rabbit's foot. "Did you know Elizabeth was ill?" His thumb caressed the fur as his keys jingled on an attached chain.

"I knew something was wrong, and I suspected she might be ill. She's ninety years old." The questions had started.

"She didn't explain further once you got here?"

"She didn't have time to tell me anything." I bit off my words.

"Interesting. As close as you say you were, she hadn't told you she had colon cancer and was signed up to receive Pawhuska Hospice next week."

I sucked in my breath. Toby Green jangled his keys and left without a good-bye.

The horsehair sofa was hard, but I didn't sit down for comfort. Elizabeth was dying. Her pain was probably unbearable. When she had said "Free me," she may have wanted to end her life. Maybe the rest—the insinuation of deep secrets— was the ravings of a sick woman, someone ready for the end to come.

The grinding of gears told me someone else had arrived. I glanced outside as an old blue Ford truck rolled up into the driveway. The window repairman I'd met earlier this afternoon lumbered up to the veranda. His bald pate shimmered in the afternoon sun; the red hair that rimmed it was tinged with gray. Instead of overalls, he now wore a jogging suit that showed off an average build and a roll of fat around his waist.

I met him at the door.

"I apologize for barging in on you again. Remember me? Bart Rourke, window repairs?" Warm, curious brown eyes surveyed my face.

"I remember you. Everything all right with the window order?"

A smile dug dimples in his wide cheeks. "They're going to pick up the window on Monday in Tulsa," he said. "I'll put it in as soon as it's here. Just wondered, though. I've been remodeling my own place. I'd like to offer my services. Thought you might need help." He nodded at the broken step.

I studied the repairman. After he had arrived, I'd left him alone to take outside measurements so I could visit Elizabeth. In spite of my intention to ask him about other local workmen, we hadn't had time to discuss any of the other projects around the house. He looked to be in good shape, although maybe a little overweight.

"I know your aunt. Sweet lady." A rosy color deepened in his cheeks. He cleared his throat. "I'm familiar with the house, and my house is about this same age. I noticed the front step when I was here earlier. Wouldn't take more than a day to make the repair. I'm only part time at the window shop, and I've got references."

"The step needs to be repaired," I agreed. "But if you're working on your own home, plus the other job, do you really have time for this?"

"I've got the time. And it would be an honor, really," the man said. "Consider it my way of helping Elizabeth one final time." He ran his fingers over some gouges around the strike plate of the front door. "Needs a little wood filler here. Locks working okay?" He rattled the doorknob and then pulled a screwdriver out of his pocket and tightened the screws in the strike plate and on the knob. "Lovely old houses do require a lot of upkeep. Bought mine about five years ago. I've been restoring the wood floor and returning the exterior to original colors."

He reached inside to run his fingers over the hinges and then used the handle end of the screwdriver to hammer a pin down into a hinge. I let him tinker with the other hinges and the doorknob.

"If you like my work on the front step, I'll be glad to help with anything else."

The step needed repair. He seemed the answer to an unspoken prayer.

"Okay. If you could just do the step for me, that would be a big help. How much would you charge?"

We negotiated the cost of the repair, and he promised to return with tools and supplies to begin the project Friday morning.

Later, I washed my soup bowl and placed it in the drainer next to the sink. Through the window, I watched low clouds in the eastern sky glow pink, then rose, and then purple as the sun set in the opposite direction. Not a leaf, branch, or twig moved. I leaned against the counter, watching the sky just beyond Trudy's little house.

Elizabeth should have told me she had cancer. Perhaps that was part of what she had been going to say when I left her to go downstairs.

My great-aunt probably *had* been asking for help with suicide—and for good reason.

It occurred to me that Toby Green had been testing me, watching to see if I was surprised by the revelation. Who had told Green that Elizabeth had cancer?

Elizabeth could have convinced someone else to help her end the pain. Whoever it was had already been in the house. My first guess was Trudy, but in the back of my head, I thought of Sam.

Something scratched at the back door. An even thumping drummed against the floor of the porch. Then came another scratch. I eased the door partially open.

A dog, low and chunky with short legs, long ears, and a whip-like tail, looked up at me. One dog parent had probably been mostly basset hound. The secondary doggy genes that resulted in a thick, curly black coat were harder to ID. Bright, intelligent brown eyes lacked the characteristic droop of a basset's. The dog lifted one big white paw and whined.

When I squatted down and extended my hand, the dog sniffed and then licked the tips of my fingers.

No collar. I checked the inside of its ears for ownership tattoos but the skin was pink and unmarred. "Who do you belong to?" I opened the door, and the dog trotted into the kitchen. After I filled a bowl with water and set it on the floor, the dog watched me as it lapped the water. It stopped drinking long enough to lick my hand again after I'd patted its head.

Sweet dog, cautious, not too energetic. Looked too healthy to be a stray. Someone was probably searching the neighborhood for it right now.

The dog dropped onto the floor next to my feet with a grunt. I tore up a piece of bread and then covered it with milk in a bowl. I set the bowl on the screened back porch and shooed the animal outside. A minute later, when I checked from the back door window, the bowl was empty, and the dog had curled up and closed its eyes.

The phone rang. My mind darted through the short list of those who might be calling. At the top of the list was the hospital. Knowing that cancer was now part of the diagnosis made it feel even more likely Elizabeth would not survive this episode.

But the caller was my daughter, Allison. Hearing her voice drained the tension from my neck and shoulders.

For a blessed hour we planned and discussed her autumn wedding. By the time our conversation ended, Allison had decided to book the glass chapel in the trees, the little classical quartet, and the caterer who didn't include fried foods.

She'd narrowed the wedding dress down to simple off-the-shoulder sheaths and would hold off shopping until I returned home, as long as that was within the next two weeks. The edge to her voice told me she was impatient with the delay.

"I'll be home soon. Promise. Hopefully with good news."

I lay on my back in the old bed, staring up at the ceiling. My mind jumped between the past and the present. Why hadn't Elizabeth identified Trudy as her niece? Why did Elizabeth hate Wells and Simpson Haugland so much? Who was Haugland anyway?

My mind moved to Vera. Elizabeth had given her a valuable car. Was she another unidentified relative?

I thought of the old baseball team photo and then limped downstairs to retrieve it. Three of us girls, the others boys. All wearing T-shirts and shorts. All but one boy had the typical buzzed haircuts of the time. None of the kids seemed to be Vera.

On the back porch, the dog barked. I returned to the kitchen and opened the door. The dog pushed past my legs, grumbling and whining. Outside, where the pools of porch light met the shadows, everything was still.

I left the light on and locked the door. When I turned around, the dog had curled up on the little rag rug in front of the kitchen sink. Her tail thumped the floor. I stooped down and stroked her backbone.

"Okay. You can stay inside. Tomorrow, we'll try to find out who you belong to."

After another tail thump, the dog's big eyes closed.

At the shadowy edge of the backyard, a small cloud of exhaled breath hangs in the cold night air for a minute before it dissipates and then is replaced by another breath cloud. The figure in the black hooded slicker stares at the back door.

So Elizabeth gave her the house. No surprise there. Not that I was expecting to be remembered in that way. Old bitch.

The dog might make things a little more difficult. Where the hell had the beast come from? Still it isn't insurmountable. An animal is hardly an obstacle. They stop breathing, just like people. Well, give her a few days to enjoy the house and the dog. Just a few days.

Chapter 18

Friday, April 5—Morning

In bed on Friday morning, I fingered the quilt and lay still, listening to the quiet. I'd actually slept well. Nothing had gone bump in the night. It would be nice if the bad things that had happened since I arrived were just a dream, and Elizabeth was downstairs making breakfast just like she had during those summers long ago. If only it were true.

When I finally sat up and started to swing my legs over the edge of the bed, every muscle in my body screamed. The past four days had not been a dream. I clenched my teeth and swung my legs off the bed. When I put half of my weight on my injured ankle, pain shot up into my forehead. The deep bruise in my shoulder throbbed.

More than anything else, I needed pain reliever and caffeine. I also needed to concentrate on two things: what was happening here now and what had happened that last summer, all those years ago. The picture of the kids playing ball might hold an answer. Trudy probably knew the answers to many of my questions, but getting her to talk about those things wasn't going to be easy.

Notes, spiders, roses. And Chief Green's involvement. Questions tumbled in my brain, and a headache started behind my left temple. Instantly, a pain shot through my heart. Ben had always been my sounding board. I needed to talk to him, to talk through these questions. My heart heaved.

I slipped on a heavy sweater and jeans and made my way slowly down the backstairs. In the kitchen, the stray dog surged to her feet and wagged her tail. I patted the top of her head with one hand as I dropped two slices of bread into the toaster. Then, with the toast and a hot cup of green tea, I dragged myself out to the swing on the front veranda. The dog padded along behind me and settled on the porch at my feet. After checking for black widow spiders, I sat on the old porch swing, my legs tucked beneath me. After a few minutes, the dog meandered down the steps to nose around the front yard.

The brilliant early morning sun warmed the back of my neck, and a southeasterly breeze played on my skin.

Maybe I'd blown everything out of proportion.

It was so difficult to see a loved one suffer. Maybe someone had tried to help Elizabeth die and had taken the locket as a keepsake. Did it really matter who? Only to Police Chief Green.

Elizabeth had cancer. They should let the idea of 'murder' go; write it off as an attempted—and unsuccessful—mercy killing.

But my mind poked at me. What if it hadn't been a mercy killing? Elizabeth's words, the comments about the past and what I "didn't know" were bothersome. So were the notes and the dead roses. I wanted answers.

"Come here, you," I called to the dog. She trotted with me into the house. "Stay on the back porch while I'm gone. We'll think about finding your owner when I get back." The dog looked up with mournful eyes as I put her and a bowl of water on the back porch and then closed and locked the door.

I drove down the shady streets and up the hill to the old city park where Elizabeth had taken us to play so long ago. Tall metal swings with rubber seats, monkey bars, and merry-go-rounds stood where they had been thirty years ago. The wide water tower, with a coat of fresh blue paint, still stood watch. Only the metal yellow, green, and orange play gym looked like a relatively new addition, circa 1975.

I pulled into a parking area and rolled down my window. A breeze blew my hair across my cheeks. The smell of wet grass hung in the warming air. I listened to the sounds of two little girls singing as their mother pushed them in the swings.

Why couldn't I remember Trudy or her father, Jasper?

Ben's smiling face, before his illness, appeared in my mind. I felt my shoulders—my entire body—sag. I could think of only one place in this town that might help me regain a sense of peace.

The parking lot at the Immaculate Conception Catholic Church was empty. Morning mass was over. I followed the sidewalk around to the south side of the church, past the rectory, and up to the double doors. When I pulled them open, the musty scent of old hymnals mixed with some type of altar incense floated out. I stepped in and waited for my eyes to dilate. Slowly, the darkness dissipated.

Sunlight glowed through the stained-glass windows and filled the church with colored light. The rich shading of blue, red, and purple in the window glass made the lifelike pictures nearly four dimensional. I sucked in my breath, remembering Sundays all those years ago. I glanced at the empty pews and then up at the altar. The silent church swelled with brilliant color and peace.

I wandered from window to window through the Stations of the Cross, just as I had as a child. I read the plaque at each of the historic windows and then let my eyes drift over the rare masterpieces. Each time we'd visited here, Elizabeth had told us about the unique windows of rare World War I-vintage glass. When I'd traveled all twelve stations, I dropped down onto a prayer bench, reached up to my throat, and pulled out the chain, letting it slip through my fingers until I found the wedding ring.

Ben had always had a possible solution for every problem or had given advice leading to answers. Now, without him, I didn't know what to do next.

Elizabeth's life in Pawhuska was a mystery. I couldn't remember Jasper. And I couldn't understand why, in the thirty-plus intervening years since my childhood, no one had ever mentioned him or Trudy. Why hadn't they come with Elizabeth to visit us in New Mexico?

Fear had kept me from coming back to Pawhuska. But what had I been afraid of?

Elizabeth had been on the verge of telling me something before she was attacked. What if someone wanted her dead to keep her quiet? If that was true, the next big question was, why? Elizabeth had so many friends, evidenced by her hospital visitors. She'd been a wonderful, caring person and a role model for me. Why would anyone want to harm her?

My thoughts circled back to the idea of a mercy killing, and then, once again, thoughts of Ben. He had been in such pain those last months. He had asked me to help him end his life, but I had been unable to do it. Kill the one I loved most in the world, or, by doing nothing, let him continue in unspeakable pain? I had been a coward. My choice would torture me forever.

Suddenly, unbelievably, in the midst of thoughts about Ben, Sam Mazie popped into my mind. He had beautiful, comforting, deep brown eyes. I felt at home with him, a sensation I wasn't used to. Could we have been friends as children? If we had, wouldn't he have reminded me of it? Now, as adults, I felt a connection to him. I wanted to know him better. Much better.

The past pressed in on me. My eyes were drawn to one of the largest windows. Osage faces glowed in this fantastic window, and I recalled the history of it, as told by Elizabeth. This window had required the Pope's approval, since living people were pictured, including the priest who had founded the Pawhuska Catholic Church.

The Osage Nation had been relocated from Missouri to these rocky hills in the 1800s. Then, in the early twentieth century, the oil boom began, followed by riches, murder, and mayhem.

Elizabeth had never talked about the traumas of those days, although she had lived here during the "Reign of Terror." If it had affected her and her family, no one had ever said.

I walked up the carpeted aisle and back out the side doors, feeling at peace yet still depressed. I didn't want to go back to the house, and so I drove up and down the hilly streets, passing houses that seemed in some ways familiar. Occasionally, I could picture my family traipsing up the steps of a wide porch and ringing the bell.

Had we really done that?

How many residents of Pawhuska did I know but couldn't remember?

I pulled into a parking space on the street just across from the old Osage County Courthouse, next to a steep hillside. Concrete steps rose from the street below. How many times when we were kids had I climbed these steps with Randy, Ellen, and Aunt Elizabeth and then sat on the steps or on the lawn above and listened to Elizabeth talk about the 1920s in the boom town of Pawhuska?

In those days, members of the Osage tribe, wrapped in their colorful blankets, waited on the courthouse lawn to receive their oil and gas royalty payments. The new millionaires had no understanding of ownership or material wealth. The money meant little to them.

"In those days, Pawhuska had more Rolls-Royces per person than anywhere in the world," Elizabeth had told us. "Instead of having the cars repaired when they broke down, the Osages would park them in their yard and go buy another. The only Rolls dealership west of the Mississippi River was right here."

I smiled, remembering the conversation like it had happened yesterday. I pulled the car door closed and drove down the curving street to the bottom of the hill and through the old downtown. During my childhood, each store had mannequins and merchandise displayed in the wide front windows. Bubble-gum machines guarded the doorways. Rows of glass-topped display cases covered the wooden floors inside the shops, forming wide aisles. Now, many of the stores were empty. Trash and loose papers littered the tattered and stained carpets of the front window displays.

In one window, the black silhouette of a coyote, molded from iron, stood guard. Coyote was the trickster of Native American legend. In every Osage story, the effects of Coyote's cunning were often thwarted in some way but only after he had caused some lasting change in the universe. Back then, I'd believed Coyote was real.

With no destination in mind, I followed the streets over hills and through neighborhoods. I slowed down as I passed the cemetery. The midmorning sun beamed down on gravestones fanning out in even rows on all sides, filling the valley between the hill and the town. Many of the people buried here were of Osage heritage. Many of them had received mineral royalties, as written in the treaty of 1872. Such wealth and joy for so many, but for others, the result had been betrayal and even murder.

I got out of the car and wandered along the rows of graves, glancing at those with fresh flowers. In the middle of one row of gravestones, spring flowers were mounded over two side-by-side graves. Lovingly tended, the grass had been clipped around the headstone. A tiny picket fence outlined the graves.

"Jasper O'Day, 1925–1985. A sweeter soul there never was" and "Nancy Hayes O'Day, cherished wife of Jasper, mother of Trudy. 1927–1990."

Trudy had already been here today.

A sense of loss filled me. This was my great-uncle and great-aunt. And I didn't remember them. They'd been living here all those summers when I visited, yet it was as if we had never met. I searched my memory, trying to break through the cobwebs. Why couldn't I remember?

A meadowlark trilled, breaking the trance I had fallen into. About a block away, a man moved among the graves, his head high, his shoulders erect. His straight black hair stirred in the breeze. He knelt at a grave.

Sam Mazie? I threaded my way through the rows toward him, but before I could get even halfway there, he stood and walked quickly in the opposite direction.

"Sam?" I called. His long strides carried him away faster than I could catch up on my sore ankle. I reached the area where he had been kneeling and scanned the grave markers until I found the depressed grassy place where he had knelt.

"Rebecca Alden Mazie. Beloved wife." She had died two years ago, just as Ben was beginning his cancer treatments.

No wonder Sam had seemed to understand my sadness. I looked up, searching the street in case he lingered nearby, but he was gone.

My fingers reached for the chain around my neck.

At Elizabeth's house, the battered blue Ford truck blocked the driveway and the sound of a saw ripped through the late-morning air. Mr. Rourke worked at a sawhorse, cutting boards and piling them near the front steps. He waved a hello in my direction and then wiped his forehead with a blue kerchief. "I'm breaking for lunch now. Be back in about an hour," he called.

I returned the wave and then skirted the front steps and went around to the back. With a happy bark, the dog greeted me from the screened-in porch. I knelt beside her and ruffled the hair around her neck and ears. She licked my chin. Laughing, I hugged her to me, losing my balance as I did and falling to the floor. She licked my cheek.

I knew I should post "Found Dog" notices, call the radio

station, and do everything possible to see if anyone was looking for the animal. Instead, I let myself into the house, tore some bread into small pieces, soaked it in milk in a bowl, and set it on the floor for the dog. She wolfed down the food, watching me.

I made a ham and cheese sandwich and carried it to the sofa in the study. The old photo of the baseball team still lay on the table. One little brown-haired girl wore a dotted-Swiss blouse and striped overall shorts. It could be Trudy. But who were the other children?

The dog padded down the front hall from the kitchen, stopped in the door to the study, and barked. A knock came at the door.

"Good dog." I stopped in the hallway to pat the dog's head and scratch her ears before I went to open the door. I could get used to having an "early warning" system. Diego, the Chihuahua that Ben and I had rescued from the animal shelter early in our marriage, had been a great little alarm but not much for follow-through. Ben's illness, just weeks after Diego died, had abruptly ended my grief for the dog.

Two men stood on the front porch when I swung the door open. Drake Goodwin's smile seemed forced. The other man stared down at me with icy eyes.

"Jamie," Drake said. "Just wanted to check on you." He frowned up at the tall man beside him.

A thin-lipped smile spread across three-fourths of the second man's thin face. "Mrs. Aldrich, I'm Simpson Haugland. At your service," he said. The chill in his eyes made me want to back away and slam the door in his face. Instead, I planted myself in the doorway.

I'd actually thought about calling Drake earlier. My shoulder still hurt, and it had been days since the accident. Was there something else I should be doing to speed my recovery?

Haugland was a whole other thing. He reminded me of

some albino cave creature without pigmentation, something that never saw daylight. Why did his name seem familiar?

"I do need to talk with you about my injury," I said to Goodwin. I pulled the door open, and both of them stepped into the hallway. "In here." I motioned toward the study. "Excuse us for a minute," I told the tall man.

Behind me, the dog stationed herself in front of the staircase. Drake and I left Simpson in the entry; I pulled the study's pocket doors shut behind us.

"May I check the shoulder?" he asked. Drake slipped the sling over my head and explored my upper arm with his fingertips, feeling the muscle and cartilage move as he lifted my arm. I winced when his thumb ran across a spot where the corner of one drawer had struck. "You're not using the arm much, are you?"

"No, but it's not much better. How much longer do you think I'll have to wear this sling?"

He slipped the sling back on and then wiped his hands on his thighs. "You can leave it off tomorrow, as long as you're careful. You had some deep bruising. The tenderness should ease in another few days." His gray eyes lingered on my face and for a few seconds, the lines on his face smoothed out.

I thought about Simpson Haugland, waiting in the hall. In a flash, I knew where I'd heard that name. Sam Mazie's office. Elizabeth's living will.

Drake seemed to read my mind. "Let's see what Haugland has up his sleeve," he said as he slid open the pocket doors.

Simpson Haugland eyed the dog warily, his tall frame leaning against the front door.

"And how can I help you?" I asked, moving toward the door. I didn't want Drake to leave me alone with this stranger.

"Mrs. Aldrich!" Haugland boomed. "Again, my name is Simpson Haugland. I am Miss Elizabeth's real estate agent. We'd been discussing putting the house on the market only a few weeks ago." He paused and cleared his throat. "That Elizabeth," he chuckled. "Loves to tease. A wonderful lady." His thin lips disappeared into a line that reminded me of a wide-mouthed bass.

"No one has mentioned the house was under contract with a real estate agent." I didn't believe for one minute Elizabeth would have written those words about Haugland in a legal document if the two of them had been doing business together. "I haven't found a copy of any such sales contract. And I've not made any decision to sell."

"I can't imagine you would want to keep a house that has fallen into such disrepair, especially when an eager buyer is waiting," Haugland said.

Drake's shoes scuffed the floor.

"You have a copy of the contract and offer?" I asked.

Simpson Haugland flashed his teeth. "A verbal agreement is hard to present. But here in Pawhuska, a man's word is good—er, and a woman's as well. We just hadn't put pen to paper yet."

"Was Mr. Mazie, her attorney, aware of this verbal agreement?" I doubted there had ever been such a conversation with Elizabeth.

"Miss Elizabeth was going to give Sam the details. Then she took to her bed and was so suddenly terribly ill." He made a futile attempt to look sorrowful. "The agreement can be between us now." He blinked, and this time I thought of a fish's cold stare, only fish didn't have eyelids.

"I need to know the appraised value of the property and the amount of the offer before I can evaluate whether this deal is in my best interest," I said.

Haugland's eyes narrowed. "Certainly," he said icily. "I understand you are, for all practical purposes, now the owner." He took a few steps over to the doorway of the study and peeked in. "Such a warm room. You've got someone lined up to fix the window? I see you're doing some repair work on the front step."

I crossed my arms and waited by the front door. The man

darted across the hall and peered into the parlor. When he focused on the stairway, the dog growled low in her throat. I hurried to stand by the dog in front of the stairs.

"Who did you say made the offer to buy, Mr. Haugland?"

He straightened to a height of at least six and a half feet. "I didn't say."

I pressed my lips together. He was playing games. *No way Elizabeth would do business with this man.* "Mr. Haugland, after you've written down the verbal contract and offer, Sam Mazie and I will look it over."

Haugland shrugged and shifted toward the door. "I'll call you." He scurried through the doorway and out to where his new white Cadillac sat at the curb.

I shoved my hair behind my ears and turned back to Drake. "Thanks for staying. Sorry to take up so much of your time."

"Not a problem," he said. His look skittered away from my face as he sidestepped past me to the front door and stepped through it.

I wondered, too late to ask, if Drake was the one who had told Toby Green about Elizabeth's cancer. Had he been Elizabeth's physician? I stepped out onto the veranda to ask him, but Drake had already rushed down the front sidewalk and was halfway to his sister's house.

I swung back around to the front door and caught sight of Trudy on the lawn at the corner of the house. Her face twisted and her shoulders hunched as she mumbled to herself.

"Trudy?"

She stalked around the veranda and up the steps and then stomped past me and into the house. I followed her down the hallway to the kitchen.

"Did you know Elizabeth had discussed selling her home and someone had already made an offer?" I called after her.

"That what he said?" Trudy leaned into the cabinet next to the sink and drummed her finger tips on the countertop.

"Did he have a verbal contract with Elizabeth?"

Trudy stared out the back window, fingers still drumming.

"Trudy?" I touched her arm. "Was there a contract?"

Trudy jerked her arm away from me. "My Liz didn't want to sell this house. Over her grave—that's what she said." Trudy's gaze darted back out the window.

"Are you sure that's what she said?"

"Sure as rain on an April day." The woman turned toward me, and her face crumpled as big tears spilled from her eyes. "My Liz didn't want to sell. But it's your house now. And she might as well be dead." She bolted out the back door and sprinted across the lawn to her cottage.

My Liz didn't want to sell. And she might as well be dead.

I eased down into a chair. The dog dropped down at my feet and rested her big head on my good foot. It was becoming more and more obvious that I didn't know squat. I didn't even know how long Elizabeth had lived here.

When had she bought this house, and from whom had she bought it?

More important, who had been trying to buy it from her?

Chapter 19

Friday, April 5—Afternoon

Mid-afternoon cravings for a candy bar and thoughts of another round of party leftovers for supper inspired me to make a list and walk the few blocks to the grocery store. Plus, I couldn't feed the dog bread and milk forever, and I had to post Found Dog notices. Someone was bound to be looking for her.

I entered the market and then circulated through the store, gathering items in my basket. Fifteen minutes later, I pushed the cart up to the front registers. Vera Peters was having a smiling conversation with the customer in her line as she rang up his groceries. I waited in Vera's line, even though the other one was shorter. It would be nice to see a friendly face for a change and to have a real conversation.

When it was my turn, I pushed the cart forward.

Vera slammed the "Lane Closed" sign down on the conveyor belt.

"Vera?"

"Break time." Vera skirted the checkouts and stalked away from me to the back of the store.

Blood rose into my face. Three customers with full carts now waited in the other line; they stared at me. I wheeled the cart into line behind them.

Ten minutes later, groceries in a bag, still red-faced, I started toward the exit but then stopped. Vera's obvious snub was unjustified. I stomped past the checkouts to the rear of the store where Vera sat eating at one of the deli tables.

"That was rude. Why did you do that?" Vera's eyes bulged as I dropped into the extra chair at her table and plopped my bags on the floor. "Have I done something to offend you?"

Vera glared and took her time chewing the final bite of her sandwich. "It's not what you've done; it's what you're thinking of doing and probably will do out of ignorance." She swallowed and took a sip of soda pop. "You're going to sell the house, even though it will surely put Elizabeth into her grave. They'll run Trudy out of her cottage and out of town, maybe even kill her to get her out. Wouldn't be the first time something like that's happened." Vera's look pierced my heart like a sword.

So, Trudy must have already told Vera about Haugland coming to the house. "Good news travels fast." I leaned across the table toward Vera. "I don't know what I'll do with the house, and I know I'm ignorant about what's happened here. Who wants to buy the house?"

Vera jerked and her eyes flashed. "That stinker Haugland's been pestering Elizabeth to sell that house for years. He's got somebody on the line. And I have my suspicions." She leaned across the table toward me.

I pulled back just a fraction and took a deep breath. I needed Vera as a friend. I didn't want to fight with her. "Haugland stopped by to pressure me to put the house on the market. Told me he and Elizabeth had a 'verbal' contract." I pushed back into the chair.

"Trudy is beside herself," Vera sighed, falling back into her chair, too. "She ought to be so happy to own the cottage outright, but she's too upset about what *you* might do. I've got to get back to work." She scooped up her trash and rolled it into a ball.

"Vera, wait. I have so many questions. Can you help me?"

Vera chewed one thumbnail. Abruptly, she clasped her

hands together. "I'm off tomorrow afternoon. I'll stop by around one."

This isn't going to be easy, I thought, as Vera sauntered away and I gathered up my grocery bags. Neither Vera nor Trudy trusted me; I was an outsider.

The phone was ringing as I came into the house through the back door. Bart Rourke was replacing boards on the front steps. I grabbed up the hall phone.

"Jamie?"

"Ellen? God, I'm glad to hear your voice."

"Before you say anything," my sister interjected, "I have to tell you Mom's going into the hospital for some tests."

"I ... I just ... just talked to her ... yesterday. She didn't say anything about this!"

"Probably because she thinks you've got too much to deal with there. Maybe I shouldn't have told you either."

Right. Ellen always loved to pass on news, good or bad, true or false. I wrote down the name and number of Mother's doctor as Ellen recited the facts. "There's nothing I can do from here, but I'll call her tonight," I said. "Even if I wanted to come home, I'm not sure they would let me leave town right now." Ellen waited. I gave her a condensed version of the past few days.

"You're in over your head, Sis," Ellen said. "I'm thankful for the Osage lawyer and the repairman. At least you've got some help."

Ellen was right. I wasn't totally alone. And there was Vera, too. Truth be known, I even had a cousin nearby. Trudy.

"Ellen, does the name Trudy O'Day mean anything to you?"

"Sort of rings a bell," Ellen finally said. "O'Day was Grandma's maiden name, wasn't it, and Elizabeth's?"

My sister had remembered the O'Day name. Why hadn't I? "Do you remember much about all those summer visits we made here?"

"Mmmm, mostly I remember playing outside. The garden,

hikes on the prairie, and the greenhouse. Oh, yeah, dancing in the gazebo. Are the greenhouse and the gazebo still there?"

Memories swelled in my mind as Ellen spoke, but something uncomfortable and dark bubbled up along with them.

"Remember that old workbench in the greenhouse?" Ellen continued. "Aunt Elizabeth's hidey-hole. Clues for treasure hunts. Candy. Remember that?"

No. I'd forgotten. But now I wondered if the old workbench was still out there, buried in the glass and metal ruins in the corner of the yard. In my mind, I saw Ellen and me, playing hide-and-seek in the greenhouse. I had loved to crawl behind the ferns and the potting table to squat beside the workbench, the air ripe with smells of earth and flowers.

Then, the room began to turn, my stomach flopped, and a sharp pain sliced into my head. I rubbed at my temples as Ellen talked.

Ten minutes later, I hung up the phone, trudged into the kitchen, and took three aspirins. Then I returned to the hallway and dialed Matt and then Allison. Answering machines picked up at both their homes. I left messages and my love and then dialed Mother's number. No answer.

Nauseous from the pain in my head, I went up the stairs and crawled onto the bed, but the room spun and my stomach hurt. I wanted fresh air.

The dog trotted outside with me and across the lawn to the gazebo. I closed my eyes and leaned my head back against one of the gazebo's roof supports, letting the slight easterly breeze caress my face.

How many hours had I spent out here, playing or sewing? Too many to count. I could see us kids, hunkered down on the floor, playing marbles or jacks. I could see us twirling, dancing while Elizabeth hummed or whistled. And I could see us playing Red Rover or Statue on the lawn.

What had happened to change it all for me? Straining to

remember brought the headache back. Those memories were too deeply buried.

Back home, a substitute teacher had led my students all week. If it took another week to clear things up here, would I still have a job? They probably all thought I was AWOL.

At least my lesson plans were complete, and the substitute had everything she needed to create the planned lessons. But in another week, it was time for nine-week tests, and the administration would not be happy with my absence. The biology sub would have to retrieve one of my old tests. Surely it wouldn't come to that.

The back porch door slammed and the dog, which had been stretched out on the floor of the gazebo, woofed and pulled herself to her feet.

"I'm over here," I called.

Bart lumbered toward me. "Done for the day. I can come back tomorrow and finish up the step. Nine o'clock good?"

I nodded, fingertips pressed into my temples. It would be nice to sleep late in the morning, to catch up on missed sleep. Rourke left.

I limped into the house through the open back door. Air moved through the room; Rourke had also left the front door standing wide open. A breeze played with the kitchen curtains, pulling them into the room, and then drawing them back against the screen. The crystal drops on the chandelier in the dining room tinkled. The moving air felt good.

The dog waited while I poured dog food into a cereal bowl. Then I sat at the kitchen table and watched her eat. The cool breeze swirled through the room, and my headache eased. I lay my head down on my folded arms.

It was nearly dark when the dog gave a low bark. I opened my eyes and raised my head. The dog had padded to the back door, and stood, nose working the air. The evening sounds of frogs and crickets echoed in from outside.

My stomach growled. I poured myself a bowl of cereal and ate it as I walked from the back of the house to the front, closing and locking both the doors. Then I climbed the stairs to get ready for bed. My legs felt so heavy.

The figure in the black slicker pulls back into the shadows as Jamie shuts the back door.

She looked so innocent sleeping there, her head on the table. So close, just the other side of the kitchen window, barely a touch away, but the risk of waking her was too great. The risk of disturbing the dog was even greater.

The timing is not yet right. But it is doubtful such an opportunity will come again. Both doors open and no one around.

The figure sighs.

A few more days. Another opportunity will present itself.

Then she'll be sorry she came and even sorrier she stayed.

Chapter 20

Saturday, April 6

I waited for Vera on the veranda as a light rain pattered on the roof. Low gray clouds had crept across the sky during the morning hours as I'd dusted and vacuumed the house, and a nippy breeze had sneaked in from the north. I tucked my hands into the pockets of my coat and watched the chickadees flitting in the trees across the street.

The figure coming down the sidewalk was wearing a slicker over jeans and carrying an umbrella. Only when the woman turned to walk up the front sidewalk could I see Vera's auburn chin-length hair.

"Thanks for coming." I smiled, but Vera smirked in response.

"You are so clueless about your family history." Sarcasm tinged Vera's words. "But I'll try to help," she added with a sigh.

Would the woman ever get rid of the chip on her shoulder? I was having a hard enough time thinking of ways to get close to Trudy, and we were related. How would it ever be possible with Vera? To make matters worse, she was obviously close to Elizabeth—my aunt had left her the old car. What was their connection?

"I think we should go to the museum," Vera added. "There are displays, old documents. History stuff you might not think to ask me about or that I can't answer for you."

"Tell me about Simpson Haugland," I said as we climbed into my Honda.

"He wasn't born here," Vera said quietly. "Left and moved back, twice now."

"Why'd he come back?"

"People back home have to take you in, don't they?" Vera shrugged. "He's doing well in real estate. That big white house up on Grandview is his."

I knew the house; I'd passed it on my drive to the park yesterday. The real estate business in Pawhuska must be profitable. "And how about you? Are you a native?" I needed to break down Vera's wall and didn't know where else to begin.

"I was raised here." Vera stared out the car window.

I steered the car into the gravel parking lot south of the county museum. As I pushed the gearshift into park, Vera pursed her lips and glared toward the museum. I followed her stare to the portico, where a tall, well-dressed man stood smoking a cigar.

Crap. Didn't the mayor of Pawhuska have anything better to do? No matter where I went, Wells appeared. Here he was, overdressed in a deep-blue silk suit, matching shirt, and tie. Who was he trying to impress?

I glanced back at Vera, a tacky comment ready, but a deadpan expression had settled on Vera's face. We opened the car doors and got out.

"Good morning, Vera! And Mrs. Jamie Aldrich!" Mayor Wells cried as we walked up the sidewalk. He tossed down his cigar and grabbed up my hands, leaning toward me. "So lovely to see you again. I'm still reeling from your aunt's unfortunate condition. Still no change?" He sighed. "We all feel her absence at this time and are so deeply afraid that her loss is imminent."

I pulled my hands away from his. *Who were the theatrics for?*

"I wonder," he continued, "might we be so lucky as to have you join us now, here in our little hamlet? Permanently?"

I pushed past him. He was probably really thinking about how he could get me to leave town. I raised my eyebrows at Vera as we entered the building. Vera grinned. It seemed like a start to forming a connection.

"He's chairman of the museum board," Vera whispered as we stepped into the entry where bookshelves and display cases held items for sale. "Guess that makes him the official greeter," she snickered. I rolled my eyes, and we chuckled.

Vera introduced me to the volunteer shopkeeper, and then led the way up a ramp into a large exhibit room. Objects from the early twentieth century filled the wood and glass cases and at one end of the room, antique furniture was arranged like a one-room log home. The musty aroma of age hung in the room, even though box fans in the corners circulated the air.

Exhibit cases held photographs and clothing, Native American objects, and ranch paraphernalia. Cards described the history of the county, both pre-statehood (1907) and during the Osage oil boom. A geology chart showed the rock layers of the earth in Osage County, illustrating how the unique sandstone and limestone uplifts sheltered the abundant pockets of oil and natural gas that had made the Osage Nation rich.

Dark, round faces stared out from old sepia photographs. I touched the cool glass sides of cases displaying Osage clothing, imagining the buttery feel of the tanned leather and the iciness of the tiny round multicolored beads sewn in such intricate designs onto the clothes.

I lost track of time as Vera and I searched the displays for photos labeled with the O'Day name. What had Elizabeth's father done for a living? Had Clara been employed?

So much I didn't know, including what these ancestors of mine looked like. Was a young Elizabeth pictured here, or my grandmother? What about their younger brother, Jasper? Was he one of the young men here in the photographs taken outside the school?

Elizabeth had probably shared stories of her childhood with

us during our summer visits—stories about riding to school in a goat-pulled cart and eating squirrel from the blackjack forest for dinner. If she had, I'd forgotten.

Someone touched my elbow. "Anything I can help you find?" an elderly lady asked.

"I'm looking for family members, the O'Day family. Are there any photographs of them here?"

The woman's eyes widened, and she blinked several times before answering. "O'Day?" She stared off at nothing.

"My great-aunt is Elizabeth O'Day Graham," I explained. "I'm looking for pictures of her family. Her father and mother, her sister and brother. Anything."

The woman's brow furrowed. She moved her hands to her hips, and her eyes flitted to the photo display racks in the center of the room. "Don't think we have any." She scurried back to the entry hall. "You can look, though."

I hurried over to the photo racks. The photographs were all of Osages, most wearing patterned shirts with leggings and moccasins or long dresses and shawls. Men and women wore their black hair long, often braided. Photos of Elizabeth's Irish dad wouldn't be here.

"Anything interesting?" Vera appeared at my side.

"In all these pictures, no people with the last name of O'Day are identified."

"I didn't find anything either. But you know, Elizabeth didn't grow up in Pawhuska," Vera said, tapping a finger on the display's plexiglass cover. "She and Darcey moved here later."

Sam had told me the property he was to sell for us, the family homestead, was near another town. "From Bigheart, right? Where the homestead was. Is that far from here?"

"About twenty miles," Vera said. "But it's not Bigheart anymore. It's Barnsdall."

I had driven through the small town on my way here. The anomaly of the old oil pumper right in the middle of a street off the highway through town intrigued me. "Do they have a museum?"

"The museum's open by appointment," Vera said. "I can take a few hours to run over there with you, maybe Monday. My shift starts at three."

"Great. You don't know how much I appreciate your help," I said. "Seems like it's been hard to get information about Elizabeth, the house, or my family." We moved back through the museum toward the door. "You know, there's a trunk in the attic full of family photos. Could you help me go through it?" I thought of the children in the team picture. Vera might know who they were.

"Why don't you ask Trudy?"

She had a point, but at this time, Trudy seemed to be avoiding me.

Back at the house, I dialed my mother in Albuquerque.

"The scheduled tests are just precautionary, honey," she said after I said hello. She clipped her words, talking in a tone that told me she was not willing to discuss her health. "I feel fine. Tell me what's happening there."

I chose my words carefully. I blamed the delay in my return home on details related to the repair of the house. Mother had enough on her mind without adding the questions with which I was struggling.

The figure in the black slicker watches from the base of the tree as the lights in the house blink out, first downstairs and then upstairs. Fingers clench into a fist, unclench, and clench again.

Six days. She's been here six days. Patience. My greatest virtue? It is going well. Moving according to plan. No need to rush. It will all unfold, just as it is meant to unfold. And in the end, justice will be served.

A full cloud slides across the moon, and in the deepened gloom, the figure disappears.

Chapter 21

Sunday, April 7—Noon

I fingered the package of smoked ham in the deli drawer. My appetite was nonexistent, even though I'd had nothing more for breakfast than a glass of orange juice and toast. For the first time since the injury, I left the sling off my arm.

The dog looked up at me and then nudged my knee. I stooped over to pet her.

"I'm glad you're here." I scratched the dog's muzzle. "But I can't get attached to you. Someone may claim you." I'd finally called Animal Control yesterday evening; they hadn't received any reports of a missing basset hound mix.

The animal raised her paw to my forearm when I stopped scratching, so I started again, this time running my fingernails down her back. "I have to call you something. You're such a lady, so dignified. I'll call you Queenie, just until your owner comes for you."

The dog rolled onto her back, showing off a pink freckled tummy. It wasn't wise of me to give her a name, like she was going to be my dog forever. Now giving her up would be even harder when the time came. I scratched the dog's ribs and then her belly. Queenie let out a contented moan and thumped her tail. Then she rolled back to her feet and trotted out of the kitchen toward the front door.

There was a knock.

Sam Mazie held out a paper bag as I pulled the door open. "Had lunch?"

I felt the smile spring onto my face. Sam's face lit up and sparkles danced in his dark eyes. Something jumped inside my chest.

"I was just feeling sorry for myself," I said with a grin. "What I have to eat doesn't look very appetizing. Come in."

"No, you come out." He stepped back and motioned for me to follow. "Let's take a drive over to the park. Come on, you too," he called to the dog. Queenie wagged her tail and raced Sam to his Ford Ranger. I pulled the door shut and followed the dog at a slower pace.

Mothers, toddlers, and babies in strollers roamed the old city park. Kids crawled over the big plastic jungle gym forts and slipped down wide slides. Sam spread the contents of his lunch sack on a concrete picnic table. The dog wandered nearby, sniffing the trees and bushes.

"Wasn't sure what you'd like. Thought I'd be safe with sliced turkey."

I forced myself to nibble at the sandwich. I still didn't have much of an appetite, partly because of the butterflies now flitting back and forth in my stomach. The sun warmed our faces as we watched the children play. I could almost hear my heart pounding, and several times, I fought the desire to reach out and touch Sam's hand. These unexpected feelings felt good.

"Jamie, we need to talk," he said, interrupting the comfortable silence that had fallen between us. Worry lines crept up around his eyes, and I resisted reaching up to smooth them away. "Police Chief Green is making a lot of inquiries. You're a suspect in your great-aunt's attempted murder."

His words stung as if he'd slapped me. "I thought he'd given up on that possibility. I thought he'd been following up on what I told him, that someone else was in the house." I wrapped my arms around myself. "You were in the house."

"They found thread fibers on her lips, teeth, and one fingernail. A small embroidered pillow was used to suffocate her."

I combed my fingers through my hair as my stomach clenched and my heartbeat quickened. "Let me guess. They found my fingerprints everywhere, and I was holding the pillow the first time Green came to the house. They don't believe anyone else was there after you left."

Sam sat quietly, his eyes locked on mine.

"But there's got to be more to this," I insisted. "Someone's been sending me taunting notes. And Green told me that Elizabeth used to get them all the time."

Sam frowned. "What kind of notes?"

"Elizabeth never mentioned them?"

"No." He rubbed his jaw line and sighed. "Jamie, I was your aunt's attorney. You haven't retained me, but I'll advise you anyway. At this time, I advise you not to talk to Chief Green without counsel."

"If I have to retain counsel, I'll ask you to represent me. Will you?"

"Yes."

"Thank you," I breathed. "You don't know me at all, but I love my aunt. I could never take her life."

Sam nodded. Then he tilted his head and looked me squarely in the face again. "There's more. Toby Green has requested more information from New Mexico about your husband's death."

His words slammed into me again. My eyes misted over.

"Someone—your police chief, probably—told Green charges should have been filed, even insinuated that they still might be, based on what's happened here," Sam continued. "People who have 'helped' someone die once often find it easier the second time."

I choked on my own saliva. Tears spilled from my eyes, and I coughed uncontrollably. Sam scooted close and gently slid an arm around my shoulders.

"Sam, he's wrong," I managed to say in a quivering voice. "But the police chief in New Mexico won't tell him that. I don't think I ever convinced him I didn't help Ben die. And the whole time I was grieving and hurting because Ben was dead, I still felt like a traitor because I *hadn't* helped him. I let him suffer. I hadn't done what he so badly wanted me to do."

Sam smoothed my hair with one hand, and I felt the comforting warmth of his shoulder pressed against mine. I closed my eyes, turned my face into him, and let him hold me.

A car passed behind us on the asphalt road and honked. I straightened and pulled away, grabbed a paper napkin, and wiped at my eyes. "It's been nearly a week since it happened. I really hoped Green might have decided there was no need for an investigation or was focusing on another suspect."

"He's been talking to neighbors, friends, acquaintances. I don't think he'll file charges against you without something more concrete. Right now, the fact you've been given one of the nicest older homes in town is about the only motive he can find. Just don't talk to him without me present."

"You can't know whether or not I'm telling the truth. If I were you, I'd walk away." I crumpled the napkin into a ball and worried it with my fingers. "There's a murderer loose out there, and Toby Green is only focused on me."

His hand rested on my shoulder. "I believe you. There's truth in your heart."

Tears pooled in my eyes again. His hand stroked my shoulder.

"Elizabeth was my blood relative too," he said softly. "You are from her line. There is a bond between us. I promise never to break that bond."

My mouth fell open. "Elizabeth was Osage?"

"You didn't know?" He sighed and moved his hand from my shoulder. "Elizabeth's mother, your great-grandmother, was a full-blood Osage with headrights."

I couldn't find my voice. An electric shock moved down my

spine and then up into my head. I scooted away from him so I could turn to see his face. His back was straight, his face unemotional. He suddenly seemed distant. "Headrights? That has something to do with tribal ownership of minerals, right?"

Sam nodded. "When the Osage bought their Oklahoma reservation, one provision of the Treaty of 1872 gave members of the tribe joint ownership of all minerals, or headrights, on the reservation forever. The royalties that tribal members receive are still based on these original headrights. The royalties are all percentages now, as the original tribal members are deceased." Sam got up and moved to the other side of the bench to face me, perching on the edge of the picnic table.

"When the oil boom hit this area in the early 1900s, oil leases throughout the county were purchased from the tribe, and royalties for all the oil and gas found here were divided equally among all tribal members," he explained. "They used the official Osage tribal role of 1906 to determine who got those royalties. Each tribal member at that time received one headright. Their heirs and descendents continue to receive the royalties today, but they are partial headrights, divided now among several generations of descendents."

"And my great-grandmother had one headright?"

"Yes, just as my great-grandfather—your great-grandmother's cousin—had a headright. They all became wealthy, with no real understanding of what 'wealth' was. At one time, there were more millionaires per capita in Pawhuska than anywhere in the United States."

The tragic stories I'd heard of how some people took advantage of the wealthy Osages now took on a new reality. And Elizabeth had told me those stories. If Elizabeth and my grandmother had been half Osage, then what was I? One-eighth?

We sat quietly in the sun. Queenie trotted over and stretched out under the picnic table in the shade. I closed my eyes and let the warmth soak into my skin, trying to stop the buzzing of my brain. I was the prime suspect in my aunt's attempted murder, and I was part Osage.

Sam's clean scent wafted on the breeze around me. We were no longer touching, but even with my eyes closed I could sense his body near. My eyes jerked open. I reached up, found my necklace, and stroked Ben's wedding ring.

A few moments later, the wind began to blow in mighty gusts, and the parents and children scattered to their cars and down the neighboring streets.

We hurried to the car and then drove back to the house in silence.

We didn't touch as he said good-bye.

My heart ached.

Chapter 22

Sunday, April 7—Afternoon

I stared out of the cracked study window. The clouds had rolled through with the blustery wind, spitting a short rain shower. Now, the sun had returned. My mind was a jumble of thoughts. What was it Vera had said the other day, when she teased me about knowing so little about my own family? Did Vera know about my Osage heritage?

No one in the family had ever mentioned Osage blood, including Elizabeth. And no one had ever said anything about headrights either. Shouldn't someone in the family be getting some royalty money? Maybe Mother and my aunt were receiving checks and had just never told me. But the will had not mentioned the headright. And Sam hadn't brought it up at the reading either. Maybe—it was possible—the Osage headright was part of the big cover-up that Elizabeth had alluded to. My teeth worried at my lower lip.

I had to get out of the house. Otherwise, my brain would go over and over the conversation with Sam and all the unknowns. In my world of scientific method, there was a "control," so you could be certain of something as you experimented. I had no control. I wasn't certain of anything.

Tomorrow, I could talk with Vera as we drove to Barnsdall and find out exactly what she knew about Elizabeth and her family. And I needed to know more about the house and more about my aunt's life. Finally, I needed to decipher what Elizabeth had meant during that last strange conversation.

Gardening always helped me pull my thoughts together. Outside, it was a beautiful spring day, and Elizabeth's flower beds were in need of spring cleaning. The feel of the warming earth on my hands and the smell of the moist soil might help me clear my head.

I rummaged in the mudroom and found a bucket already filled with gardening supplies. Armed with the bucket and a roll of garbage bags, I traipsed out into the backyard. Purple buds clustered on the branches of the redbud trees and yellow blooms bent the long, spindly branches of the forsythia bushes.

After pulling on a pair of blue cotton gardening gloves, I grabbed handfuls of last fall's leaves from around the blossoming tulips, uncovering mounds of magenta phlox that bordered the flower beds and circled the trees. I crammed the leaves into a bag and let my mind move through the things I knew for certain.

Elizabeth's mother—my great-grandmother—was full-blood Osage. She'd had a headright that my family never mentioned. Did that have anything to do with Elizabeth's near death?

If Sam was right, Police Chief Green still considered me a suspect. He very likely might charge me with attempted murder if I didn't find out who had wanted Elizabeth dead—and why. The police might even reopen the investigation into Ben's death back home.

Was there no end to the nightmare?

As I worked, I glanced at the neat little cottage on the edge of the back lawn. I hadn't seen Trudy since Friday morning; the shades and curtains on the windows were drawn, as usual. And then I looked next door to Rory and Daniel's house. I'd heard the children playing outside the last few days, but they stayed in their yard, minding the property line as if there was an electric fence between the two yards. Still no sign of Drake's sister or her husband.

Toby Green had said that Elizabeth had been getting nasty notes for a long time. Why? And for how long?

I scooted from one flower bed to the next, pulling out the dead leaves and stuffing them into the yard bags. With small trimmers, I pruned dead branches. I used the weed popper from the bucket to pull dandelions from the lawn. Gradually, my mind slipped into neutral. The sun grew hot and the breeze stiffened. Soon, three trash bags were stuffed full, and perspiration had beaded on my forehead and trickled down my sides.

I slipped off my windbreaker. There was probably a compost bin or at least a compost pile somewhere. Aunt Elizabeth was a gardener, too. It was unlikely that she would have sent the yard waste to the landfill when it could so easily be turned into fertilizer for the flower beds. I glanced at the greenhouse ruin squatting in the far northeast corner of the yard.

"Ring around the rosy, pocket full of posies. Ashes, ashes, we all fall down!" The childhood game popped into my mind, along with vaporous memories of children playing in the yard, in the greenhouse, in the gazebo. I wondered when the greenhouse had fallen apart. And I wondered why Elizabeth hadn't torn it down.

I dragged the leaf bags across the yard toward the twisted frame of the dilapidated greenhouse. The ceiling had crashed in, pinning scattered twigs and branches beneath the metal framework and broken glass panes. Rubble had buried a wooden stepladder. Broken clay pots and saucers littered the ground, and rusted garden tools protruded from cubbies in the corner workbench. Vines clung to the remaining walls, and although the stems were bare now, swelling leaf buds were ready to burst open.

I set the bags down and stepped into the wreckage, picking my way toward the far corner. Ellen had remembered the hidey-hole in the workbench. I doubted that Elizabeth would have left the notes Toby Green had mentioned in the bench's hidey-hole where anyone might find them. *But then again,* I thought, as the remaining ceiling panels creaked above me, *who would be stupid enough to come into this dangerous ruin?* Maybe it was the safest possible place to hide something.

The mockingbird perched on the remaining frame started through his repertoire of birdsong as he flicked his long black and white tail feathers.

Someone called my name.

Across the yard, Drake held up one hand to shade his eyes from the midday sun as he searched the yard. I stepped out of the greenhouse, avoiding fallen glass shards and sharp metal window frames. We met halfway across the lawn.

"Out doing yard work? That's not exactly taking it easy," he scolded, glancing toward the nearby flower bed and the bucket of tools I'd left there and then back toward the greenhouse ruin and the stuffed garbage bags.

"Such a beautiful day. Who could stay inside?" I rubbed my gloved hands together to loosen the soil and then slipped the gloves off as we moved toward the house. "So you're one of those doctors who make house calls?"

He cocked his head. "Don't let anyone else know, okay?"

I smiled, thinking he might be joking, but his face was solemn. His forehead creased in his permanent frown.

"Just in the neighborhood, visiting your sister, right?" I tried again, smiling. "I still haven't met her. I hear and see the children but no grown-ups. Are you sure she lives over there?" I teased.

Drake stopped at the back steps, hands deep in his pants pockets, his face grim. "You haven't seen Susan because she's a paraplegic. Doesn't go out much in her wheelchair."

Saliva balled up in my throat and made me cough. For the first time, the ramp that angled off the back porch and down to the garage registered in my brain.

"And Susan's husband? Where is he?"

"He's in sales, on the road for weeks at a time. Steve's due back midweek. I'll ask him to stop over and see if you need any help, if you're still here when he returns."

"Thanks, but Bart Rourke is doing some repairs for me," I said. "He's finishing the front steps tomorrow and installing the new window midweek." I glanced again at the house next door. "I should go over to say hello. I'll do that in the next day or so."

"A word of caution about Bart," Drake said, glancing at his wristwatch. "He means well, and he'll do his best for you, being family, but sometimes his results leave something to be desired." He waved good-bye. "Easy on that arm, now."

I slouched against the back door as Drake crossed the lawn and disappeared around the corner of his sister's house. Family? It hit me that Rourke was the last name of Elizabeth's second husband.

Early in the evening, Allison called. My bubbly daughter's conversation flitted from one topic to the next, explaining the latest dress she had seen and the cake flavor she had tasted at the bakery on Saturday. *Damn. This is such an important time in Allison's life. I should be there.* But I couldn't be, not until I found out what Elizabeth meant in that last conversation and whether someone had tried to kill her—and why.

And then there was Sam Mazie.

He had been such a comfort earlier today. And there had been such a look of compassion in the depths of his beautiful eyes. Since Ben's death, no one had stirred my heart like Sam. Was his attentiveness simply because of my aunt ... and because of our Osage relatives?

Chapter 23

Monday, April 8—Morning

Monday morning, after a quick call to Sam's office, I left the house. The northwesterly wind blew a chill over the town. I sucked in my breath and puffed the cold air back out again as I walked past blooming redbud trees, purple and yellow pansies, and nodding red tulips.

I hoped that in a few hours I would know much more about Aunt Elizabeth's house. The house dated to the twenties. Had she bought the house with one of her husbands or in between marriages?

I parked at the bottom of the hill below the courthouse. Halfway up the steep stairway on Grandview Street, I paused to catch my breath before climbing up the final set of stairs and going into the building. As the center of the white man's government in Osage County, the notorious Osage murder trials had taken place here in the late 1920s. Had my family experienced that terror?

Sam was waiting for me in front of the wide glass doors. My heart stuttered.

"Thank you for meeting me," I called up to him. A smile popped onto my face.

He opened the door and returned the smile before leading me down a short hall to the County Clerk's office.

"I've got a few things to do elsewhere in the building, but

I'll catch up with you in an hour or so. They can tell you where to start your search." He motioned to the information desk inside the office and then held the door open as I slipped through.

The young clerk was talking on the phone and staring out the window.

After at least a minute, I rapped on the counter. "Excuse me?"

The girl glanced at me and quickly ended the conversation. When I had her undivided attention, I gave her the legal description of Elizabeth's property that Sam had provided. With a sour expression, the clerk led me to a room filled with shelves and filing cabinets. Then she left.

I scanned the legal descriptions on the spines of the bound volumes and finally found the one that indicated the correct township and range for the property. I thumbed through the pages, looking for the entry on Great-Aunt Elizabeth's house.

When the door behind me opened, I glanced over my shoulder, expecting to see Sam. Instead, Martin Wells stood in the doorway.

"Jamie! How delightful to see you!" Wells drawled. "I was just passing by. Anything I can help with?" He stepped into the narrow room, leaving the door slightly ajar.

"I was looking for information about Aunt Elizabeth's house," I said. "It will be a while before I get the updated abstract." I turned back to the pages, ignoring the mayor's leer. I tucked a stray strand of hair behind one ear. *Damn. I hate the way he makes me feel self-conscious and uneasy.*

"You are sleuthing. The house has an interesting—but short—history. I can cover it all in just one sentence. My great grandfather build it in 1922, arts-and-crafts style." He stepped over to me and stood close.

I reacted with a start. Now, I thought about how comfortable the mayor had seemed there and how he had disappeared during the dinner following the funeral. He had probably been reliving his childhood visits, just like I had been doing for the past week.

"When did Elizabeth buy it?" I took several steps sideways and moved behind a small table before I turned to face him.

Dimples poked into his cheeks as he smiled. "Let's investigate that together, Jamie. I only returned to Pawhuska after my mother passed on in '90." Wells reached across the table to pat my arm. "Someone will remember. I'll ask around. Meanwhile, I hope to see more of you," he said, winking. "You are the breath of spring itself here in our little town." He pulled out his pocket watch and sighed.

The door opened wider, and Sam Mazie stepped in.

"Samuel," Wells grunted. Then he straightened the watch chain and nodded at me. "We'll talk soon, my dear." He slipped out the door with a quick nod and a wide grin.

I sank into a wooden chair next to the small table, and Sam dropped into the chair across from me. His eyes locked on mine, and my face grew warm.

"I just found out that Elizabeth's home was built by Martin Wells's family," I said.

Sam nodded, still gazing deeply into my eyes.

"You knew?" I said. "Why didn't you just tell me?" I probably should have felt angry, but I couldn't manage it. His eyes pulled me in, and I didn't feel anything but thankful that he had come and found me so quickly. It was crazy.

"It was still called The Wells' House when I was a child," Sam explained, letting his eyes roam over my hair. "That's the logical conclusion."

Obviously. I pushed back in the chair, suddenly aware how this might look to anyone who passed by in the hall—the two of us gazing at one another, leaning across the table. I cleared my throat. "Any idea who wants to buy it?"

Sam pulled back too and then looked thoughtful. His expression changed, and I wondered if he was feeling the same butterflies in his stomach that I was. I had thought I was too old for such feelings.

His lawyer face slid back on again. Whatever he was about to say, he clearly had now changed his mind. He was all business again. "I'll search for the abstract and let you know what I find out."

Driving home, the butterflies still flitted in my stomach. Thoughts tumbled in my brain—The Wells' House, Sam, Martin, Sam, Trudy, Sam. If I let Simpson sell the house, I wouldn't have to make repairs. *I could go home to New Mexico*, one part of my brain said. But what about all the questions concerning Elizabeth's attempted murder? What about Trudy? And what about this crazy feeling I had for Sam? Going home right now wasn't an option.

And something about the two notes I received last week was bothersome. Toby Green said my aunt had been receiving similar notes for years. From whom and why? Possibly, the two notes I received were only a prank. There had only been two and nothing more since. No more accidents, either.

My mind spun into full investigative gear, arguing with me. Deep down inside, I didn't really believe that Elizabeth's near death a week ago had been an assisted suicide attempt, even if she did have cancer. My vivacious aunt would never consider suicide; it would have been the cowardly way out. I was off base to even consider that was what she wanted. I had let what had happened with Ben keep me from thinking sensibly. Elizabeth had nearly been murdered for a more sinister reason, something to do with the house and her past. That's what she'd been trying to tell me.

Back in the house, the dust motes shimmered in the air, and the layer of dust on the hallstand seemed glaringly apparent. That dust would not go away by itself, but Trudy had apparently decided not to help with the cleaning.

In the mudroom, I found a smock hanging on a peg and

slipped it on over my clothes before I raided the storage cabinets for cleaning supplies.

As I began to run the duster over the hallstand, a saw's buzz ripped through the late-morning air. Through the parlor window, I could see Bart Rourke, wearing a denim carpentry apron and standing at the table saw on the front sidewalk. An orange extension cord snaked its way across the yard toward the driveway. I had no idea where an outside electrical outlet was, but Rourke obviously did. I continued to rub the hallstand with the dusting cloth. I had hours to kill before it was time to meet Vera at her home. If nothing panned out from our visit to Barnsdall, I'd think again about the possibility of leaving for New Mexico midweek. I had to focus on my life and not on Sam Mazie.

After eating a sandwich, I walked the few short blocks to Vera's address. The white frame house sat in the middle of a small lot; ivy covered much of the shaded yard around large oak trees and climbed up the east end of the house. I went up the front steps, punched the round doorbell, and rapped on the screen doorframe. The drapes on the front windows were tightly closed.

I knocked again, waited, and knocked again. A minute or so later, I took the stepping-stone path that led around the house.

A two-sided shed protected the back stoop from the north and westerly winds. "Vera?" I called. I started up the back steps; messy spider webs hung from the corners of the shed. I backed down the steps. Four glistening black bodies, emblazoned with red hourglasses, scurried with long legs through the mess of spider silk.

I sprinted around the side of the house, heart galloping. I tripped, fell, caught myself with my right arm, and then let myself fall to the pavement. *Damn!* Pain stabbed from my previously injured shoulder. I pulled myself up and headed for home, focusing on putting one foot in front of the other, grimacing with pain, out of breath, heart pounding.

I turned the corner and pushed on down the sidewalk. Bart's saw buzzed from the front sidewalk, and his bulky frame bent over the sawhorse. I skirted the house to the back door, where Queenie greeted me.

Inside, I slumped into a chair at the kitchen table. Had Vera sent the notes? If so, I couldn't trust her. My only other information sources were Sam, Drake, or Trudy. I already knew Sam was not telling me everything he knew. Drake was so withdrawn it seemed unlikely he would tell me anything willingly. The only possible help now would have to come from Trudy.

Chapter 24

Monday, April 8—Evening

The clouds broke apart as the sun dropped below the western horizon. In the east, a high bank of clouds glowed pink and then violet. I rinsed my soup bowl and silverware and then peered through the kitchen window toward Trudy's cottage. Lamplight glowed behind the curtains. I had to build an alliance with Trudy; otherwise, I might as well consider my investigation here finished. It was only a matter of time before Chief Green served me with an arrest warrant.

Queenie and I crossed the back lawn at a slow pace. I sniffed the fresh, rain-scented air and felt the damp breeze caress my skin. Queenie snuffled along, nose to the ground.

Trudy swung the door open, glanced at me, and then smiled down at the dog. I was again struck by the radical difference between the two sides of the woman's face and the bent place in her jawbone. I thought of what little my mother had said about Trudy and wondered if her facial deformity had been caused by an accident during one of our family's summer visits. Worse yet, what if Ellen and I had somehow been responsible?

Trudy motioned me inside.

The tiny home was comfortably furnished with colorful braided rugs on the floors, a padded rocker, and a blue plaid loveseat. Through a door on the right wall of the cozy room, I could see into a small kitchen with a table and two chairs in the center. Most likely, the closed door on the left opened into a bedroom with an adjoining bath.

"Your home is darling, Trudy," I said, settling down into the loveseat with one leg tucked beneath me. "So cozy and cute."

Trudy dropped into the rocker, her face blank. Queenie plopped down between us on the rug, big head resting on her front paws. We sat quietly for several seconds as my discomfort grew.

"I know Jasper was Elizabeth's brother," I finally said, "and that you are his daughter. You and I are cousins." Trudy rocked back and forth. "I would imagine you're worried I'll sell the house. But you need to know that this cottage is yours; no one can take it away."

The squeaky rocking continued. The start of a smile played on Trudy's lips.

"You'll be the first to know if I decide to sell the big house. And if you want to live there, to own that house, we'll work it out. I won't sell the house to anyone outside the family if you don't think Elizabeth wants that."

Trudy moved one eye back to my face and kept rocking.

Squeak. Squeak.

A floorboard creaked in the bedroom.

I stood up as a shiver ran down my back. "I'd like for us to be friends. Elizabeth would want that, too. Please come over to visit."

Trudy scratched Queenie's ears, and the dog grunted softly.

I moved toward the door. "And one last thing. Those pictures in the attic—can you go through them with me? My grandmother, Elizabeth's sister, is probably in some of those pictures. And her parents. I have no idea what they looked like."

Trudy nodded but kept rocking. Our conversation, such as it was, was over. I closed the door softly as Queenie and I left.

I spied something white on the back steps as I walked toward the house. A white envelope protruded from beneath the screen door. I tore off the end and pulled out the folded paper.

The black, bold words read: "*Whore. Murderer.*"

With my heart thumping, I scanned the edges of the yard and then glanced back at the cottage. Fingers of night mist stroked at the outside walls of the cottage, and light radiated from the windows. Beyond the house, the pink glow in the eastern clouds had faded to a dull gray. Shadows clung to the trees and bushes.

Hands shaking, I unlocked the door and stepped in. Queenie trotted through the kitchen and disappeared into the front hall. I threw the back door deadbolt closed and flipped on the kitchen light. I laid the note on the counter.

I'd thought there'd be no more notes. Clearly, I was wrong. And now, the message was directed at me. Why?

Toby Green had suggested I look for the notes Elizabeth had received, perhaps to determine if he had received duplicates of each one. I wanted to find them too. I wanted to know what they said. Elizabeth had hidden these notes from everyone. The notes either frightened her or embarrassed her. Maybe the sender was blackmailing her in some way. Only Elizabeth knew, and for now, she wasn't able to give anyone the answer.

I moved through the house, closing all the blinds and drapes and turning on all the lights. Then, I began a systematic search through every drawer, closet, and shelf in the house. Slowly, I moved through the first floor rooms. In the study, I checked behind all the books, as well as on top of the wall cabinets. I searched the kitchen and pantry and then the mudroom. An hour later, all that was left downstairs was the basement.

Spider-panic crept with a shiver up my spine. I did remember the basement—dark, musty, full of old spider webs and shelves filled with preserve jars. Not a likely place to hide paper notes. That fact alone made it a good place to search.

I crept down the stairs, peering into the darkness behind

the dancing shadows of the bare overhead light bulb. From the bottom of the stairs, I couldn't see any boxes or hidden alcoves, just the four stone walls of the old basement, forming the square foundation of the house, and the heater unit. And all I felt was a giant case of claustrophobia, a vibrant, living thing pushing in on my lungs so I couldn't breathe. An ache started at the back of my head and tightened like a cinch.

I climbed back up the basement stairs, turned off the light, and locked the basement door. Pulling air into my lungs, I rubbed at my temples. My claustrophobia had come back full force. It had been years since I'd struggled with this much irrational fear.

When I could breathe normally again, I climbed the backstairs to the second floor. Methodically, I searched the three bedrooms and the two bathrooms, including the window benches, the nightstands and armoires, and all the cabinets. I looked through the hall closets, investigating every storage box and moving every pile of linen to look beneath it.

Finally, armed with my flashlight, I fought off my arachnophobia again and searched the attic. I tried to ignore the sound of scampering creatures in the corners as I ducked under dusty cobwebs. The large attic would take days to search completely, so for now, I concentrated on old trunks, suitcases, and boxes, as well as any furniture that had drawers that might hide a bundle of notes or letters.

My head filled with dust, and the grit coated my hands and face. Eventually, much later, I had come full circle, back to the attic stairs. I turned off my flashlight and stomped down them.

The small electric alarm clock in my bedroom read 11:30. I'd spent more than four hours searching.

Vera had not called. She owed me an explanation for not being at home. When we did connect, I wondered how Vera would explain the nasty spiders she seemed to be cultivating.

I couldn't count on her to help with the investigation into either this house or Elizabeth's past.

I was completely alone.

The figure paces in the deep shadows beneath a tree, occasionally glancing up at the steady small light now shining from the attic window. The light had progressed from main floor, to basement, to second floor, glowing behind the drawn curtains and blinds.

What is she doing? She is smart, smarter than expected, and she is not backing down.

A long sigh escapes chapped lips.

It is time for it to begin, then. The preliminaries are over. She is beautiful, and she will be a beautiful atonement.

Chapter 25

Tuesday, April 9—Morning

A cool northwesterly breeze carried moist air into the house through cracks in the walls and beside the windows. Clammy with moist cold, I traipsed down the backstairs to the kitchen. My ankle twinged when I put too much weight on it, and I'd put my aching shoulder into the sling again. I couldn't seem to get warm, even wearing a long-sleeved T-shirt and a sweater over it. I pulled a cardigan off the wall peg in the kitchen before pouring myself a bowl of cereal.

I felt as if I was sleepwalking. Problem was, I hadn't slept much last night, or if I had, it had been a light, half sleep that left me feeling like I'd not slept at all. It had not been a productive half sleep either. Three thoughts had kept rising to the forefront of my tired mind. Vera and the spiders. The third note. And the possibility someone had been in Trudy's cottage with her last night. Someone else had watched me go to Trudy's and then left the message.

Was someone watching every time I left the house?

The buzz of Bart's saw floated in from outside. I hoped the porch repairs would be finished this morning and that the new window would come in from Tulsa and be installed this afternoon. I would be a little closer to going home.

During my sleepless night, I had decided I should not think about Sam or use him as an excuse to stay. The idea of a romance with him was ridiculous. We lived hundreds of miles apart and had little in common.

After breakfast, I settled at the desk in the study to go through Elizabeth's bills and papers and make a list of the places where she had accounts, so I could e-mail them an update about her status and provide my contact information. I also made myself a note to e-mail change of address to the subscription departments at *Reader's Digest*, *Better Homes and Gardens* and *Time* magazines and request magazines be sent to my home.

About midafternoon, Queenie and I took a walk in the neighborhood. I needed to stretch my legs and clear my head after all the clerical work. When I returned, Bart had finished installing the new window and was caulking around the edges.

I climbed the front steps onto the veranda, stepping heavily on the newly replaced boards. "Looks great!" I called to Bart.

Inside, the house seemed stuffy, the air stale. My head immediately began to pound. I tugged at the parlor windows to let fresh air in, but the windows were sealed with paint and wouldn't budge. I went down the hall to the kitchen, took a couple of aspirins, and sat down at the table.

Footsteps pounded as Bart crossed the front hall and entered the room. "Finished the steps, and your window is in. Want me to check things in the basement before I go? I'm wondering about the wiring and the furnace. Don't suppose you know if Elizabeth and Herbert redid the wiring?"

"No idea," I said, my fingers rubbing circles over my temples. At the moment, I couldn't even remember for sure which husband Herbert was.

"I should take a quick look then. Maybe get the electrician to come by tomorrow and give you an estimate."

I followed Bart as he strode over to the basement door and

pulled it open. The sight of the yawning black doorway, like the dark at the top of the attic stairs, made my head pound harder.

Bart flicked the light switch inside the door and started down the steps. "I'll be up in just a minute," he said. "Don't bother to come down."

In the basement, the single light bulb swung from a chain in the center of the room, and shadows danced in the corners as Bart stomped down the narrow stairs. I stepped back into the well-lighted kitchen, stomach roiling. This felt like more than loony claustrophobia. Maybe I was coming down with the flu.

Bart climbed back up the stairs to the kitchen.

"Well, what I can see of the wiring looks okay, but the whole thing should be redone. Most likely your homeowner's insurance will require rewiring the next time you renew. I'll change the heater filter tomorrow morning. Looks filthy."

"Seemed cold in here this morning, like maybe it wasn't working right." I focused on Bart's plump face and brown eyes. If we were related, as Drake said, he might be another source of family history information. "How well did you know Aunt Elizabeth and Herbert?" I asked.

Bart glanced at me and then clasped his hands together. "Well," he began, "I grew up here. Moved back about the time Herbert passed away." He took a deep breath. "Your great-aunt's second husband was my great-uncle." He studied his clasped hands and then looked at me again. "I should have told you before."

"Doesn't really matter. I appreciate your help. There's a lot I don't know about Elizabeth or her family."

"Glad to give the help. We're family, after all." Bart thrust out his hand. When I shook it, he wrapped my hand in both of his and pumped up and down. "Time for me to call it a day. I'll get my friend Deke to come look at the wiring. Be back with him in the morning." Beads of sweat glistened on his temples. He swiped at them with a red bandana, wiped his mouth, and trudged out the front door.

As I walked over to shut the basement door, cool, damp air rose up and touched my face. I dragged myself into the study and collapsed on the sofa, completely devoid of energy. Queenie plopped down nearby on the floor.

I closed my eyes. Sam's arms around me on Sunday had felt so good. He seemed to be a very gentle, sympathetic, and understanding man. As nice as his offer had been to represent me, I felt sure, after not hearing from him for two days, that he was having second thoughts about any involvement with me. Maybe he believed I had killed Ben and had tried to kill Aunt Elizabeth too.

Chief Clay back in New Mexico certainly believed it. And probably Toby Green as well.

How could I prove Sam had not been the only person besides Elizabeth in the house when I arrived?

I groaned and clutched my stomach. No way could I go to the hospital to see Elizabeth today, feeling like this. Was it the flu? Most likely, if I went home now, Sam Mazie would be out of my life forever. My heart gave a heavy lurch.

Queenie barked. Someone knocked.

I opened the front door to Chief Green. Behind him, the red sun met the tops of the western hills on the far side of town, five miles distant.

"Mrs. Aldrich, I have a few questions. Do you have a minute?" His forehead was pinched with wrinkles, and his turned-down mouth had the look of a man faced with an unpleasant task. I led him into the study. He sat back against the cushions on the sofa.

I remembered Sam's warning. I shouldn't talk to him without counsel present. But I didn't want to turn this into an ordeal. The room had an odd tilt to it, and my stomach churned.

"Fact is, your aunt's not getting any better. I have been

instructed to pursue an arrest in her attempted murder. The doctors have confirmed it is likely her coma was induced by brain damage, possibly caused by asphyxiation," Green stated, eyes on my face.

I braced myself against the door jam.

"The small embroidered pillow we took into our possession was used to try to suffocate your aunt." He leaned forward. "You were holding the pillow when the police and the medical examiner arrived."

"I picked the pillow up off the floor in her room. I told you that." I reached out for the door frame.

"When you and I spoke just after your aunt went to the hospital, you said your husband died at home. Was there an inquest?"

I took a step into the room, and the walls lurched. I grabbed the back of the chair to steady myself. "Chief, I've been advised not to answer any questions without Sam Mazie here."

"Your husband was terminally ill. Did you feel a responsibility to end his suffering? Did you feel a responsibility to end Elizabeth's suffering?"

I closed my eyes and took a deep breath. When I opened them, the walls were steady. "If you insist on questioning me, you'll have to take me in and call Sam Mazie."

Chief Green's left hand flapped up and down against the sofa cushions as his look flitted around the room.

"There was someone else here in the house, someone who tried to kill her while I was downstairs," I repeated.

"She wasn't acting like a woman who wanted to take her own life? Didn't ask for help ending it?" he challenged. I crossed the room and stepped into the hall. When he spoke again, he was standing beside me. "You said your aunt called and asked you to come," Green continued. "She didn't tell you why? She didn't mention she had refused treatment for her cancer?"

"Take me in for questioning and call Sam," I said. "There's no way to know if her illness even figured in what happened. Drake Goodwin hasn't mentioned her illness to me at all."

Police Chief Green ran his fingers through his sandy hair and cocked his head. "Goodwin may not have known. He wasn't her medical doctor. He's a psychiatrist."

Drake had treated my arm. He'd been there in his white coat at the hospital. I had only assumed ... "Please go. Now. I'm not well." I jerked open the front door and stood to one side.

Toby Green's face softened. He thrust one hand into his pants pocket, and I knew he was fingering the rabbit's foot. His expression grew thoughtful. For a few seconds, he looked more like a close friend discussing a problem with me than the local badgering lawman. Then, his facial muscles stiffened, and he was the police chief again.

"Officially," he ordered, "don't leave town."

The lights flickered. I nibbled some wheat crackers and tried to watch the television in the study. Queenie lay at my feet. The constant flickering and rolling of the television screen made it impossible to watch any program. My head hurt too much to read.

Sam Mazie should have been here. Green wouldn't have acted so tough if Sam had been here. I turned the set off and stumbled to the hall phone.

I left a message on Sam's answering machine; I called my mother. No answer there either. My pounding head kept me from remembering the schedule for Mom's hospital tests. Maybe she was already in the hospital.

I climbed the stairs to bed, working to pull my aching legs up each step. My skull was splitting. Worst headache I'd had in years. I felt truly ill, and Pawhuska was the last place I wanted to be sick. I'd been ordered to stay in town. So much for helping Allison.

I'd just climbed into bed when a crack of thunder shook the house. Queenie whined and trotted out into the hall. I grabbed my glasses off the night table, rolled out of bed, and then stepped into the upstairs hallway just in time to see the end of Queenie's tail disappear into Elizabeth's room.

When I looked into her room, I halfway expected to see Elizabeth in the bed. Then I reminded myself she was still in a coma, still in the hospital.

I was no closer to understanding what had happened now than I had been a week ago.

The dog stood at the window, front paws on the window seat, looking outside. Fingers of lightning stretched across the sky. The house shuddered with each corresponding boom of thunder.

"Queenie, come on. Let's go back to bed. It's cold."

The dog whined. I peered out through the rain-splattered windowpane. Lightning flashed. I could just make out a dark shape standing close to the trunk of the old elm tree across the street.

The lightning flashed again, this time illuminating a face. Heavy rain smeared the window, blurring the world outside. I backed away, my heart pounding in my ears.

Chills rippled up and down my back and arms.

Above the house, the thunder crashed again.

There she is, in the window. Huge eyes, beautiful hair. Is she frightened yet? Does she know enough—or has she guessed enough—to be truly frightened? She thinks she is hot on the trail of something.

Thunder drowns out the low cackling laugh.

It won't be long now. So many possibilities, hard to choose the best way to take care of it.

The greenhouse. Now that is an option to consider, although certainly the most distasteful. No way to know if she will still be beautiful when it is all over.

No need for a decision quite yet. Time will tell.

A police car rolls down the street, and the figure moves back into deep shadows. By the time the vehicle parks farther down the street, the figure has moved in the opposite direction, slinking beneath the shadowy shelter of the trees.

Chapter 26

Wednesday, April 10—Morning

Whatever direction I moved, some muscle complained. An ache thudded in my head. Neither my eyes nor my brain would focus. I pulled on some clothes and stumbled downstairs, grasping the banister.

God, my head was killing me. I rubbed my temples frantically as I reached for the aspirin bottle in the cabinet above the kitchen sink. Something pinged down in the basement. Bart? Had to be, but how had he come in? I'd left him a key yesterday, when he'd installed the window. Had he returned it? I couldn't remember. I slumped over the kitchen table and stared out the back window, waiting for my head to explode.

The front doorbell rang.

"Bart? I think the electrician is here." I called as I stood. The floor came up to meet my face.

Queenie whined and poked her nose into my cheek.

"Jamie! Thank goodness," Bart said, his face only a few inches from mine. "I was fixin' to call 911."

The pounding at the front door continued.

"Just a dang minute, Deke!" Bart boomed. My head seemed to split in two. He surged to his feet and charged out of the room. The walls flipped as I tried to sit up.

The front door slammed. When Bart scurried back in, a man in coveralls trailed behind him.

"I'm Deke Edwards, the electrician," the man said.

Bart rushed to the sink, filled a glass with water, and brought it to me where I lay on the floor. After I'd had a few sips, he helped me up and led me to the kitchen table.

I tried to focus on Bart's face without success.

"We'll slip on down to the basement and have a look at the wiring," Bart said. "You sure you're okay? Not going to faint again?"

Faint? Had I fainted? Stress? Flu? "I'll be okay," I said, and took another sip of water, blinking to clear the fuzz from my vision. What I needed was fresh air.

The men crossed the kitchen and clattered down the basement steps. I eased up from the table and teetered through the front hall and out onto the veranda. Then I settled into the porch swing in the shadowy corner.

A cardinal trilled his melody. After a few minutes of listening to the repeated song and breathing deep and steady, the horizon settled and held itself flat. I stared across the street at the old elm tree.

Someone had stood there last night in the storm. I hadn't imagined it.

A car motor shifted into idle in front of the house. Voices floated on the breeze.

I scooted over on the swing and saw the white Cadillac. A magnetic Simpson Haugland Realty sign clung to the passenger door. Simpson Haugland himself was leaning into the front passenger window of a second car, a black Lexus parked in front of the Cadillac. A For Sale sign lay on the sidewalk at his feet.

Haugland pulled his head out of the window of the Lexus and stood back to watch as it rolled down the street. I could see the car's license tag clearly: "WellsOne."

Simpson traipsed out into the middle of the front yard and pushed the For Sale sign down into the moist earth.

"Haugland? What are you doing?" I yelled.

"Jamie!" he called back up toward the house. "I have the papers ready for you to sign. I'll get them." He turned back to his car.

I mustered my energy and stalked out into the yard. "I'm not selling!" I jerked the sign out of the grass and heaved it toward the sidewalk. "Take your sign, and stick it somewhere else."

Haugland's mouth dropped open.

I marched back up the steps and into the house, slamming the door behind me. My head reeled; I leaned against the door, dizzy and unbalanced. Haugland's car roared away.

By noon, my dizziness was worse, even though I'd rested either on the veranda or in the gazebo most of the morning with my face turned toward the breeze. Two trucks were still parked in the drive. When I finally stepped inside the house, the headache returned full force.

Bart walked into the front hall and then stopped. "Say, you don't look so good. You're white as a sheet." He motioned toward the hall bench, and I sank down into it. "Something wrong?"

My shoulder throbbed. My head pounded. I could hardly breathe. "This house is so stuffy. Help me open some windows, will you?" I made my way into the parlor and tugged at one of the tall old windows. Bart poked and pried at the paint with his pocketknife until he could jerk the sash up.

"By next winter, you'll be sealing this window up again so the wind can't squeeze its way in," he grumbled.

"Maybe so," I griped back. "Just get the damned thing open."

He clicked his pocketknife closed and then picked up his toolbox from the hallway. "Done for the day anyway. I'll get out of your hair." He rushed out of the house. Deke followed close behind.

The ring of the phone woke me from a fitful nap on the sofa. I stumbled to the hallway and grabbed the receiver.

"Jamie?" Sam said. "I found the abstract on the house. There've only been two owners, the Wells family and your aunt."

"She bought the house from the Wells family?" I rubbed my forehead.

"In a manner of speaking. According to the records, the house was sold to her for one dollar."

Even in my confused state of mind, it sounded like a pay off.

"Jamie? Are you there?"

"I'm just surprised," I said. But it was more than that. I had to be honest with Sam. He seemed to be my likeliest ally now. "I'm a little under the weather," I added. "Stomach flu, I think. You got my message last night? Have you talked with Toby Green today?"

"I got your message. Tried to call you a couple times when I had a break from court," Sam said. "If Toby had anything new, I'd have heard from him today."

I couldn't detect any emotion in his voice. *He's my lawyer,* I reminded myself. *I'm just a client.*

"Toby's a thorough cop," Sam continued. "He doesn't jump to conclusions. Once he's as certain as I am that you're telling the truth, he won't bother you anymore."

I hoped Sam was right.

When he hung up, I stared down at the phone. Maybe I should have invited him over to dinner or at least have suggested he stop by. He was the only possible bright spot in my life. But our relationship was professional, not personal. The personal one existed only in my mind. It had been so long since I'd gone through the dating process, I didn't even know how to begin. I wasn't even sure I should. *Maybe the only real connection Sam and I have is Great-Aunt Elizabeth.*

I warmed up a can of potato soup and then went out to the back porch with Queenie. Twilight was settling; shades of rose, pink, and gray swirled and blended in the thin clouds. I tugged my sweater closer. My headache had worsened, in spite of four aspirin. I felt only slightly better out in the cool, fresh air.

I glanced over at the house next door. I needed to meet Drake's sister officially, but it was too late in the day now, and besides, I didn't feel like being friendly. I felt lousy.

And I couldn't stop thinking about the spiders on Vera's porch. She still had not called. She had to know I had seen the spiders. She obviously didn't care. I had really been wrong about her. She looked honest, and she'd always been straight about her feelings; rather, I thought she had been.

I plodded across the lawn toward the greenhouse. Drake had interrupted when I'd been about to check the hidey-hole. Now was as good a time as any to check it out, before it got any darker. The back of my neck prickled as I stepped into the ruin and picked my way across the littered floor to the debris-covered workbench. I pulled open the bottom left cubbyhole.

The cubby was full of leaves, bits of paper, hair, and mouse droppings. I picked up a metal scrap from the floor and used it to shovel out the debris. Then I poked at what I knew was a false drawer bottom. The wood popped up to reveal the small recess and a stack of smudged, faded papers bound together by string.

I snatched the notes and shook them making sure no eight-legged creatures had nested between the pages. Then I hurried back to the house. In the kitchen, I dropped the grimy bundle onto the table. Over the years, something had chewed most of the edges. I unfolded the top note.

Black widow!

The two bold, black words seemed to jump toward me from the page. I unfolded another note: *Murderer.* And then another: *Who killed Robert?* One by one, I opened and read each note and added it to the pile.

You're going to hell

Who killed Dodie?

Leave! Else die for your sins!

The accusations continued. Each message was printed in thick, black pen or marker in grade school letters—Big Chief tablet style. The notes from the bottom of the pile were yellowed and brittle.

More than thirty of them. I thought of my aunt's serene face and sparkling eyes. What had she ever done to warrant such hate?

I retrieved the notes I'd received from beneath the counter and laid the short stack next to the pile from the greenhouse. The grade-school-style printing could have been done by the same person. My hands shook, and my head pounded mercilessly. I pushed back from the table and staggered into the hallway.

I pulled Police Chief Toby Green's business card from where it remained stuck between the mirror and the frame. But Green wasn't the first one I needed to talk to. I picked up the phone.

"Mom? How are you?" I tried to push energy I did not feel into my voice.

Mother's voice sounded tired and strained. "I'm all right. I'll have to go back to the hospital for more tests in a day or two. So far, they're telling me the results are inconclusive."

"I have more questions about Elizabeth, Mom. I need more family history." I rubbed at my temples again, but the relentless headache pounded harder and harder. I could hardly focus my eyes.

"Well, if you don't get the facts from me now, you may never get them." Mother's voice sounded suddenly strong. "Not that I'm going anywhere. Just that my sister wouldn't be one to let skeletons out of the closet. If there were any," she added quickly.

"Why didn't anyone ever say Great-Grandmother O'Day was a full-blood Osage?" I pinched the bridge of my nose.

My mother cleared her throat. "Someone told you." There was a long pause. "When I was growing up, Indian blood wasn't something to brag on," she finally said. "Didn't see any need to discuss it when you were little. Why now?"

"We have relatives here I've never heard of. Some are Osage. Seems a little odd no one ever mentioned that heritage or these relatives."

"Does it make any difference?" she asked. "Elizabeth didn't want to be a half-breed, and neither did your grandmother. They both married white men."

My skull pounded and my stomach tightened. Racial bias remained alive and well.

"Yes, my grandmother was a full-blood," Mother sighed. "Married Grandfather after he came to Oklahoma from St. Louis for the oil boom. He was an Irish carpenter. Had a job with the lumber company over in Bigheart, where they lived. They both died long before I was born. Your grandmother was just a child when they both passed."

"Huh," I muttered. My mother should have told me this years ago. But now, feeling as ill as I did, and with Mother's health issues, arguing about it seemed pointless. "Were Elizabeth's marriages happy?" *Black widow.* "Did she have anything to do with her first two husbands' deaths?" *Murderer.*

"Of course not! Her marriage to Dodie lasted a good long while," Mother said. "They had two babies, both stillborn. She was devoted to him, and he was quite handsome." She paused. "There were rumors—other women, gambling." Ice clinked in a glass.

"How did Dodie die, Mom?"

"Somebody shot him after a poker game."

"How did Elizabeth take it?"

"She was devastated. But Rourke came along and swept her off her feet. Elizabeth was still beautiful, still lots of living to do."

"What about her marriage to Rourke?"

"He was another handsome one. After she married him, she fell into a real doozy of a pity party. I heard he had a much younger mistress and refused to give the woman up. He had children with that woman, while Elizabeth couldn't conceive again. It was terribly hard for her." My mother clucked her tongue. "Rourke died in a terrible accident. Elizabeth shut herself off from everyone for a time."

Two marriages. Two husbands dead of unnatural causes. *Black widow.*

"Thankfully, Herbert brought her out of that slump." My mother cleared her throat. "They had some wonderful years together."

"Herbert is the only one I remember. But that was later, when they'd come visit us in New Mexico. I don't remember Robert Rourke at all, but he was alive when I was little, wasn't he? Do you know anything more about Rourke's mistress? Her name? Her children's names?"

"No. Names were never mentioned. What a miserable situation! We were glad Herbert stepped into her life."

"I'm thankful she had Herbert too, Mom, but this still doesn't tell me what I need to know. Who hated her?"

"Of course there were people who didn't like her. You don't like everyone, do you?"

I thought of Haugland and Wells. And I was sure there were those who didn't care for me, both here in Pawhuska and back home. I couldn't bring myself to believe Aunt Elizabeth had played any part in the deaths of either of her husbands, yet she had kept the notes hidden away. Had she been afraid? Ashamed?

An hour later, Sam and I sat in the kitchen at the little table.

"Who else knows about these notes?" Sam asked, closing the last one and laying it on the table with the others.

"Only Chief Green, as far as I know. He told me about them last weekend," I explained. "I've received a couple of notes just like these since I've been here, and someone even copied Chief Green on one. He seems to think Elizabeth's been getting notes like these for years."

We both stared at the notes on the table. Ever since Sam had walked in the front door, all I could seem to think about, aside from my headache and the nausea I was experiencing, was the feel of his arm around me last Sunday and how gently he had stroked my hair. Damn. I wanted his arms around me again. I'd called him because I needed comfort. I didn't feel well. But I'd also called him because I was starting to wonder if I was in over my head. Someone had wanted Elizabeth dead, but I had no idea how to figure out who it was.

Sam shot out of the chair and crossed the room. "Put the notes away somewhere safe," he said, pacing in front of the window. "I'll call Toby first thing tomorrow." He rubbed the back of his neck and then combed through his long hair with his fingers. "I should go."

I followed him to the door. After a sudden, quick kiss on my cheek, he was gone.

I closed and bolted the front door behind him and then slumped against it. My body and my heart ached. I had wanted him to stay—I needed to talk through all of this with him. My stomach clenched and an unpleasant taste filled my mouth.

When the nausea passed, I went back to the kitchen and gathered the notes. I put them in the only hiding place I could think of: the bin in the pantry. Then I pulled myself up the steep back stairway.

I'd never felt quite this ill—or this uncertain about so many things.

Chapter 27

Thursday, April 11—Early Morning

I twisted in the bed covers and struggled to pull open my eyes. Something was wrong. My stomach flipped and then flopped. The walls, floor, and ceiling of the room spun around and around again.

Vaporous light swirled across the blurred room like mist, and the bed rolled as if floating on a gentle sea.

A shape loomed at the door. I reached for my glasses on the nightstand, but my fingers closed on empty air. I pulled myself up and out of the bed, and frantically felt for my lenses across the top of the little table, knocking over my water glass in the process. The electric clock radio crashed to the floor. When I glanced back at the doorway, the fuzzy shape had melted from the fuzzy doorway and into the fuzzy hall.

Something seemed to be squeezing my chest. I tried to suck in a deep breath of air, but coughed instead. Bile rose up in my throat. I lurched across the room and out into the hallway, gagging. Hands in front of me, I staggered forward, reaching for the banister in the dim light.

"Queenie?" my voice croaked.

I reached the top of the stairs and gripped the banister. Colored lights floated up from the entry hall. Downstairs, someone was singing the gazebo waltz.

"Elizabeth?" I called. *No, not Elizabeth. Aunt Elizabeth was in a coma, wasn't she?* But it had to be Elizabeth down there, singing the song we'd danced to as children.

"Casey would waltz with the strawberry blonde," a clear voice sang out from the entry hall below.

The colors in the air swirled like kaleidoscope crystals. I swayed against the banister, and when I closed my eyes, the nausea got worse. I opened them. The voice had stopped singing.

"Casey would waltz ..." I sang out in an unsteady, off-key voice. Below, a door banged.

Gripping the rail, I inched down the stairs, my stomach roiling. The thudding behind my eyes shook my skull.

A dog barked.

"Queenie?" I stumbled off the last step and down into the entry hall. The rhythm pounded faster in my head. A dog barked again. From outside? On the front porch?

Pound.

Pound. Pound.

I wove my way across the hall, dodging prisms of color. I reached out to grasp the front doorknob.

Pound. Pound.

It pounded me into blackness.

Quiet voices and beeping machinery stirred my brain into consciousness. Something irritated my nostrils and the end of my nose, where sweet air poured in. I opened my eyes to a white world, fuzzy in my myopic vision.

A blurred face loomed over me. I blinked but couldn't focus the image. Another face crowded near and leaned close.

"Jamie?" The voice was familiar.

"Drake?" My tongue was a giant wad of cotton.

Someone leaned close but didn't touch me. "It's good to have you back. Another few minutes and it would have been too late."

"What happened?" The pounding in my head was softer, and the brain fog had thinned.

"Carbon monoxide," the voice stated. "If you hadn't come to the front door, I'm quite sure you would be dead by now."

I tried to remember. The shape at the bedroom door, the swirling lights, the music, Queenie barking.

"Where's the dog?"

"I found you lying inside your open front door about 6:30 this morning," the voice said slowly. "There was no dog."

"I opened the door to let her in."

He stepped away from the bed. "If not for that bit of fresh air ..." He sighed and stuffed his hands deep in the pockets of the white lab coat.

"You were there?" I struggled to piece it together.

"I stopped over to fix breakfast for Susan and the kids. Steve didn't make it in last night." He leaned toward me again, peering at my eyes.

Steve didn't get home. Susan's husband, Steve. Drake's sister, Susan.

"Carbon monoxide," I breathed. "The heater?"

"Yes. I've got somebody over there right now, checking the heater. Those old numbers are notorious."

Carbon monoxide. My science teacher self searched my mind and then clicked off the symptoms I'd always discussed in the science lab: dizziness, nausea, confusion, and headache. I had been blaming my own symptoms on stress or the flu and lack of sleep.

"Odorless," I mumbled. Bart had been working in the basement yesterday. Why hadn't he complained of any symptoms?

"Very dangerous," Drake announced. "A monitor would have indicated it, but there isn't one in the house."

When I woke again, the nurse was checking the oxygen monitor clipped to the end of my finger. The nurse's face, like everything else in my world, was blurred without the benefit of my corrective lenses.

"Hello, again," another familiar voice said. "I hope you're not planning to make a habit of these visits."

I squinted. It might be the nurse from last week's visit, but I couldn't be sure.

"Heaven forbid." I tried a smile. The oxygen tube pinched into the end of my nose.

The nurse smoothed the light blanket over me.

"I'm glad it's you. Not too many friendly faces around here," I said. Drake had seemed emotionally dead this morning, more so than just physician detachment.

The nurse might have nodded her head, but the blurred movement was slight. Her name badge was only a white smear with dim black lines across it.

"I'm Janice Green. Toby Green is my husband."

I closed my eyes and felt suddenly choked up. The chief's wife. Janice plumped another pillow and stuffed it behind my head.

"If you need anything, Jamie, just push your button. I'm here until three this afternoon. Drake asked you be kept over-night for observation. Phil Sims, our on-call internist, agreed. He'll check on you later. Rest now." The door closed.

When I woke again, someone had pulled a chair close to the bed. I could make out chin-length auburn hair. "Vera?"

"Jamie, are you all right?" the woman whispered.

I pulled the oxygen tube away from my nose and pushed the plastic yoke up to my forehead. "According to Drake, I could have died." I looked at blurred Vera. My mind worked, slowly. The image of plump black spiders crept in. "Where were you Monday?"

"You need to know ..."

Martin Wells burst into the room, carrying an enormous bouquet of flowers. "My goodness, dear Jamie! I hear we almost lost you!" His cologne cloud rolled in with him. Wells set the vase on the bedside table and moved opposite Vera to the other side of the bed.

I tucked the oxygen tube back into my nose, not wanting to smell the scent of Ben's favorite cologne. Martin leaned over the bed and stared into my eyes.

"For heaven's sake, Jamie, carbon monoxide," Martin groaned. "That old house is a dangerous place. All the systems need a thorough review. Thank goodness you are still here with us." He straightened and turned toward Vera. Vera pushed out of her chair and jerked toward the door, mumbling.

"What did you say?" I pulled the oxygen tube out again. "Vera, you're going?"

"I'm due at work. Rest." The door swung shut behind her.

Wells sidled around the bed to the chair. "Seriously, Jamie, I do hope you will rethink what you're going to do with that house. You shouldn't stay there any longer. I can get you a room at the B and B. I'll even cover the expense."

I replaced the tube and drew in pure oxygen. The pounding in my head was now only a persistent heartbeat. I closed my eyes. I wanted him gone. I wanted to feel well, so I could get out of here.

"You're exhausted," Wells cooed. "You think about that room at the B and B. Soft bed, people nearby. Meanwhile, please call me if you need anything at all. Advice, a shoulder to lean on ... I'm here for you, Jamie, always." He planted a wet kiss on my forehead.

I sucked in the pure, sweet oxygen. *Get out, please,* I prayed. The smell of the man's cologne brought tears to my eyes. *How many days had I been breathing poison air?* I kept my eyes scrunched closed, and eventually I heard the door to my room shut.

Some time later, when I opened my eyes again, someone with glossy dark hair stood beside the bed. Sam Mazie. My heart tightened and tears welled up again.

"Hi," he said. He laid a small bouquet of flowers on the

white hospital blanket near my hand. I fumbled for the bed control and pushed the button to raise my upper body. "Do you need anything?" Sam asked in a soft, worried tone.

"I'm feeling better," I whispered. "I'll be able to go home tomorrow morning. Drake ordered I be 'observed' for the night."

Worry lines deepened around Sam's eyes. "Have you seen the internist? Drake's practice is psychology, you know."

"I heard. He seems to be pulling double duty. Every time I've been in, he's here, and he takes charge. Janice Green is one of the nurses on duty."

Sam nodded, fingering the blanket. "I was there last night, in your house." Guilt edged his voice. "Why didn't I feel something?"

"There is no way you could have known. There's no smell to the gas. I'm the only one who's been sleeping there. It's just been me and that little stray dog, Queenie, and I don't know where she is." I sniffed. "I heard her outside and went downstairs to let her in," I continued. "I had some strange notion Elizabeth was hosting a dance downstairs. Someone was singing "And the Band Played On"—that old waltz about Casey and the strawberry blonde. Elizabeth used to sing it, and we'd dance in the gazebo."

Sam placed his hand on my shoulder and stroked with his thumb as I let the story spill out. "Uh-umm." He moved his hand to my cheek.

I turned my face into his open palm and closed my eyes. I wanted his hand to stay there. I wanted him to sit down and stay with me while I slept. I just needed to sleep.

Minutes passed, and he stood close, his hand on my cheek, not saying a word. His other hand touched my forehead and smoothed back my hair. I sighed and opened my eyes again.

"I'll check the neighborhood for the dog," he said, patting my shoulder. "Maybe Trudy's seen her. Meanwhile, I'll make sure that heater is being repaired."

"Drake said he would have someone check it out," I said, looking up at him. Butterflies invaded my stomach.

"*I'll* check into it," he said. "You need rest. Don't worry

about anything. I'll be back in the morning to take you home."
He stroked my cheek with the backs of his fingers and then
moved his flowers to the table next to Wells's extravagant
bouquet. I followed his blurred shape as he crossed the room,
stopped at the door, and looked back. Then he was gone.

After the aide removed my supper tray and the internist, Dr.
Sims, checked my chart and looked me over, a tap came at the
door. I recognized the visitor by his light coloring, stocky size,
and athletic posture, even though he, like everything else, was
a blur.

"Chief Green." I had been expecting him.

"Sorry to hear what happened. You're lucky to be alive.
Can you tell me about it?"

I described the blurred figure I'd seen in my doorway,
the hallucination of music and light, and Queenie's barking.
I explained how Drake had said he'd found me. Then I told
him about finding the stack of Elizabeth's notes earlier in the
evening.

"Where are they now?" The police chief leaned so close that
his freckles came into focus.

"Hidden. You can go over to the house and get them," I
suggested.

"Where?" he asked. His fingers jingled the coins in his front
pocket.

"In a favorite hiding place of Aunt Elizabeth's. The kitchen
pantry flour bin."

"Should have known," he muttered. "I think I'll go get
them." He rushed toward the door, calling over his shoulder,
"I'll be back."

Thirty minutes turned into an hour as I waited for Green
to return. I'd listened to a blurry television program on the
monitor suspended above the bed. The floor nurses dispensed
the night meds. The lights dimmed. Finally, just as the edges of

the room were beginning to fade away and my eyelids drooped, the room phone rang.

"The flour bin is empty."

I sank back on the hard bed. Questions nagged like the faint ache remaining in my head. Anyone could have taken the notes; the house had been open all day. But who, besides Sam, had known where they were?

Chapter 28

Friday, April 12—Morning

Nurses came and went all night. By morning, all that remained of my carbon monoxide experience was a dull headache. After Janice Green brought in my dismissal papers, I dressed in borrowed hospital scrubs, laid back down on the bed, and waited for Sam.

I would have died if not for the crazy dream/hallucination that had drawn me downstairs in the early dawn. Had there really been someone upstairs at the bedroom door and then someone singing downstairs? If not, how did Queenie get outside?

Always swirling in the back of my mind was the thought that the notes were gone.

Trudy probably knew the pantry hiding place. But I hadn't seen Trudy since Monday evening. Had she come into the house without permission again? And if she had, why would she take the notes?

Then there was the old heater. Had Bart or the repairman done something in the basement that created the leak or made an existing leak worse?

I sensed someone had entered the room and I was no longer alone.

"Ready to go?" Sam asked. His hands rubbed my shoulders. I turned to face him, feeling flushed and self-conscious. I hadn't felt so vulnerable in years. His arms slid around me in a slow, easy hug. He kissed my forehead, but I stopped myself before I stepped into his unexpected embrace.

Could I really trust this man?

"The repairman is still at the house," Sam said as he opened the passenger door so I could climb into the dark-blue Ford Ranger.

I faked a smile. This handsome man was the only person who had known I had found the stash of old notes and where I had hidden them. He could have returned to the house that night and taken them. But why would he do that?

"Do you feel well enough to go for a drive?" Sam asked as we pulled into Great-Aunt Elizabeth's driveway and parked behind the two work trucks.

I wanted to know him better, to give him a chance to disprove what I feared about him, but part of me didn't. I wasn't sure I could trust him. This might be a chance to find out. And my body cried out for fresh country air.

"I'd like that," I finally said. "Just let me freshen up a bit. You want to wait inside?"

"I have something I need to do," he said with a solemn face, but then a smile began at the corners of his mouth. "I'm going to get Queenie."

"Where is she?" My spirit lifted, and Sam grinned. I had been worried about the stray dog's whereabouts and had told myself I would probably never see her again.

"Trudy found her," Sam said. "I'll run over and get her."

Grinning, I shuffled up the new steps and shoved the front door open. Banging noises echoed up from the basement. Hand on the banister, I stopped. I'd seen swirling lights ... heard music. Someone had been singing the gazebo waltz. That voice couldn't have just been a figment of the poison in my system.

I hurried up the stairs, discarded the borrowed hospital scrubs, and slipped into a pair of jeans, a light sweater, and boots. A few minutes later as I inserted my contact lenses, I heard a low woof and dog claws scrambling on the hardwood floor of the entry.

"Queenie!" I called.

The dog charged up the stairs and into the bathroom, threw herself at my legs, and licked whatever her tongue could reach.

Sam shouted below. "Come on!"

I brushed a stray strand of hair back off my forehead and moved to the stairs. My knees weren't holding me up very well, but my head was clear.

"I appreciate your help in getting that heater fixed, and thanks for getting Queenie back," I said as the three of us climbed into Sam's truck. My voice sounded formal; had Sam noticed? If he had, would he care?

Crap. I had to stop thinking like a teenager.

Sam drove the truck north on Grandview. Scraggly black-jacks and post oaks lined the road as it curved past ranch-style homes set in the middle of fenced acreages. He tuned the radio to a Tulsa country-western station. The volume level was low enough for conversation, but we drove in silence. Wind from the open windows whipped my face as we entered the rolling, rocky hills covered with stubby oak trees. Birds chased each other from tree to tree.

"Any place in particular you'd like to drive?" Sam asked.

My heart lurched unexpectedly as I looked at his face, prominent cheekbones, shining dark hair and eyes. I turned back to the window. I was too old to feel this way. Like everyone else at this point, Sam was a suspect.

"Something wrong? You feeling ill again?" he asked, reaching out to touch my knee.

I wanted to believe the concern in his voice was genuine. I turned back to him and lay one arm along the back of the front seat behind Queenie. The truck turned off the pavement and bounced along a wash-boarded dirt road.

"You sure you got time for this? It's a workday." I shoved my suspicions away. The sunlight changed everything. Out here, on this perfect spring day, Sam seemed an unlikely suspect.

"It's a beautiful day, and I'm due a day off. I'm so relieved you're all right." He reached over, touched my hand, and then blew out a big breath. His look swept across the countryside around us. "April is the time of the Just-Doing-That Moon and everything is turning green."

"The Just-Doing-That-Moon. I've heard that before." My memory twitched, and I imagined a large tree with an old rope swing hanging down, the dangling seat board chipped and lopsided. Heaviness pressed on my chest. What was I remembering?

"It's the Osage Planting Moon, the moon of promise," Sam said. "Each month has a special Osage name, having to do with Mother Earth and the Moon Woman, the natural world, and Grandfather Sun."

I nodded. I remembered. Great-Aunt Elizabeth had told us those names as we worked in the garden. We'd never been here for spring planting. By the time we came for summer visits, the seedlings Elizabeth had planted were growing tall.

"Little Flower ... something Little Flower," I said. "That was May, right? We would come then, right after school was out, and stay through June. Buffalo Paw month or something like that," I laughed. "It didn't make much sense when I was little."

"Probably not," he chuckled. "May is Little Flower Killer Moon, and June is Buffalo Pawing Earth Moon."

I tried hard to remember the reasoning behind the names. Sam grinned at me.

"Little Flower Killer Moon because the first little spring flowers, the ones that come up even before the last frost, like bluets, are low and close to the ground," he explained. "As May comes and the weather gets warmer, these little flowers go away. So, Little Flower Killer Moon."

"And the Buffalo Pawing Earth Moon?"

Sam shrugged his shoulders and tossed his head. His hair

flipped and then fell back into place. "Buffalo Pawing Earth Moon. The male buffalo struts his stuff, getting ready for the mating season in July. Practicing his bluff and establishing his territory."

Sam glanced sideways at me with a pinched grin that made a little dimple pop up in his right cheek. I cleared my throat. Sam reached over and folded his hand around mine. My palm started to sweat.

I still had no idea where we were going when Sam turned the truck onto a paved highway. It didn't matter. It felt good to be out driving with Sam, laughing and talking. It was something normal, and not much had felt normal in the last twelve days. But it was also something more than normal. I'd never thought I'd have these feeling about anyone again.

"Did you grow up around here?" I asked, still wondering if I had known Sam as a child. How could I have ever forgotten someone like Sam?

"My family still lives in the house where I was born," he answered. "We're on our way there."

"I'd love to see it." I couldn't stop the grin from spreading across my face.

He chuckled. "It's on the way to another place you need to see again," he added. "You've been there before, picnicking with friends and family."

"And how would you know that?" I asked.

"I was with you."

I shifted my body so I could face him. He reached over behind my left shoulder, jabbed the door lock button down, and then gave me a quick, parental frown.

"Tell me more," I demanded.

"You really don't remember?"

I shook my head.

"It wasn't often I got to picnic with little white girls. Back when we were growing up, white people and Osage didn't socialize much. Your Aunt Elizabeth was one of the few white people in town who treated me just like the other kids. But then, she was half Osage."

I remembered what my mother had said. Apparently, I'd had much more contact with my Osage relatives in Pawhuska than my mother knew.

"When your family came to town in the summers, Elizabeth wanted you to have playmates," Sam explained. "She'd have us over; we'd picnic or play baseball and other games. I'm hurt that you don't remember. I think I was about ten when I fell in love with you." A blush crept up my neck. He reached over and chucked me under the chin. "Seriously, whenever you came to visit—that was my favorite time of year. Then, when my voice started changing and I was *really* looking forward to seeing you, you stopped coming. Broke my heart." He frowned at me, but his eyes twinkled.

"Sam, I don't remember much about those summers. I remember Elizabeth loved to entertain. The grownups would play cards or play records and dance while we kids would spy on them. Remember that?"

"Mostly, I remember Osage stories and dancing," he said. "The playing cards and records must have been the 'white' side of the family." There was a hint of hurt in his voice. Who was he talking about? There had been no other family members here, except, as I'd recently learned, Jasper and Trudy.

The truck lurched as it crept off the highway onto a dirt road. I thought about the headright again as we passed an oil pump jack. Maybe Elizabeth had traded the headright for the house. Had my grandmother and Jasper known what she had done? Was that the secret she'd hidden all these years?

"Not much farther," Sam said. "Look familiar?"

I looked for recognizable landmarks. Thick groves of oak trees crowded the rolling hills, and cattle grazed on the rocky pastures. Bluebirds flashed by. Mockingbirds dipped their long black and white tail feathers as they swooped from tree to tree. Wispy clouds smeared the blue dome above sprouting emerald grass.

The truck slowed and stopped in front of a gravel driveway. At the end of the drive, a wide grassy lawn surrounded a small blue house. Chickens pecked around the front stoop.

"The family homestead. Mom and Dad must be in town shopping."

"I'd love to come back another time to meet them," I said. Sam had wanted me to meet his family. Surely that was a sign of something.

"You will meet them—and soon. I promise." He smiled and then shifted the truck into drive.

A few minutes farther down the rutted road, he eased the truck as far to the right as he could and parked. "This look familiar?" he asked, looking north across the barbed wire fence. We got out of the car.

I scanned the area as I stepped through knee-high brown grass to the fence. Old trees and overgrown bushes dotted the acreage and lined the fence row.

Queenie woofed, crawled under the lowest wire, and took off at a lope toward a hedgerow, skirting naturalized daffodils and iris clumps. Birds fluttered up and a rabbit dashed for cover.

Sam spread two stands of the wire fence apart and motioned for me to crawl through. My heartbeat quickened, and the air was suddenly thin. Time seemed suspended. My feet felt rooted to the ground, but I forced them to move, forced my body to stoop over and step through the opening between the wire strands. We looked across the acreage.

The grass-choked foundation of a house was centered in the weedy lot. A tumbled-down brick pile might have been a chimney. A few charred timbers littered the yard. Metal pieces poked up from hillocks of last year's tall grass.

Fifty yards away, limb fingers of a huge tree jabbed at the sky. One side of the trunk had split and fallen away, but new leaves clung to living branches. Remnants of an old rope swing hung from one of the biggest limbs. Sam walked toward it.

"A wise old owl sat in an oak. The more he saw, the less he spoke. The less he spoke, the more he heard. Why can't we ..." He paused and looked over his shoulder at me.

"Be like that wise old bird?" I finished slowly. "We used to recite that when we were swinging," I said. The memory reel ran: I had soared over the people below like a hawk.

"The white man's rhyme seemed appropriate here, even for an Osage." Sam's voice interrupted the summer scene rising up in my mind from thirty years before.

Sam led the way as we wandered, stepping around rusted household debris. My ears rang, and the landscape seemed fuzzy. Queenie loped past, nose to the ground, and then charged off, ears flopping.

I stopped and fingered the branch of a small tree. "Everything looks strange. I know this place, yet I don't."

"Thirty years is a long time." Sam stopped beside me. "What kind of tree is this?"

I let go of the branch and peered down at the scattered dry remnants of last fall's mitten-shaped leaves. "Mulberry."

Sam nodded. "As in, 'Here We Go 'Round ...'"

"This was our little mulberry bush?" I pulled away from the tree as I remembered Elizabeth humming the nursery rhyme the day I arrived here. A breeze blew an icy breath on my neck, and a chill settled over me.

"Remember that cavity in the trunk," he asked, "where we'd leave clues for treasure hunts?"

I remembered fingering the smooth edges of that hole, low on the trunk, just above a branch.

Sam stepped away from the tree and over to a small earth mound covered by a piece of rusted metal. A cement block held the metal to the ground. "Remember this?" He shoved the concrete block to one side and pulled the metal door open.

My skin prickled. The breeze carried the musty, damp

smell from the hole to where I stood. I closed my eyes, nause-ated. Spiders. Darkness. Damp stink.

"After you," he offered.

I shook my head. "I let you all drag me down there when I was a kid, but I'm not falling for it now." I stepped back as claustrophobia pressed in. Unpleasant memories jammed into my mind.

"Great place to hide. Remember?"

"I don't remember the cellar as being so great. All I remember is being trapped, unable to get out." My hand reached up to grab my necklace.

The metal door clanged shut. Sam walked over to the old cabin's foundation.

Queenie emerged from a clump of staghorn sumac and trotted toward me. Eyes closed, I took a few deep, slow breaths of the grass-scented air.

"How long did Elizabeth's family live here?" I called, trailing after him. "The house was already gone when we were kids."

"Elizabeth's father died in the fire that destroyed the cabin," he said. "Didn't she ever talk about that?"

Another bit of family history no one had ever mentioned. Sam and I skirted the cabin foundation. Queenie panted along beside us. A few yards ahead, a bluebird flitted from the bushes near the road. Behind us, two crows cawed at each other.

"Elizabeth was born here," Sam said. "She always talked about being innocent and happy here with her family. She'd tell stories of her childhood but never talked about the fire or her dad's death."

I glanced back at the foundation. A flash of brown-orange moved through the still-bare sumac bushes. The coyote sat down and stared. And then it came to me. "This is the Bigheart property."

We drove back to town in silence. A chill had crept into my bones and my head felt heavy. Sam seemed preoccupied. I didn't want to deal with his moodiness or probe his thoughts as I often had when Ben was in a similar mood.

Sam's right hand felt warm on top of mine.

When we got back to Elizabeth's house, the front door was locked and the repairmen were gone. I let Sam lead me down into the basement to inspect the new heater unit. Everything looked clean and shiny. The heater hummed.

Moments later, after we had climbed the stairs and walked back into the front hall, Sam squeezed my hand and pulled me to him. His kiss was sweet and warm, and he lingered, tasting my lips. I wrapped my arms around his neck and clung to him, wanting him to stay, needing to be held. It had been so long since I'd let anyone that near. Eventually, we pulled apart; he smiled and then slipped out the front door.

From the veranda, I watched the taillights as the little truck moved down the street. My heart was still pounding. *Maybe I should have responded more to his kiss. Drawn him back into the house. Taken him upstairs.* I had wanted to.

He wanted me to meet his family.

The clock in the study ticked loudly, and the refrigerator whirred behind me in the kitchen. Queenie whined. I wandered through the house to the dining room window. The silent house seemed to be breathing down my neck.

Queenie and I went out the back door. The dog rushed out into the yard and then ambled from flower bed to flower bed, sticking her nose into everything and snorting at the smells.

The hair on my neck prickled. I whirled and looked from tree to house to shrub to the windows of the house next door. Nothing moved.

This place was getting to me.

I walked out to the gazebo and sat down. I needed time to think. About Aunt Elizabeth. About Sam.

The sun was hanging low in the afternoon sky when I returned to the house. Darkness had settled in the corners of the hallway. I walked from room to room, turning on all the downstairs lamps, hoping I would feel safe and cozy with the extra light, but the lights didn't help. Sam's presence would have done much more, especially if the two of us were having a glass of wine while the aroma of baking bread swirled in the air, as well as some garlicky concoction bubbling on the stove.

I grabbed a book from a shelf in the study, curled up in the wingback chair under a crocheted afghan, and tried to read. After the first few pages, I couldn't have told a soul what the book was about. My mind kept tumbling my thoughts as if it was polishing stones, not hunting for answers.

I laid the book down and called Allison. Minutes later, as we talked, I heard the disappointment in her voice when I told her I wouldn't be home this weekend to help her select a wedding gown. She didn't demand an explanation or pout, and when I told her there were still matters to be taken care of here, Allison didn't pry. In some ways, I wished she would have. I needed to bounce all of this off someone, but Allison was too young to understand why it all mattered so much to me.

To Allison, Elizabeth had been an elderly woman she hardly knew. I had never told her how much I had relied on Elizabeth for the emotional support my own mother hadn't been willing to provide. Now, I didn't want to fail Elizabeth. Somewhere inside her head, I felt sure, my great-aunt was cheering me on. If only I had some idea what she wanted me to do.

I called Mother's number and then Ellen's, but there was no answer at either place and no answering machine. I opened the book again, but instead of reading, I thought about my high school class back home. What was this week's lab experiment and assignment supposed to be? I couldn't remember. Life as a teacher in New Mexico seemed hundreds of years ago.

Queenie growled. A soft rap came at the front door.

The porch light shone on Vera's wide-eyed face. As I

opened the door, the woman slipped in, peering back over her shoulder. "How are you feeling?" Vera asked softly.

I remembered all too clearly the black widow spiders Vera was growing on her back porch and didn't invite her to come any farther in than the front hall. For all I knew, Vera was the enemy.

"I'm really sorry about Monday," Vera whispered. "I need to explain. When can we talk?" She peered out the door to the yard and the street beyond.

"We're talking now," I said.

"No, not here. There might be ... just ... not here, please."

"In the car? Outside? Where, then?"

"Tomorrow? Lunchtime." Vera pulled her jacket tight and stepped back out to the veranda.

"Okay. Nice of you to stop by." I swung the door shut and locked it. Vera had seemed ... frightened. I turned the lamps off in the study and in the parlor, and then went to the front parlor window, drawing aside the sheers to peek outside.

The figure stands close to the tree, blending into the shadows, watching the house.

She is home again. Close call.

A gloved hand reaches up to stifle the low chuckle.

Better things yet to come.

Chapter 29

Saturday, April 13—Morning

An insistent ringing cut into my dream. Queenie padded to the bedroom door and then back to my bedside, whining, but I didn't want to open my eyes. The quilts mounded over me in the soft warm bed, creating a safe, warm sleeve. The ringing continued. I stirred and finally reached for my glasses so I could see the alarm clock in the early morning light.

I lay there another few seconds, hoping the ringing would stop. Seven o'clock? Who was calling on the phone at seven in the morning on Saturday? I jerked on a robe and plodded downstairs.

"Jamie! Caller ID said I missed your call last night. Were you still in bed?" Ellen sounded chipper for this time of the morning. It was an hour earlier in her time zone.

"It's been a rough week." I yawned. "I spent Thursday in the hospital." I told her what had happened since we'd last spoken. Ellen listened without comment. Maybe she wasn't listening. Finally, I asked her what I really wanted to know. "Do you remember summer picnics out in the country at a place with a rope swing? And an old root cellar?"

After a pause, she answered. "Yes. There was a whole gang of us kids. We went out there to picnic. Have you run into any of them in Pawhuska?"

"Sam Mazie was one of those kids. I don't know about the

others." I *was* certain, after what he said yesterday, that Sam was one of those kids.

If Ellen remembered the home site, she remembered the cellar. I wouldn't go there again. Sam could sell the place as Elizabeth had instructed.

"I remember waltzing in the gazebo while Elizabeth sang," Ellen said, cutting into my thoughts. "She was always humming old songs. Didn't she tell us her dad played the fiddle while she and Grandma fell asleep at night?"

I pictured the burned timbers at the home site and changed the subject. "What about Trudy O'Day? Did you remember anything?"

"I do remember another little girl about my age," Ellen said. "But mostly little boys. I wish Randy could ..." Ellen began. We both knew Randy couldn't remember. He sometimes didn't know who Ellen or I was when we visited him at the Veterans Hospital.

"One with dark hair, Indian-looking, was Sam," I prodded.

"Two of the boys had dark hair. Both of them were shy. And I remember another boy who danced with us in the gazebo. Kind of chubby with blondish-red hair. Freckles. He was 'Casey' when we were waltzing. You know how the song went. 'Casey would waltz with the strawberry blonde...'" Ellen sang, off-key.

"I remember," I interrupted. All too well—and recently.

"That kid would drag one of us out and waltz around, remember? Was Trudy's hair sort of a dark blonde?"

I could picture a boy and a girl waltzing in the old gazebo. "What were the other kids' names?" The baseball team picture was on the table in the kitchen, and the cord on this phone didn't reach that far.

"I don't remember. And all I remember about Trudy was that she stopped playing with us that last summer." Ellen sighed. "Enough of that. Let me update you on Mom. She's going back in the hospital Monday for more tests and is scheduled to be home on Wednesday. She's not accepting phone calls from anyone, so don't try to contact her. If it's an emergency, I can pass something on when I stop in each day to see her."

I heard the self-important tone in Ellen's voice and knew there was a message there. I longed for the day when the two of us would no longer feel sibling rivalry. "Okay. I don't have anything to tell her, really. Just tell her I love her and I'm thinking about her. I really do hope to get home next week, maybe by Thursday."

As I said the words, I had no idea whether the situation would be resolved by then. Green wasn't pushing me, but his investigation was underway.

"Sis, you won't believe what's going on right now with me and Harry," Ellen rushed on. "Seems like we just get something worked out when he goes and pulls some crazy stunt. He's driving me batty." Ellen turned the conversation into an exposé of her own marital problems. I tried to listen, but as the complaints dragged on and on, I fell silent. I liked Harry—admired him, even—for putting up with Ellen. He had a heart of gold, and my sister couldn't see it.

I squirmed on the hall bench and finally broke in when she paused. "If you remember anything else or have news, please call me. I've got to go now. I'll call you in a few days." The line buzzed as the connection broke.

I set down the receiver and stared toward the front door. Soft morning light sifted through the frosted side windows and glowed on the wood floor. I breathed deeply and felt the air charge into my lungs. Good, sweet air.

After taking my time with a breakfast of pancakes and bacon, I pulled a hoodie over my light sweater and walked to the house next door. If those kids were anything like mine had been, they were up early, watching Saturday morning cartoons. I'd just take a minute of time to introduce myself. I had been living next door to this family for nearly two weeks.

A buzzer rang somewhere inside when I pushed the doorbell. Someone fumbled with the knob, and the door swung inward a few inches. A television set blared in the background. I dropped my gaze to the woman in the wheelchair.

"I know who you are," the woman snapped. Long blonde and gray hairs had been loosely pulled back into a ponytail. Small brown eyes glared at me from a pale face. She had Drake's cheekbones and high forehead.

"I'm Jamie Aldrich, Mrs. Graham's great-niece," I said anyway. "From next door."

Susan glowered at me. She glanced over her shoulder into the house and then at me again.

"We haven't officially met, although I know your brother. He's been very helpful." The woman scowled. "Your kids are cute," I forged on with a half smile. "I'd like to bring them some cookies. Snickerdoodles were always my kids' favorites. What do Rory and Daniel like?"

"They get all the sweets they need. Don't bother." The door swung shut in my face.

"Nice to meet you, too," I grumbled as the latch clicked. Drake wasn't exactly friendly, but he was nothing like his sister. I could feel the woman's glare on my back as I trekked down the sidewalk to the street.

I settled in on the weathered gazebo bench in the backyard, eyes closed, and let the warm breeze play on my face. Queenie stretched out in an ivy bed. I reran my brief conversation with Drake's sister, Susan. The woman had no reason to be so hostile. Had she treated Elizabeth the same way? What could have caused such bad feelings?

Catches of a melody drifted past. Someone was humming "And the Band Played On" just like Elizabeth used to do. I opened my eyes and saw Trudy strolling across the lawn.

"*His brain was so loaded, it nearly exploded, the poor girl would shake with alarm,*" Trudy sang out. "*But he'd ne'er leave the girl with the strawberry curls, and the band played on.*"

My mouth dropped open. Trudy's rich voice didn't match her uneven features and odd way of speaking. She had perfect pitch.

And I had heard her voice before.

Trudy stepped up into the gazebo wearing a pretty pink sweater. The bill of her striped cap still protruded from her jean pocket. Her eyes had lost their usual cautious look.

"I haven't seen you for nearly a week," I began with a friendly smile. "Have you been all right?"

"I've been all right," Trudy said. "I'm sorry about what happened to you."

I knew I had heard Trudy singing early Thursday morning. Had she also been the blurred shape in my bedroom doorway? "Trudy, did you come in the house that night?"

She ducked her head.

"Trudy, it's all right if you did," I murmured. "That's what woke me up. If it *was* you, you saved my life."

Trudy looked me full in the face, and one eye focused.

"I saw you in the greenhouse, just like I saw my Liz when she hid the notes," Trudy said. "They made her cry. She didn't want anybody to see them. You found them, and you showed Sam."

Had Trudy been in the house when Sam came over?

Trudy looked off toward the house and started to hum "Do You Know the Muffin Man?"

The cookie signal. She had guessed where I had hidden the notes. I squirmed. Her uneven face didn't necessarily mean she had a low intelligence.

"Trudy, why did you come upstairs?"

Trudy picked at her pink sweater and then stroked the bill of the hat in her pocket. She looked closely at me. "I miss her. I wanted to read her story again."

"What do you mean?"

"Her story, in her room. But I couldn't breathe up there, and you were asleep."

The saliva evaporated in my mouth. "Are you talking about a diary? Her story?" Diary entries might answer all my questions, including the "truth" that Elizabeth had been raving about before she fell into a coma. "Did you find the diaries in Elizabeth's room that night?"

"Queenie and I found them."

"Did Queenie go outside with you?"

"She barked and barked. I told her no, but she wouldn't quiet down. I took her outside with me."

"Did you sing the waltz that night?"

"Elizabeth used to let me sing in the front hall. I'd pretend there were people dancing." Trudy swayed, singing the first bar of the old waltz one more time.

I waited until she finished singing. My heart pounded.

"Trudy, I love Elizabeth too. Could I see her diaries?"

Chapter 30

Saturday, April 13—Late Morning

Trudy stopped singing, shrugged her shoulders, and motioned for me to follow her as she walked toward the cottage.

Once inside, Trudy turned the dead bolt. "People try to get in," she stated and then disappeared into the little bedroom, closing the door behind her. Seconds later, she returned with a small cedar box. Trudy inserted a key and the lid sprang open.

She handed me four small homemade books tied together by twine. I fingered the thick paper covers and the rough, scissor-cut edges. I opened the top volume to the first page.

1928. Elizabeth Darcey—age 19.

"Read out loud," Trudy urged.

I read: "*May 15. Dodie Darcey and I were married yesterday! The little house that he and I share will be a love nest (!) for he is besotted with me! (What a lovely word!) Today we spent the day like a little honeymoon, and I laid a picnic lunch on a quilt in the yard. He is a good man and will provide well for me and for our children. He has shaved off his moustache, though, and I liked the way it looked before, although I'm sure it would have tickled. I am feeling happy. Hard to believe. However, I miss Little J. Will see him in a few days.*"

"Little J. That's my daddy." Trudy's face beamed.

The short entries detailed a newlywed's daily life in the Great Depression; life was hard. Elizabeth's sister Sarah and

Little J. (Jasper) had lived with the young couple. Sarah had worked in a café. The primary care for their younger brother, Jasper, fell on Elizabeth. She never mentioned her mother or father.

As I read Elizabeth's sporadic entries, Trudy listened, spellbound, as if she'd never heard the words before. She tapped my arm whenever one of the entries mentioned her father. About one-third of the way through the first book, I found record of my grandmother's marriage.

"*1933, September 15. Sarah married Kenneth Jamison today!* That was my Grandma," I explained to Trudy, scanning pages full of entries about everyday life. Then, "*1934, July 2— Sarah had little Martha today!* My aunt was born." I flipped through the diary, reading some entries aloud, others silently. "*1935, April 12—Our daughter, Agnes, was born two days ago. We will bury her on the hill, next to Daddy. I am 24. Will there be another child?*

"Elizabeth's first baby," I whispered. My aunt's penmanship was shaky. I came to the last entry in the first volume. "*1936, Oct. 10—Sarah had little Mary today!*" Trudy listened as I read about my mother's birth and how Sarah almost died before the midwife could get there and deliver the baby, who was turned wrong in the womb.

Trudy patted my leg when I closed the book and then nudged me, nodding at the pile of diaries. I opened another.

"*1938, January 18. A week ago (I still can hardly write), I lost our second baby. Cruel, cruel day. I can write no more. I sleep, and I wake up and am still alive. J. is thirteen and still with us.*" Tears welled up in my eyes. I'd known about the babies, but it had never seemed real. Now, with the words written in my great-aunt's own hand, it suddenly became the tragedy that it had really been. Trudy sniffed. I stopped reading aloud.

I turned page after page. Elizabeth's entries noted weather and eventually, as the years passed, who had gone off to the war. Occasionally, she mentioned Jasper, describing his sweet nature or detailing his work as a delivery boy. She mentioned moving to Pawhuska but gave few details.

A short, shocking entry began the third volume. *Aug. 16, 1956— Robert "Dodie" Darcey died today. The numbness I feel is a relief.*

I flipped past several blank pages before the simple entries began again, detailing Elizabeth's mundane life. In late 1959, she made note of someone new in her life, another Robert.

On December 15, 1960, she wrote: *I married Robert Rourke today. He has bewitched me with his good looks. Jasper doesn't like him.*

I turned through the remaining pages of the little book. My mother and Aunt Martha were mentioned and then we began our summer visits. Elizabeth gave no details of how we spent our days.

I didn't remember Robert Rourke being around during those visits or even what the man looked like. "Do you remember Robert Rourke, Trudy?" I asked.

Trudy shook her head back and forth and then looked out the window, her jaw muscles tight.

I flipped through the remaining pages of the third volume. My eyes burned from reading the faint, small script. Trudy had begun to rock back and forth, humming the gazebo waltz.

I read the next entry. *July 16, 1964. Somebody killed Robert. Will I go to hell for being happy?* I read it again and then looked at the date. We always came for June and stayed into July. When this was written, we must have just gone home after that summer visit. Why had I never heard anything about his death? Why had I never seen him while we were here?

The next several pages were blank, and then Elizabeth's weekly entries began. The third volume ended.

I fingered the fourth volume. I couldn't read anymore right now. My heart and my head ached. My great-aunt's life was here, in these little books, but so far, I'd found no answers.

"Trudy, I'd like to read this one later. Can I take these over to the house?"

Trudy chewed on a fingernail. "Will you keep them in a safe place?"

"Like the flour bin?"

Trudy shrugged. "Guess so."

"The same place where I hid those notes?" I asked. Trudy ducked her head. "You have the notes now, don't you?" I watched my cousin closely.

Trudy sat on her hands and stared at the floor. "My Liz cried every time someone sent her something mean. She couldn't stand to have those letters in the house. The only time she cried even more was one rainy day when me and Daddy were with her in the attic, and we found the first book she wrote. She got so sad; she had my daddy put it away for good right then. Said no one should ever see it. It made my daddy sad, too."

I tried to read Trudy's face and decipher her cryptic talk. "Her first book? Did she have a diary from when she was a little girl and her parents were alive?"

Trudy stood up abruptly. "Daddy put it away, safe as could be, where nobody'd ever find it," she said. She hummed again as she pulled the striped cap out of her pocket and jammed it down onto her head, cocking the bill to one side.

I needed that first book. The answers to everything lay in those early years, before she married Dodie. Trudy probably knew where Jasper had hidden the diary. Now, I just had to get Trudy to get it for me.

"Chief Green needs to see those notes. Maybe we can figure out who sent them. Will you get them for me?"

Trudy swayed, licked her lips, and then hurried into the bedroom. Minutes passed without any sound. I finally went to the door and peeked into the bedroom. Trudy sat motionless on the bed, her look focused on the ceiling.

"Trudy? Are you all right?"

Trudy began to cry. "He took them."

"Who?" I touched her shoulder.

Trudy buried her face in her hands and sobbed. She seemed to have forgotten I was there.

Back in the big house, I sat at the kitchen table and stared at the flowered wallpaper, unable to eat any lunch. My mind jumped in all directions.

Two husbands dead, two babies dead. Poison-pen notes missing again. Someone had thought Elizabeth was responsible for the deaths of her husbands. Someone thought I was now responsible for Elizabeth's near death.

The Elizabeth I knew had not been capable of murder. But why were the tragedies not explained in her diaries? Why had the entries been so short and emotionless? Elizabeth had mourned over her babies. She hadn't had much to say when her husbands were murdered.

Maybe Elizabeth had been right and I didn't really know her. Maybe I had only seen the Elizabeth she wanted her family to see.

What had happened to make her that way?

If there were answers, they'd be in that first diary.

Trudy had to know where it was.

Chapter 31

The screen door on the back porch slammed, and I jerked open the back door before Vera could knock. With a quick glance back over her shoulder, Vera pulled me outside and then dashed across the yard to the alley. I followed at a jog.

"You okay?" Vera asked, slowing down to wait for me in the alleyway.

"Getting there," I said, closing my eyes and taking a deep breath of fresh air.

"There's something suspicious about this carbon monoxide thing," Vera blurted. "Elizabeth never had any problem." She started off again at a fast walk. "Elizabeth replaced that heater not long ago," Vera said, stopping again on the sidewalk. "She had to start buying a different size filter. I helped her find the right one at the grocery store. Couldn't have been but two years ago, maybe three."

Bart Rourke had told me the furnace was old and filthy. He had lied. And he'd been down in the basement several times since last week. Heat crept up my neck and onto my face.

Vera pounded down the sidewalk; I trailed behind. Then I sped up, feeling a rush of adrenaline. I gritted my teeth and glared at her back. I caught up to Vera, grabbed her, and spun her around.

"Why did you miss our trip to Barnsdall?"

Startled, Vera pulled in a quick breath. "Someone left me a

message at work to meet you in Barnsdall at twelve. You didn't show." Vera frowned. She met my stare, shrugged, and then walked stiffly down the sidewalk.

I remembered the way Vera had looked over her shoulder last night when she came to the house and made this date for today—as if someone might be listening. Had someone been listening last week, when we had made our plans to go to Barnsdall?

Vera turned up her driveway. "Just need to grab a thicker shirt," she said.

I watched Vera hop onto the porch and try the front door and then pat the pockets of her jeans.

"No key. Shoot." Vera felt under the doormat and then called out to me on the driveway. "I've locked myself out. I'll go 'round back."

Vera charged around the house. I trudged after her, my hands going clammy.

"*Shit!*" Vera cried from the back steps as I rounded the corner. "Geez, the place is crawling with spiders! Would you look at this?"

Backing down the steps, Vera pointed at the messy webs and fleshy bodies hanging in the corner, her face contorted with revulsion. She snatched a stick from the yard and jabbed at the webs, stomping on the spiders where they fell.

"Damn," Vera muttered. She examined the little shed and then tossed the stick away. I followed when Vera cautiously climbed up the steps and entered the house.

If Vera hadn't planted the spiders in the dead roses, who had? Bart? Could it have been Bart who broke the window? Bart who left the flowers? Bart who came to my house to repair the window and the porch and check the heater?

I needed to have a talk with Bart.

I waited for Vera at the kitchen table. A theory about Elizabeth's past and her assault simmered in the back of my mind. I needed a sounding board. Could I trust Vera?

"Vera, what do you know about the Osage murders?" I called to her.

"Not as much as I should," Vera shouted back from somewhere else in the house. "That's ancient history around here. Nobody talks about it much anymore."

"I need to know about headrights."

Vera rushed back into the kitchen, buttoning up a flannel shirt. "Why? That has nothing to do with the house, finding out why Elizabeth owned that property, or learning more about your family." She lowered herself into a chair across the table.

"I think it does. Elizabeth's mother was a full-blood."

"Huh," Vera said. "Elizabeth never referred to any Osages as relatives." Vera seemed to be thinking out loud. "She had Osage friends, including Sam's family."

"Her parents died when she was young, about the time of those murders in the twenties."

Vera went to the sink and peered out the window. "We should go to the museum and look again."

"I don't want to tell anyone what I'm really looking for," I said. "Not until I know if I'm really on to something."

"Works for me."

A huge weight seemed to lift from my shoulders. She didn't think my idea was crazy. And her smile seemed genuine.

The curator at the front desk was reading an old book when we walked into the museum.

"I need some help." I gave her one of my best smiles.

"What do you need, my dear?" the woman drawled through pursed lips.

"Pictures of my aunt's house. Wells House," I said. "I'm thinking of restoring some of the original trim work when I repaint the house."

The woman carefully placed a bookmark in the book, closed it, and stowed it under the counter before she led us to the photograph display in the middle exhibit room. "Check here.

And maybe in here." She dragged out a crate stowed beneath the display. "Seems like there's one of the Wells' House somewhere. Now, where did I see that?"

I helped her pull out three cigar boxes stacked inside the crate. The curator opened one and began to thumb through a stack of photographs. Vera and I each took one of the boxes and flipped through more photographs.

"Anything else?" the woman asked curtly, her eyes focused on the photographs she held.

"Aunt Elizabeth's parents, the O'Days. Mrs. O'Day was an Osage. Which of these photographs is of her?" I pointed at the racks of old photographs.

The curator stopped flipping through the photographs in the cigar box and looked at me. "There's no picture of your great-grandmother here. Fact is, it's her brother and his family we have a picture of. The Mazies. There." She nodded toward the far end of the photo rack and then went back to the photos in the cigar box.

Vera and I set down our boxes and turned to the photo display. Vera pointed to a picture of an Osage family. "May I?" she asked the curator. When the older woman nodded, Vera pulled it off the display and handed it to me.

"Matthew Mazie, wife, and children." I read the faded label aloud and then studied the photograph. This was Sam's great-grandfather. Sam had his straight black hair, stoic features, and dark eyes.

"Here." The curator closed the cigar box lid and turned to us, holding out an old sepia-tone photograph. "The Wells' House."

A couple and three children stood in front of Elizabeth's house. The two girls had dark hair, unlike the rest of the family, but all of them were neat, clean, and well dressed. I turned the photo over.

"1923. Wells House. Josiah Wells, Lily, Spencer, Elizabeth, and Sarah."

The two little girls held hands and stood together but were

separated by a few feet from the others. The boy stood between his parents. Both had a hand on his shoulder. I did the math. In that year, Great-Aunt Elizabeth and Sarah, my grandmother, would have been twelve and eight. The girls in the picture could easily have been those ages.

"Do you know these people?" I handed the picture back to the curator, pointing at the children.

The woman studied the photo and then flipped it over and read aloud. "The Wells Family. Josiah, Lily, and Spencer, Elizabeth and Sarah. These two must be visiting relatives or something." She paused. "Unless you suppose this is your great-aunt Elizabeth?"

"It's an interesting coincidence, since she ended up owning the house." I reached for the photograph, and the curator handed it back. "Would you mind if I kept this picture?"

The curator shrugged. "Since it's not on display right now, I don't suppose it matters. Bring the picture back, though, when you're done." The curator drummed her fingers on the nearby display case.

"One other thing," I said. "Do you have the 1906 Osage tribal role or a list of the original allottees who received headrights?"

The curator looked blank. "The original allottees, 1906. The Tribal Museum might have the list. We don't."

"But I thought I remembered ..." I stepped over to one of the exhibit cases. "There's a partial list here, identified as the '2,229 Osages, and one white woman, who received allotments.' And a note that says, 'An actual royalty payment, paid quarterly to each allottee for their equal share of all the royalties collected from the oil and gas fields in Osage County. In July 1923, this single payment for three headrights came to $10,258.68.'" I forced a smile and walked back to Vera and the elderly curator. "My great-grandmother would have been an allottee, but I'm still looking for information about when she died. Nobody seems to know."

The curator's look flicked toward the museum entrance.

"We should look through some old newspapers," Vera said. "There would have been an obituary. You have old newspapers, don't you?"

The curator shook her head. "Not from the twenties. Maybe the library has some on microfilm."

The bell on the front door jingled.

"Excuse me." The curator hurried across the room and down the ramp into the entry hall.

Vera stared at me with wide eyes. "I'm following your train of thought. Let's go."

The two of us slipped past the new visitors. Outside, we dashed up the sidewalk along Lynn Street.

"I know what you're thinking," Vera whispered, although there was no one within hearing range. "You may be right. The Wells family somehow got control of the half headrights belonging to your grandmother and Elizabeth because their mother was a full-blood Osage. The house must have been a guilt payment to Elizabeth later. But how can we prove it?"

"Find the list of allottees. If Clara O'Day's name is there, it proves Clara had a headright, and we *know* something illegal happened to it."

We angled across Lynn and back into the neighborhoods.

"Jamie, do you realize how dangerous this could be? Martin Wells is an important man around here. His family owns half the town, and he's been mayor for more than ten years."

We hurried down the sidewalk. My mind clicked back to the afternoon I arrived at Elizabeth's house. I had thought she was ranting, wanting to die. She had wanted to tell me something. *"My life has been a sham. I should have told,"* she had moaned. Had Elizabeth suspected—or known—the Wells family had stolen her mother's headright?

We turned up the hill to the library.

Chapter 32

Saturday, April 13—Late Afternoon

The librarian grumbled to herself as she set Vera and I up at two microfilm machines and brought over microfilm spools of the Pawhuska newspaper from the early decades of the 1900s. I settled in a chair at one machine, Vera at another. The box of film spools rested on a small table between us.

We had two hours until the library closed. Was that enough time to find what we were looking for? Rolling through microfiche was much more time consuming than a simple CD would have been.

"The girls were pictured with the Wells family in 1923," I said. "Their parents must have died before then. I know that my great-granddad died when fire destroyed the old homestead at Bigheart. We ought to be able to find something about the fire in the years before 1923, and something about what happened to my great-grandmother Clara O'Day."

The microfilm readers clicked and whirred. I struggled to focus when a page settled on the screen. As I scanned the old issues of the *Osage Journal*, the constant blur of moving words brought on a headache and nausea. Every few minutes, I stopped turning the wheel and rested, eyes closed, rubbing my temples.

Vera's machine stopped whirring. I glanced at her. Vera was slumped in her chair, head resting on the table.

"Vera? You okay?"

"I found something about the fire," she said as she straightened up.

I scooted my chair close to Vera's machine and leaned in.

March 19, 1922—Bigheart Man Dies in Blaze

A blaze has destroyed the former homestead of the James O'Day family, northwest of Bigheart, and has taken the life of Mr. O'Day. Firefighters report the home was engulfed in flames upon their arrival last night.

Police speculate the fire started when a kerosene lamp overturned, spilling oil that ignited and caught fire.

O'Day had recently moved from the homestead into town, following his wife, Clara's, disappearance last December.

Anyone having additional information about the fire or information about Mrs. O'Day's whereabouts may contact the Osage County Sheriff's Department, Pawhuska."

A brief obituary followed on the next page in the "Deaths" column.

James Michael O'Day

James Michael O'Day died Monday, March 18, 1922. Mr. O'Day was employed at Wells's Lumber Yard in Bigheart for the past five years. He is survived by two daughters, Elizabeth and Sarah.

Friends are invited to a wake at St. Luke's Catholic Church, Bigheart, on Wednesday evening, and to the burial service in the Bigheart Cemetery on Thursday afternoon at 1:00.

March 1922. I rolled my chair back to my machine. So Clara had disappeared. My brain whirred like the microfiche reader. The Osage Reign of Terror had begun, but it was years before anyone was brought to justice for all of the murders. Had Clara O'Day been an early victim? I turned the microfilm reader dial so the pages from November/December 1921 moved across the screen.

"Got it!"

Bigheart Woman Disappears

Police are investigating the disappearance of local woman, Clara O'Day. Mrs. O'Day was last seen on Tuesday morning at the courthouse during the quarterly Osage royalty check distribution.

Mrs. O'Day was reported missing when her husband returned from work at Wells Lumber Yard and found their two daughters, Elizabeth and Sarah, at home alone. The girls last saw their mother before going to school.

Mrs. O'Day, a cook for a local café, had not reported to work that day.

Anyone with information as to the whereabouts of Mrs. Clara O'Day should contact the Osage County Sheriff's Office immediately.

I rolled the reader through the remaining issues of December 1921 but found no other references to Clara O'Day or her disappearance.

Vera turned off her microfilm reader; I leaned back in my chair. The timing of Clara's disappearance fit right in with the Osage Reign of Terror. But it had been years and many murders and disappearances later before the men were brought to justice. It was possible that other perpetrators were never caught. But something wasn't quite right. I touched Vera's arm. "Neither story mentioned the girls' younger brother, Jasper. And he wasn't in the photograph at Wells house either."

Vera chewed her lip. "Maybe he wasn't their brother."

"Then who was he?" We threaded our way through the stacks and the checkout area to the front doors.

I trudged down the sidewalk alone after dropping Vera off at her house. Then I cut through the yards and alleys to the house that had once belonged to the Wells family. A family photograph with no Jasper. An obituary that didn't mention him, as well as an article about his mother's disappearance. Could my mother have been wrong about who Jasper was? Elizabeth had not referred to Trudy as her niece in the will. Maybe it was because she wasn't her niece.

I stepped up to the veranda. Bart Rourke slouched on the front-porch swing. He pulled himself up and stumbled towards me. "Hel-lo. And where have you been ou' walkin' this fine day?"

He looked innocent enough. But he was a liar. And he reeked of alcohol. The man was drunk. I stepped around him and grabbed at the front doorknob. I didn't want to get into it with a drunk, especially a drunk who might have tried to kill me.

Bart reached around me and put his hand on the knob. As I looked over at him, his big brown eyes blinked and tried to focus.

"Figure'd you'd be restin' up today. No idea the heater was bad. Shoulda got to 'er first thang. 'Course, I'd been workin' on the steps and the winder."

I squinted at him. Shouldn't I be able to read the lie in his eyes? His look shifted away.

"What'll go wrong next? Ol' pipes, mebbee. I'll be here early and bring my plumber friend. 'Kay?"

How had he known the pipes thudded when I turned on a faucet, and water ran at a lukewarm trickle upstairs? Had he been up there?

"See you to-murra," he muttered, turning to the front steps. "Af'rnoon."

You bet he'd see me tomorrow, if he showed. And if he was sober, I'd have some questions for him.

Bart stepped off the porch and then weaved from side to side down the sidewalk with careful little steps. He'd probably forget he had agreed to work on the pipes. Drake had warned me about him.

I glanced at the telephone as I walked down the front hall. I wanted it to ring, and I wanted Sam to be the caller. The newspaper articles Vera and I had found supported my theory. But why, during all these years, had no one ever asked questions about Clara and her headright?

Somebody in this town had to know something about my family's history, something he or she didn't want revealed. Was that why Elizabeth was in a coma?

I settled down in the leather wingback in the study with the fourth diary. My eyes grew heavy as I read, and by the time I had turned the last page, I felt disoriented, caught up in that previous time. But the diary told me nothing new.

My mind drifted off to thoughts of the fire and Clara's disappearance. I thought about Bart and the furnace. And behind everything else, I thought of Sam Mazie.

Had it really only been yesterday we'd spent the afternoon together? I wanted to talk to him, to tell him what I'd found out about Clara and about James. But then, maybe he already knew. They were part of his family.

Why had he not told me about Clara's disappearance?

I scolded myself for being so taken with him. I was not being sensible. Ben had always balanced me out, endorsed my methodical, fact-based way of solving problems. He had always made sure I kept emotions out of things, except when it came to our romance.

What would Elizabeth say if she knew what I was feeling for Sam? I pictured my aunt's snapping eyes and the lift of her chin. It wasn't right to imagine Elizabeth endorsing my feelings. Elizabeth was not present, and I was beginning to suspect why. I had to keep my focus on finding the answers.

A sharp bang from downstairs jerked me awake. Queenie barked and dashed out to the hallway.

I pulled on my robe, grabbed my glasses and, heart hammering, hurried downstairs. Queenie's nose was pressed to the crack of the front door. I switched on the porch light and peered through the peephole. The porch was empty. I unlocked the dead bolt and pulled the door open. Queenie darted out, plumed tail wagging.

I scanned the yard and saw Queenie nosing something near the porch swing.

"Queenie! Leave it," I hollered as the dog latched on to a large bone and dragged it toward the front door. I grabbed the dog. Then I reached down and pulled at an envelope smeared with animal blood and gore and attached to the bone with a rubber band.

I shooed the dog back into the house, dashed inside and rammed the dead bolt into place. My heart pumped in my ears. In the kitchen, by the nightlight's yellow glow, I pulled a folded sheet of paper from inside the blood-smeared envelope.

Get out now. Or die.

It was written in the same black, heavy-handed, thick-lettered print of the previous notes. A black widow spider was sketched into one corner.

A low growl rumbled in Queenie's throat. Somewhere in the house, something creaked. The dog sniffed.

I tucked the note under the sink and listened. Queenie didn't growl again. I grabbed a butcher knife and slowly climbed the backstairs. After locking us into my bedroom, I slipped the knife under my pillow.

For a long time, I stared at the ceiling and listened. Like the note said, I probably should get out. But after what I'd learned today, I couldn't. I was close to the answers. For Great-Aunt Elizabeth's sake, I would find out the truth.

Somewhere in the house, a floorboard or a door creaked.

Queenie stayed quiet at the foot of the bed.

I waited in the dark.

The cackling laughter rings out in the night and is quickly silenced.

It was amusing to see her startled eyes, to see her jerk the dog away from the bone. Too bad, though. The dog hadn't even had a chance to bite off enough of the poisoned meat to do more than cause a bellyache. Now, the bone will have to be retrieved.

It is almost time.

The figure shivers with anticipation.

The house can be entered now. It can be done tonight.

But no. That isn't the way I've planned. Personal sacrifices still have to be made, but it will be worth it in the end.

After all this time.

Finally.

Chapter 33

Sunday, April 14—Morning

The darkness outside the window was fading into morning gray. Thoughts of last night's gruesome gift had haunted me all night, and I had been aware of every tick of the clock as well as every creak and groan of the old house. I must have dozed some, but the fog in my mind told me I'd had no quality sleep. I needed coffee.

Get out now. Or die.

Had that been the intent the other night with the carbon monoxide poisoning?

The water ran slower than ever in the upstairs bath, and when I flushed the commode, a terrible banging began and went on and on. I gritted my teeth.

Queenie barked, and someone pounded at the front door. I pulled on jeans and a T-shirt and stomped down the stairs.

"Hey there, cuz," Bart Rourke said. "I'm early but might as well get to it. No rest for the weary!"

A strong westerly wind blew the front door into the doorstop. The trees leaned toward the house. The creaks I had heard in the night had most likely only been the wind, shifting. I glanced past Bart and onto the porch, looking for the bone. It was gone. Another dog had probably dragged it away.

Bart bustled past me and into the house. I followed him into the kitchen, where he drained his plastic coffee mug with a long swallow and then set it on the counter next to the sink.

I cleared my throat and thought about how to start this

conversation. I didn't want to see this big man turn angry. I wondered if I should delay the conversation until we weren't alone. "You're tackling the pipes just in time," I said. "Lots of banging when I turned on the water just now."

Bart stared toward the basement door, avoiding my eyes.

"And how's everything else? No more headaches?" He folded his arms and settled back against the counter, watching the floor.

"No. The new heater seems to work fine," I said. I moved to the other side of the little kitchen table, placing it between him and me. "Funny thing, though. Vera remembers that Elizabeth had a new heater installed not all that long ago. You sure the unit was old?" I stared at him.

Bart studied his shoes. "Hell, Vera's worked at that store for twenty years. Might've been longer than she remembers. The unit sure was dusty. Defective, most likely." He cleared his throat and looked out the window. "You plannin' on hangin' around here today? It's Sunday. Ought to take ya a drive or somethin'. We'll clean out the flues. Might need to ream out the vents and put in a sewer trap. Water'll be off. Hope you don't need some new pipes."

I followed Bart's gaze out the window to where the dilapidated greenhouse hunched in the corner of the yard. He had neatly sidestepped my question.

"I might look at the greenhouse, see what it will take to repair it or get rid of it," I said.

"It's been that way since Rourke died. Happened right out there, you know. Elizabeth never had it repaired."

No one had mentioned Rourke's dying out in the greenhouse. Not even Elizabeth, in her diary.

"Quite a mess. Dangerous. Ought to get someone to haul the rubble off. I can hook you up with somebody." Bart turned from the window and lumbered toward the basement door. "Don't mess around out there." He looked back at me. "Leave it alone, okay?"

"Right." I didn't intend to listen to Bart. I'd look at the

greenhouse later, in spite of his warning, but first, I had an errand to run. I grabbed my jacket from the coat hook.

At the Osage Tribal Museum, I pounded on the door until a woman in a long skirt and cowboy boots finally opened the door a crack.

"The sign says you're open at ten. I'm a little early, but I won't take much of your time. Just need to look something up."

I explained what I needed, and the woman pointed to the photo panels covering all four walls of the room. Photos of members of The Roll of 1906, used to determine who received headrights for the oil and gas royalties, had been collected and placed on the Museum's walls.

She handed me an alphabetized index.

I flipped through the pages listing the names and photograph locations. Clara O'Day was not listed as an allottee.

I stared at the index. What if James and Clara had married after 1906? If so, she would have been listed under her maiden name, Mazie.

I scanned back up a few lines and found her name.

At the police station, the desk clerk motioned toward Green's dark office and said, "He's not usually here on Sunday. Want to leave a message?"

I wrote on a notepad: *Need to talk to you. Jamie Aldrich.* I tapped the end of the pen against my teeth for a moment and then wrote "Urgent" at the top of the page.

Billy Ray, the plumber, had turned the water off at the meter. Five minutes of constant banging and the plumber's colorful language drove Queenie and me out of the house to the gazebo. I sat on the bench and stared at the greenhouse. Elizabeth had mentioned Rourke's death in her journal only on the day he died. The tumbled-down frame had been setting there like some kind of shrine for nearly forty years. And Elizabeth had kept the poison-pen notes hidden inside the ruin.

Mother had said Rourke had a younger mistress and children by her. Did the family still live around Pawhuska?

The wind stroked my face. Almost two weeks had passed since Aunt Elizabeth's call and my trip here. If I had listened when Elizabeth had wanted to talk that first day, would she still have been here at the house with me? Could I have prevented her coma or merely postponed the assault?

It was pointless to speculate on what might have been. I fingered the wedding ring hanging over my heart and then dropped my hand into my lap. Ben was always with me, but something was different now about the way I thought about Ben and about life. It had to do with Sam Mazie.

Between my house and the house next door, Drake scurried past on the front sidewalk, his head down, shoulders hunched, probably heading next door to Susan's.

I looked again at the dilapidated greenhouse.

"Come on, Queenie." The dog and I crossed the yard.

Only one intact greenhouse wall remained. On each end, metal pieces hung together in what had once been a framework for the adjacent glass-paned walls. Some glass shards still dangled from the metal frame, and only a few lower panes remained unbroken. Cautiously, I stepped out onto the old cement floor, looking down. Were there bloodstains or any evidence of Rourke's death? The wind rustled in the dried skeletons of weeds growing in the ruin, and a mockingbird began a soliloquy from a nearby oak.

Abruptly, the bird squawked and flew away as something snapped. I threw up my arms, covered my head, and then dropped to my knees as metal and glass crashed down. Queenie yelped.

When I raised my head, bits of glass and metal slid off my back and struck the floor around me. I straightened, brushing off bits and pieces. Blood smeared the backs of my hands, and

I sat for a moment, trying to slow my breathing and my heart. The few ceiling beams that had remained had crashed onto the floor directly in front of me.

Voices called. When I turned, I saw Bart and Drake running across the lawn.

"My God, Jamie, are you all right?" Bart roared.

Drake reached me first and squatted near, scrutinizing my face and hands. He pulled latex gloves from one pocket, slipped them on, and then gently probed my scalp with his fingers. With a tissue, he swiped at the blood oozing from a scalp wound above my hairline.

"Let's get out of here before the rest of this glass and steel comes down," Drake growled.

"Elizabeth should have pulled it down years ago," Bart muttered as he grabbed my elbow. "And I told you to stay away just this morning. Not only kids get hurt."

"What were you doing out here?" Drake asked through clenched teeth as we stepped across the yard.

Behind me, Queenie whined.

I turned and saw the dog struggling to get to her feet, her hindquarters caught beneath a long piece of metal. Bart hurried over to lift the framework away. Queenie lay still.

Drake moved over to the dog, knelt, and felt along Queenie's back and hind legs.

"You should call the vet."

I rushed back to the dog. Queenie's chest heaved, and she gave a pitiful whine. Two pairs of hands pulled me up.

"Come on," Drake insisted. "It's not safe here." Reluctantly, I let the men help me toward the house.

"Odd the structure fell at just that moment, after all these years," I said. The words of last night's note blazed in my mind.

Drake swabbed the gashes on my hands and head with a sterile liquid cleanser.

"Doesn't matter." Drake's voice was cold and angry. "It fell. I hope you won't be as stupid as Elizabeth and let the ruin stand any longer. One man lost his life in that greenhouse, and now you and that dog had a really close call. My sister's kids live right next door. Too bad Elizabeth didn't fall victim herself." The muscles worked in his clenched jaw. He picked up the unused items and put them back in the packages. He washed his hands.

"You don't like Elizabeth, do you?"

Drake continued to clean up. "A man was killed when the greenhouse fell. Robert Rourke, Elizabeth's second husband," he barked. "Her second *dead* husband." He snapped the lid of the bandage box shut and washed his hands for a second time. "She was responsible. It was her greenhouse, and she wanted him dead. Figure it out yourself."

He closed the door of the medicine cabinet, then washed his hands for the third time. I could hear Drake's teeth grinding against one another. Elizabeth's diary entry had not expressed much sorrow. Maybe Drake was right.

"He bled to death, you know." Drake spat the words. "Lying out there, in the greenhouse, all night long. Elizabeth didn't even go look for him." His pale face had turned into an angry mask, and his hands trembled.

I took a step away from Drake and toward the bathroom door. He looked ready to kill somebody. "Thank you," I managed to say. "I'm okay now. You don't have to stay. The vet will be here soon to check on Queenie." I heard his steps behind me as I walked to the front door. Once he was on the front sidewalk, I locked the door.

Drake had always been cool and distant. Detached, even. But beneath his exterior was an angry man who hated my great-aunt. Had he been angry enough to try to kill her and then to carry his vendetta on to me? Even as the thought crossed my mind, I realized it didn't make sense. He'd been right there to help me every single time something happened.

Dr. Nelson, the new young vet on weekend emergency call for the local animal clinic, arrived ten minutes later. I let him carry Queenie into the house and lay her on a pallet of towels piled in the corner of the kitchen.

"Is she going to be okay?"

The vet checked the dog's eyes one more time and ran his hand over her spine.

"No bones broken that I can tell. Her back's just badly bruised," he said. "Here are a few samples. It's like aspirin, one three times a day with food and water ought to help her through this. She'll be fine in a few days." He squatted beside Queenie, stroked her, and then turned to me. "You had this dog long?"

"She's a stray. Came to the back door, little over a week ago."

"I'd swear I've seen her before," he said. "You haven't seen any Lost Dog notices about her or posted one?" He asked as he slipped on a hunting jacket and gathered his equipment into his bag.

"Haven't seen any notices. I left signs at the grocery store and called Animal Control. You think she belongs to someone who lives around here?"

"Wouldn't swear to it. I'll have a look at my records. See if I can jog my memory." He stuck out his hand and shook mine. "Call and let me know if she isn't back to herself in two or three days."

I called Toby Green's office. This time I left a message on the answering machine: "Chief Green, it's Jamie Aldrich. Call me. It's urgent. Please."

In one of the desk drawers in the study, I had seen files of household papers bound together with rubber bands, according to year. I rifled through the receipts and folders. In the folder marked "Household Warranties," I found a receipt and warranty for a new furnace, installed five years ago. Had that been enough time for the furnace to get as filthy as Bart claimed? Perhaps it had been defective. Maybe Elizabeth had never had the unit serviced.

"Mrs. Aldrich?" Chief Toby Green's voice had an edge to it. "I'm at home. Just checked my messages. What's wrong?"

"There was an accident here this afternoon, and I've gotten another of those nasty notes," I stated. "A threat. And I've uncovered something interesting, related to the carbon monoxide incident."

"I have a meeting in Tulsa with the district attorney tomorrow. Won't be home until late. Would you like someone else to come out to talk with you?"

I thought about it. "No. Tuesday should be soon enough, I hope." I wanted to believe the greenhouse had collapsed because of a wind gust. Why else?

After supper, I gave Queenie her pain medicine and gave myself another dose of my own before I went upstairs and crawled into bed. My muscles relaxed as a fog crept through my mind.

A few hours later, Queenie's soft "woof" from downstairs woke me. Groggy from medication, my eyes wouldn't open.

The house creaked. Another muted "woof," and then a *pop*.

The wind pushed against the house, whistling into the cracks.

I fell back to sleep.

Chapter 34

Monday, April 15—Morning

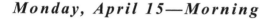

The carpet runner at the bottom of the stairs was rumpled and askew. Still in my pajamas and at the bottom of the front stairs, I scrutinized the hall in the early morning light. Had Queenie been roaming last night and caught a toenail on one of the carpet loops? Slightly groggy from last night's pain medicine, I vaguely remembered hearing something.

Queenie staggered out from the kitchen, wagging her tail, and crossed the hall to me. Queenie's bark last night had been soft, playful. Not an alarm. I squatted to stroke the dog's curly black fur. I remembered a strange popping sound. The plastic sheeting over the mudroom screens again? Louder than that.

I stepped off the carpet and lifted the runner until I could see the floor and then the first and second steps. Scratch marks marred the center edge of the first step. I laid the folded carpet on the stairs and then pushed and prodded at the step. When I pulled upward on the center edge, a board shifted. When I pulled harder, a small section dropped down into the step, revealing a clean empty space about eight inches square. I felt around inside it, prodding and pushing the sides to see if another space would pop open, but nothing happened.

When I pushed the board back down, it popped into place. The same sound I had heard last night. Someone had been here. What had they found in the stair?

I eased down onto the floor and sat cross-legged. Queenie

tottered over and stuck her nose onto my neck. The dog stared up into my eyes. I scratched her ears. Queenie had not been disturbed by the intruder. It might have been Trudy again. But why hadn't she knocked on the door or called to tell me what she was doing?

I stepped outside just as Billy Ray clambered up onto the house. Bart stabilized the base of the ladder, and Billy Ray worked around the vent pipes on the roof. Every other sentence he uttered started with "F—."

My legs and back muscles twanged as I moved; I was lucky. I could have been back in the hospital or even dead, sliced to pieces by falling glass. I began walking down the sidewalk without any destination in mind. A long, easy walk could work out the stiffness and help me think.

Drake's anger at Aunt Elizabeth gnawed at me. The diary entry after Robert Rourke's death made it seem Elizabeth had not been sorry he died, perhaps because of the mistress.

Damn. Guilt shot through me. Mother was in the hospital, having tests. And I didn't even know what symptoms she was experiencing or how long she'd been feeling ill. I'd been too wrapped up in things here. Then, I had to admit I was still peeved that no one had ever mentioned my great-grandmother's Osage heritage.

I headed west down the sidewalk past pink and rose azaleas. Green leaf-bud clouds blurred the branches of the old trees. Today's overcast sky looked like rain. I walked past a few houses, warming up the muscles in my legs and rolling my shoulders. My hands looked terrible, with swollen red skin surrounding numerous cuts.

Counting the garage accident and the front step, the greenhouse was my third accident in the two weeks since I'd arrived. I'd never been accident-prone before. And I rarely even took an aspirin.

A black Cadillac pulled into the driveway of the two-story stucco just ahead of me and an elderly white-haired man eased out of the driver's seat. He slammed the car door. Stooped over and obviously arthritic, he limped around the car and up the porch steps.

I recognized the volunteer who had driven me home from the hospital. "Hello!" I called.

He glanced over his shoulder and then stepped inside, closing the door quickly behind him. The curtains parted in a wide front window, and a shadow moved behind the glass. The curtains dropped back down.

Maybe he hadn't recognized me.

An hour later, I paused on the front steps of Elizabeth's house to stretch. The clouds had thickened, and the air was heavy with the scent of rain. The ladder was gone and so were the men, but Bart's truck was still in the side drive.

I plopped down onto the porch swing, inhaling moist air laced with the scent of spring. Through the open parlor window, I heard Bart on the entry hall phone. He sounded angry. I moved closer to the window.

"I hear you, and I'm tellin' you, *no*! What I've already done is bad enough. Next time she might get killed! Can't have that on my conscience, and no amount of money in the world will make that right."

The blood drained from my face.

"Ain't ... gonna ... do ... it." Each word was clipped and louder than the one before. "No way!" Bart shouted into the phone. "Find yourself another stooge!"

I raced down the veranda to the front door and threw it open. Bart stood in the hallway, phone to his ear. He swung around toward the door and then quickly put the receiver down onto the cradle.

"You set up my accidents?" My voice quaked. Bart Rourke stared at the floor. "Get out of this house!"

Bart grabbed his cap from the hallstand. He scooted past

me and out the front door, eyes to the floor. Sweat trickled down his cheeks. I slammed and locked the door behind him.

My face felt numb, and my heartbeat thudded.

But who had hired Bart to get to me? I should have questioned him right then and there. As guilty as he had looked, he might have told me. Damn. I grabbed at the phone. It was an old rotary dial, with no caller ID or redial. I paced the hall and then stomped into the kitchen.

I made a pot of tea and sat at the kitchen table. Rain began to pelt the kitchen window and drum a soothing rhythm on the roof of the back porch. I didn't feel comforted.

Someone was planning another accident. And someone *had* been in the house last night. If Trudy could get in, who else could? And then I remembered. Bart had a key. Locked doors didn't mean anything.

With a whine of pain, Queenie gingerly got up from her pallet to rest her head on my knee. I scratched the dog's muzzle.

Someone had taken something from the hidey-hole under the stairs.

Time was running out. Bart had betrayed me. There was going to be another attempt to persuade me to leave—or kill me in the process.

I raced back to the hall, picked up the phone, and dialed Sam's office number. The secretary answered. He was in court. Would I like to leave a message?

I left a long-winded voice-mail message, starting with my questions about the headright and ending with Bart and the phone conversation I'd overheard. His recorder cut me off in mid-sentence, and the line disconnected.

I hoped he'd check his messages soon.

I dialed Mother's number, hoping she hadn't gone to the hospital yet. My questions couldn't wait any longer. She answered on the fifth ring, speaking softly and slowly, sounding tired.

"Mom? Are you okay?" I asked about her health and the tests. No results yet. She was heading back to the hospital in another hour. No reason to worry or get upset or come home.

"How's everything coming with the house? Are you getting it ready to sell?" Mother asked.

"I'm doing some repairs." I heard a slight tremor in my voice. I should have said I *was* having repairs made. I couldn't very well say, *"You see, Mom, my repairman cousin has been trying to kill me."*

My mother started to speak, but I cut her off. "I'm dealing with family history here." I used my teacher tone. "I need you to answer some questions about Aunt Elizabeth's family background. If I tell you what I think I know, will you fill in the gaps? Will you tell me if I'm off base somewhere?"

"Jamie, I didn't want you going there to that old town. I was afraid all the old trouble would get stirred up. Are *you* in trouble?"

"What *old* trouble?" I put a hand to my forehead, where the ache was beginning again. "I think I'll be in worse trouble if you don't tell me the truth. Here's what I think I know." I summarized what I had learned and what I suspected. Mother listened, so quietly that twice I asked if she was still there before I continued.

"Here's where I have gaps. Great-Grandma Clara disappeared. Did anyone ever find out what happened to her? She had a headright as Clara Mazie. Did anyone investigate her disappearance as part of the Reign of Terror?"

Mother didn't know.

"What happened to the headright? It should have passed on to her husband, James. When he died in that fire, the headright should have passed to the girls. As orphans, they would have had a guardian appointed. Who was their guardian? Why did they not receive the headright when they came of legal age? And what about Jasper? Why was he not mentioned in any of the newspaper articles? Or the obituary? Who was he?"

"Jamie, Jamie, Jamie. I see where you're going with this. I don't have an answer for the omission of Jasper, only that perhaps because he was retarded, he wasn't listed. It wasn't acceptable to have a retarded child back then. People put them away in institutions and never talked about them. That's just the way things were." Mother paused, and I waited. "As far as the headright, I'm sure nothing illegal happened. Elizabeth and Sarah would have done something about it when they got older if someone had cheated them."

I remembered my aunt's last words before the coma. Elizabeth had wanted to tell me the truth.

"That's just it," I insisted. "I think Aunt Elizabeth *did* want to do something about it, but now she's in a coma. Someone stands to lose a lot if this is uncovered now."

"Jamie, I find it hard to believe." Mother's voice was soft and soothing. "Elizabeth would never have let someone cover up something like that. She would have gone after the truth a long time ago, and so would your grandma. I don't think there is anything to your theory. Just let it go."

"And what about Rourke and the greenhouse? Why did I never meet him, and why did I never know how and where he died? Ellen, Randy, and I were here that summer!"

"You were all so young and impressionable," my mother sighed. "You'd already had your summer visit. There was no need to scare you with that awful story."

"Was there an investigation? Was Aunt Elizabeth a suspect?"

"Oh, you know small towns. Such rumor mills. Maybe some people suspected her, but she was never charged. Some people thought she killed her first husband, but nobody could ever prove anything then, either."

"Someone thought she killed Dodie Darcey?"

"In 1956. Murdered in a back alley, after a poker game." Mom's voice was getting softer, fading.

Elizabeth had bought this house in 1956 for one dollar.

My mother cleared her throat and sighed. "Elizabeth had a temper. Don't we all? Talk was that he was seeing someone else, and she couldn't stand it. I never believed it. Elizabeth loved Dodie. He was fun-loving, probably a philanderer, but she loved him. Never, ever would she have killed him, no matter what he'd done."

What had the entry in the diary said? Something about "numbness" and "relief." What had Aunt Elizabeth been feeling *before* he died? Had she wanted him dead? Someone *had* believed her guilty and sent her notes by the dozens so she would never forget.

"Enough of this now, honey," Mother suddenly said. "I think it's best you just let it go. There's nothing to be done about any of it now anyway."

As soon as I hung up from Mother, I called Vera. I had a plan.

I made the short drive to the library and then drove to the museum. The curator was busy with other visitors, so I waved at her and continued into the exhibit room. Five minutes later, I was back in my car, driving home.

I paced from room to room as the evening wore on. Sam never called back. I needed to talk to him now, before Vera and I started things in motion.

Chapter 35

Monday, April 15—Night

At 11:00 PM, with stars glittering in the night sky, Vera joined me on the cracked sidewalk outside her house. We power-walked together through the cool night, camouflaged by black sweat pants and hooded sweatshirts.

Pools of yellow light from the street lamps on Lynn Street illuminated the west side of the museum. We crossed the street to the deep shadows on the south end but didn't slow our pace until we reached the darkness beneath a post oak tree in the adjoining field. We turned back to the building and waited. A moth fluttered by and something scurried through the grass.

Roof shadows hid the small window of the ladies' restroom. We stepped closer. Behind the small screen I had loosened that afternoon, the lower sash window stood open two inches.

I stretched up on tiptoe, leaned toward the shadowy wall, and reached for the edges of the screen. Using a small pocket-knife, I popped the screen away. When it dropped into the tall grass below the window, one corner thumped into the side of the building. We both held our breath and listened. An insect chorus rose and ebbed in the field next door.

I reached in and pushed the window up another ten inches.

"Vera! Boost me up!" I put my left foot into the basket Vera made of her hands and fingers and propelled myself upward. I shoved the window up even more, wriggled onto the sill, and pulled myself through the opening. Vera pushed from behind.

One small slit of moonlight illuminated the small bathroom. I reached down for the tank of the commode below the window. I hoped it would hold my weight and not pull away from the wall.

Slowly, I worked more of my body over the sill, holding tightly onto the commode. I pulled my legs inside and then eased myself down to the floor.

"I'm in!" I whispered over my shoulder. I picked up the small crate by the commode and handed it through the window to Vera. With the extra height, Vera would be able to climb through the window without a boost.

Vera's upper body appeared in the window opening, and I pulled on her shoulders as she grunted and groaned her way in.

After Vera collapsed onto the floor beside me, we waited in the dark, listening. Vera pulled open the bathroom door. The old Regulator clock in the adjacent exhibit room ticked. A light left on in the entry hall two rooms away cast eerie shadows onto the walls from mannequins dressed in clothing from the early twentieth century.

The heavy silence breathed.

"Down this way. In the office. If they have any public records about headrights and royalties that aren't in exhibit cases, they would be in here," Vera said.

We felt our way along the short wall to the corner office.

The door opened soundlessly into blackness, and we stepped into the stuffy room. Vera moved into the darkness to the left. My heart pounded.

The air vibrated with movement, and then I heard a groan. Something pushed against my leg and then thudded to the floor.

Lights flashed in my head.

Then, darkness.

The acrid smell of smoke stirred me awake and seeped, stinging, under my eyelids.

I coughed and tried to pull in good air. In flickering light, I saw Vera crumpled beside me on the floor. Fire blazed from two paper-filled boxes by the desk.

I crouched over her, struggling to breathe, coughing in the smoke-thick air. A dark stain oozed from Vera's forehead down onto her face.

"Vera!" I shook her shoulder. "Vera!"

With a pop, another box caught on fire. Smoke licked around and over the edges of book piles and boxes on the lower shelves. I pulled off my sweatshirt and swatted at the flaming boxes but did little more than fan the flames. The fire crawled and crackled up into the storage shelves.

I stepped to the closed door and grabbed and twisted the doorknob. The door didn't budge. I kicked at the latch. Nothing.

The room erupted into an inferno.

I scanned the room, searching for something to use to break off the doorknob. On the floor, next to a wall shelf, a long, heavy iron tool protruded from a box. I grabbed it and battered at the door until the knob, the plate, and the latch all broke off and fell to the floor.

The door swung open.

"Vera! Wake up!" I grabbed her under the arms and dragged her from the room, pulling her through the eerie half light as smoke billowed out of the corner office. The world began to spin as I reached the incline leading up into the smaller exhibit room and finally into the entryway. Behind me, the fire roared and snapped.

Outside, a siren wailed and strobing red and white lights danced across the walls of the smoke-filled entry. The front doors burst open.

The first firemen rushed past me toward the big south

exhibit hall and the corner office. When arms reached for me a few seconds later, they were clothed in a blue pinstriped suit.

"Jamie?" Martin Wells asked. The doorway framed a crowd of faces behind him.

"Help me!" I screamed.

Wells grabbed my arms and pulled me outside. Coughing, I kicked and shoved at him.

"It's all right, Jamie. You're safe with me."

"Let me go!" I was far from safe with Martin Wells.

He held tightly onto my arms as he dragged me away from the museum toward the street. I choked and coughed as he lowered me onto the lawn.

My eyes smarted. When I closed them, bile rose up in my throat. I retched.

The scene swirled with flashing lights. Tears blurred my vision.

Martin held me so tightly that I couldn't get away from him.

Another fire truck and an ambulance screeched into the parking lot.

I tried to focus on three figures separating from the crowd; they moved toward us. Faces in shadow, their bodies were backlit by the fire and billowing smoke.

"Setting the museum on fire was bad enough, but why'd you have to kill Vera?" Chief Green asked in a harsh voice as he leaned over me.

Chapter 36

Tuesday, April 16—Morning

Light from the small, barred window, high in the wall of the holding cell, slowly turned from black to shades of gray. Hugging my knees, I had stared up at the window all night long, my back to the guard who was slumped in the desk chair in the office behind me.

I clasped Ben's wedding ring and rocked back and forth. My clothing and hair stank of smoke, and my mouth tasted of it. A lump the size of a goose egg on my forehead throbbed. If wishes could come true, I'd wake up and be in bed, at home in New Mexico. But all too well I knew that wishes rarely came true. I couldn't wake up because I'd never been asleep.

The museum was partially—if not totally—destroyed. I was sitting in jail.

Vera was dead.

And it was my fault.

Other than the night guard who had offered me food and water, I'd seen no one else since they brought me in. I'd asked the guard to call Sam Mazie. His only response had been to shake his head and say in a gruff voice, "You just sit there and be quiet."

No one knew I was in jail. And I didn't have the proof I'd gone to the museum to get, the evidence I needed to contest the headright ownership. Now, I'd probably never have the chance to get it. I'd been crazy to think I could do anything about something illegal that had taken place so long ago.

It might have turned out differently if I'd had a chance to talk to Sam or Toby Green before Vera and I went to the museum. That hadn't happened.

Somewhere close by, a door slammed.

My eyes burned. Tears spilled onto my cheeks as I squeezed my eyelids together. I knew there was a law about how long they could hold me in jail without charging me. And I was supposed to have had one phone call, wasn't I? Not that it mattered. I couldn't deny it was my fault Vera was dead, and the museum fire had destroyed irreplaceable historical items.

The holding cell door slid open, and footsteps crossed the little room. Warm arms engulfed me. Sam. I turned my face into his shirt and sucked in a deep breath of him. Then my whole body began to shake.

Sam pried my fingers away from their grip around my knees and then laced his fingers through mine. He held me close and rocked me. "Toby shouldn't have put you here."

"What will happen to me, Sam? It's my fault. I needed to find proof, and we thought it would be at the museum. Someone was waiting for us."

"Shhhh," he soothed. "I'm taking you out of here." He tried to pull me to my feet, but my legs wouldn't support me. Sam slipped his arm around me and together, we walked out of the cell and over to the desk. The uniformed man shoved some papers over, and Sam signed them.

His truck was parked in front of the door. When Queenie peered out at me through the open passenger window and barked, my eyes filled with tears again. The dog licked my face as I climbed into the truck, and then she settled herself half onto my lap.

Sam's truck roared out of Pawhuska on the deserted pre-dawn streets.

The sun broke above the horizon as we bounced along the

gravel roads. Outside my car window, yellow daffodils waved in the morning breeze. My stomach roiled. I yelled for Sam to stop the car, and when he did, I opened the door and tried to throw up. Dry heaves.

Sam handed me a bottle of water. I rinsed and spat and then slumped against the seat.

As the truck bumped along, I relived the fire, felt the heat, and smelled the smoke. So helpless. Martin Wells had held me, kept me from helping Vera. Tears rolled down my cheeks. I hugged Queenie.

The truck stopped. Sam brushed a wisp of hair off my forehead and tenderly touched the aching bump above my left eye.

"You'll be safe here," he said. "You can clean up and rest. Get a bite to eat. Then we'll figure out what to do." He got out of the truck and came around to open my door.

I'd seen the little blue house with the gravel drive on Sunday. This time a maroon Chevy Impala was parked in the drive. White and brown chickens squawked and flapped away from the front door steps.

"Why did you bring me here?"

"Your house is not safe," Sam said. "I'll get you anything you need from town. Just make a list." With one arm around my waist, he propelled me up the steps to the front door.

Sam shoved the door open, and we stepped in and onto a floor covered with bright woven rugs. Native American art hung on oak-paneled walls, and carved animal figures cluttered the tabletops. The scent of cedar wood wafted from the fireplace.

A sixty-ish woman rushed into the room, wiping her hands on a blue plaid dish towel. She threw her arms around me in a bear hug. Then she held me away and peered into my face. I knew she was Sam's mother.

Concern filled her warm brown eyes. "My sweet Jamie," she cooed. "Tell me what you want first: a bath or food? Then we'll take care of the rest, and you will sleep. You are exhausted." Her white hair was coiled in thick braids around the back of her head.

A memory flashed as she said my name. This house, this woman, the aroma of homemade bread. Safety.

"Thank you so much. And thank you, Sam." I squeezed his hand and then followed Mrs. Mazie into the kitchen. The walls rolled, and I staggered. Sam grabbed me and led me to a chair near the table.

"Just something small. I don't want to be any trouble."

"You never were any trouble. Sam, get the juice from the icebox." Sam obeyed his mother, moving with her around the room.

The two of them sat with me at the table while I ate, and then Mrs. Mazie stood and motioned for me to follow. She led the way down the hall to a bedroom with an adjoining bath.

"Nightshirt's on the bed. You take a nice bath and then sleep. Sam will be waiting for you." Mrs. Mazie turned on the water in the tub and poured in bath oil. The room filled with a musky fragrance; the scent reminded me of a New Mexico forest—the aromas of cedar and mesquite.

"I think I've been here before."

"It was a long time ago, those summers when you would visit Elizabeth," Mrs. Mazie said. "You would come and have supper with us. We'd tell stories." Her wide smile was comforting and familiar.

I didn't know how I could ever have forgotten this kind woman and this comfortable home. But I had.

Hours later, after a bath and a deep, dreamless nap, I tucked the soft flannel nightshirt into a pair of jeans and thick socks that had been left on the rocking chair.

Sam sat alone in the living room, eyes closed, with Queenie at his feet. When I came into the room, he got up and took my hands. I leaned into him. His kiss was gentle.

"You look much better. I was so worried." His eyes shone. "What a horrible night you've had."

"Why did Green release me? I'm surprised he would let a hardened, repetitive murderer out of jail after just one night and with no bond." My throat clogged.

"Toby put you there to protect you."

"Because people were angry that I torched the museum and killed Vera?"

He pulled me to him, holding me, letting me sob. "What were you looking for in the museum, Jamie?" He stroked my hair.

I took a few deep breaths. "Didn't any of your family wonder what happened to Clara's headright after she disappeared? It should have gone to Elizabeth and my grandmother. Why didn't it?" I questioned him with my eyes and pulled slightly away from him. "Nobody around here, including you, will tell me anything!"

Sam looked at me, frowning.

I couldn't stop the words from coming once I'd started. "The carbon monoxide poisoning and the greenhouse collapse were not accidents," I blurted. "I overheard Bart on the phone, refusing to set up another accident."

The muscles in Sam's jaw twitched. "All the more reason you need to stay here." He pulled me against him and stroked my hair with one hand. "I'm sorry I wasn't open about our family relationship. I didn't know how you'd take it, or what you would be like." The look in his eyes softened my anger.

"But what about the headright?"

Sam held the palm of my right hand up and traced the outline of my fingers with the fingers of his other hand. "I will tell you the only answer I know. After Clara O'Day disappeared, James O'Day sold her headright to the Wells family," he said. "He wanted to move back to St. Louis and needed a stake to set up business. Unfortunately, he died before he could move the girls there and carry out his plans."

My heart sank. "You knew this?" A great heaviness pressed against my heart. I had created a scenario in my mind, blaming the Wells family for the lost headright, but none of it was true.

Worst of all, I had dragged Vera into it. "Dear God, Sam. Vera's dead."

Sam stroked my hair. "Vera's in the hospital. She'll pull through."

I bounded up off the sofa. "We've got to go see her. I'm responsible!"

Sam grabbed my hands. "She chose to get involved in your witch hunt, too."

I pulled my hands away from him.

"Sam, somebody else was there in the museum. That person started the fire and locked us in. If there's no truth to my theory, then why try to kill us?"

"I don't know. I told you what the family has always been told about Elizabeth's headright. Maybe it has something to do with the notes and the accidents. A different matter entirely."

"Somebody wants me out of here badly enough to kill me. And somebody *did* try to kill Aunt Elizabeth."

"Somebody wants you scared enough to leave town." Sam planted his feet and grabbed at my hands again. "Jamie, listen. If Bart was behind the accidents at the house, then you can't go back there. No telling what may have been booby-trapped. You shouldn't even go into town. Right now, everyone thinks you are in jail. Let them keep thinking that, okay? There's nothing you can do for Vera now, except pray."

Sam released my hands, and I dropped back down into a chair.

"I have a message for you from Trudy," Sam said, turning back to the sofa. "Something about Elizabeth's old book. She says not to worry; she's got it, safe and sound."

"She's talking about Aunt Elizabeth's first diary. It could explain everything."

"Then we'll go into town in a few hours, just after dark. Less likely anyone will see us then."

Chapter 37

Tuesday, April 16—Evening

The twilight sky turned pinks to grays and reds to purples as Sam parked near the alley to Trudy's cottage. We made our way through side yards, keeping to the shadows of the hedges and tall old elms.

Trudy opened the cottage door wearing her usual overalls with a pink and white checked shirt. Her striped hat peeked from the large center pouch. She stood stiffly when I tried to hug her.

"I thought you was in jail. Vera's in the hospital." Trudy's look flitted around the room and then to the table and a small square metal box banded with leather. "Here's Elizabeth's book."

I picked up the box. "Where was it?"

"'Up two, down one, up three, down two.' We always landed there."

Stormy days in the dark entry hall, playing on the stairs, our sing-song voices repeating the phrase over and over again as we leapt up and down the lower stairs. Of course.

"Why didn't you come up and tell me you were in the house the other night, Trudy?" I sank down onto the edge of the blue loveseat.

"He was outside watching. Didn't want any lights coming on. And you and Queenie had been hurt in the greenhouse. You needed to rest."

"Who was watching?"

Trudy turned her body sideways toward Sam, forcing me out of her line of sight.

I sank back into the soft cushions, the metal box in my lap. Sam and Trudy moved to the kitchen doorway. I pushed at the metal clasp and opened the box.

The simple journal was scraps of paper folded together into a thick booklet. Knotted cotton twine had been wrapped between and around the pages to hold them together.

On the front page, in a looping script, Elizabeth had written, "1921—age eleven—diary of Miss Elizabeth O'Day, Bigheart, Oklahoma."

Sept. 9, 1921. Miss Pembrooke wants us to keep a diary. I am writing this so I can remember how it is to be eleven and number one in the sixth-grade class. She says I should go on to high school so I can be a teacher, but Daddy says that's highfalutin. We aren't that kind of people. Daddy runs the lumber yard for Wells, and Mama cooks in the café for the cot house men from sunup to sunset. How would I ever get to high school? Daddy thinks that since he wasn't educated beyond third grade and we only have a cow, some chickens, a horse, and a cart, there isn't a chance for me to get educated. He's wrong.

I kept reading. Elizabeth described the box suppers and church meetings that made up the social life of an eleven-year-old in rural Oklahoma in the oil boom of the early twenties. The entries were usually short; Elizabeth wrote only a few sentences every few days. With the earnest voice of a preteen, she had recorded the main events of her life. The girls had filled kerosene lamps, so they would have light in the evening, and hauled water from the well for laundry, cleaning, and cooking.

They kept the woodpile stacked with the logs that their father chopped for firewood.

I scanned the pages—1921 was the year Elizabeth's mother disappeared. I flipped forward in the journal.

Nov. 7. Mama came home tonight and had a cleaning fit. One of the men from the cot house came into the kitchen at the café with bedbug bites all over, and Mama says she's been itching ever since. Daddy drew water for a hot bath, and we waited on the front porch while she washed. Mama thinks the bedbugs followed her home. Daddy put kerosene in jars and set the bed legs in them to keep the bugs from crawling up into the mattresses.

I turned a few pages farther into the book.

Dec. 14. Sarah and I got home from school today, but Mama wasn't here. I milked the cow, and Martha fed the chickens. I made biscuits and gravy for supper. Wish Mama or Daddy would get home.

Dec. 15. Mama hasn't come home. Daddy looked for her at Grandma's and at Uncle's, but no one has seen her. Everyone is searching. Sarah and I are praying that she'll be home tonight.

Dec. 24. Sarah and I made ornaments for a little tree and decorated the house. It's Christmas Eve. Mama, please come home tonight.

The water's gone bad. Daddy says it tastes like death. Daddy found us another house closer to town, but how will Mama find us if we move?

I read the entries quickly, and my heart began to race.

January 5, 1922. We're in a new house. I guess this one is nicer, but it isn't like Mama anymore. Sarah and I tried to fix things like we thought she would. Mr. Wells and his family helped us move. Their son, Spencer, is mighty handsome. He smiled at me once. Daddy doesn't talk about Mama, but he watches out the window, just like Sarah and me.

Her next entry was two months later.

March 17. Dance tomorrow night, and Daddy says I can go! Got some new ribbon at the store and have sewn it on the hem of my old dress. I'll make a bow for my hair with the extra. Maybe W. C. will ask me to dance, or J. L. Would I just faint if S. W. did?

Two blank pages followed, then:

March 25. I haven't been able to write. Daddy died. He went to the old home place. They say he set it on fire. Why would he do that? Sarah and I are with the Wells'.

April 10. Mr. Wells told Sarah and me that he is our guardian now, and his family will take care of us until we are old enough to be on our own. We eat in the kitchen. Mrs. Wells mostly tells us what to do. Sarah gets tired of chores and getting up early to do them before school. I miss Daddy. I miss Mama. (Mama, if you're out there, please come home. Please.)

April 30. Mrs. Wells made Sarah and me go to the church supper with her. S. stared at me all the way there, but I didn't talk to him or anybody. I just wanted to come home. I take the exams for high school tomorrow. How can I even think?

My heart hurt. Sam had said that James O'Day sold the headright to the Wells Family to get money to move back to St. Louis. If he had, Elizabeth hadn't known anything of the planned move to Missouri.

I opened the diary to a new year—1925.

June 17. J. is not crawling. Sarah and I want him to be, but he's happy to be carried. When I cook at the diner in the evenings, Sarah keeps him. Last week when we all went into town, Mrs. Hudson patted his head and said, "Poor orphan." Mrs. Wells says it's best if no one—not even Sarah—knows he's mine. She thinks the Wellses adopted him from Mrs. Wells's cousin so that we could have a brother after Mama disappeared and Daddy died. Later, we'll be glad to have a brother, Mrs. Wells says. I saw S. outside the café yesterday, but he didn't come in. Would he have, if he'd known I was there?

I looked up. Sam and Trudy had stepped into the kitchen. Their quiet voices hummed.

Jasper was Elizabeth's son.

I flipped back, looking for 1924, the year that Jasper must have been born.

March 13, 1924. I'm so anxious about the dance tonight. I've been working on my dress, adding ribbons, making it beautiful. I want him to notice me for real, as a woman. I am not the housemaid.

March 14, 1924. I have shredded the dress. How could he? He made me swear never to tell anyone. Said that he was sorry, and he just loves me so much, he couldn't stop. I feel so ashamed. We should have gotten married first.

It was three months later before she wrote again.

*June 10. I can't keep it to myself any longer. I think
there's a baby! I have to tell Mrs. Wells. I can't go on to
high school. I can't stay here. Where will I go?*

I closed my eyes and laid the book in my lap. I waited until
my heart stopped pounding before I read on.

*June 12. I am going to live with Mrs. Wells's sister in
Sallisaw until the baby comes. Sarah is not to know that
I'm having a child. Mrs. Wells thinks the secret will be
easier to keep if not even Sarah knows. I want to tell her.
How can I not tell my own sister that I am in love, and
I am having his baby? She knows I love him, but she
doesn't know what we did. They will not let S. talk to
me. He is staying with his grandparents.*

More blank pages.

*Aug. 4. S. married A. C. today. I would kill myself, but
then, there's the baby. Would our baby go to hell with
me?*

My knotted stomach churned, and my face felt hot and
clammy at the same time.

*September 11. Mrs. Wells's sister Josephine is kind to
me, and so is her husband, Stephen. There's too much to
do. Their farm is so big—320 acres. I have a room in the
loft to myself, but climbing the ladder gets harder every
day. I'm so tired.*

December 18. J. was born two days ago. He is so sweet

and never cries. The midwife says my labor was hard. I just want to sleep. J. is nursing fine.

December 23. Mrs. Wells is coming after the New Year and bringing Sarah. We'll all go home to Pawhuska to live in the big house.

I rubbed my temples, where a small ache had begun to pound. I thought of the hateful notes. *Slut. Whore. Jezebel. The wages of sin are* death*!*

Someone knew the truth and wouldn't let Elizabeth forget— as if the shattered innocence of a fourteen-year-old could ever be forgotten.

No wonder Elizabeth had not told anyone about the notes. She would have had to explain the implications. A young woman with an illegitimate child in the twenties didn't have much hope for bettering her future. But somehow, Elizabeth had bettered her fortune. Robert "Dodie" Darcey had loved her and married her in 1928.

I flipped farther into the book until I reached the pages dated 1925 again and skimmed the entries I had already read. Sam and Trudy were still in the kitchen. I was alone with the diary and with the reality of Elizabeth's early life. Had my grandmother ever realized that Jasper was really her nephew?

Oct. 14, 1925. S. W. slipped me a note under his plate today at the diner! He loves me and J. He's sorry he married A.

Nov. 1. Mr. Wells told me that Sarah and I had to find another place. He gave me money and said he'd help move us Saturday. I've never had this much money before. Tomorrow, I'll find the three of us a place. Mrs. Harris has rooms, and she won't take oil workers.

Maybe she'll take us. J. is hardly any trouble. Maybe she'd even watch him during the day when I'm at the diner. Mr. Wells said that S. won't ever leave A. I don't want to believe it. Will it always be just the three of us— Sarah, J., and me?

Dec. 17. J. is one year old today. I made him a little cake and some sugar icing. We sang and lit a match, since we didn't have a candle.

Dec. 31. J. hasn't pulled himself up yet. Mrs. Harris says something's wrong. How can something be wrong? He smiles all the time. He's so happy. I'm so tired. More and more men crowd into the diner for lunch and supper. It's such a relief to have Mrs. Harris watching J. while Sarah and I work. Some days, I wonder if I'm as old as I feel. If so, I must be nearly one hundred.

I closed the little book, and tried to imagine what Elizabeth's life had been like.

Sam and Trudy's voices broke into my thoughts as they stepped back into the living room. I swiped at my wet cheeks. Sam crossed the room and slid his arm around me.

"Are you all right?"

Trudy stared at me. She pulled the striped cap out of her pocket and fingered the edge of the bill. I stared back, wondering how much she really knew and wondering why Elizabeth had not identified her correctly in the legal document Sam had read to us.

S. W. was probably Spencer Wells, Martin's father. So Martin was Jasper's half brother. If Jasper had been acknowledged, the two of them would have shared the family's wealth, including the royalties from the headright that Joseph O'Day had supposedly sold them.

"Jamie?" Sam touched my shoulder again.

"Have you read all of this?" I asked Trudy. "Do you know what it says?" The family secrets needed to end now. I wouldn't be part of keeping secrets any longer. Everyone needed to know the truth.

"My Liz and I read it together," Trudy said, raising her chin. "I know it by heart."

"You know it in your heart, but you can't read?"

Trudy's chin jutted out. "I know some words. I'm not stupid."

I winced. Trudy couldn't read. Who would take care of her if Elizabeth never recovered?

"Trudy, do you know who Jasper was to Elizabeth?"

Trudy smiled and nodded. "He was her special boy. Her J. She loved him. Said he was her special blessing." Trudy grinned. "He stayed right here, close, so they could help each other." She screwed her mouth around and focused one eye on me.

"I know Elizabeth loved him, Trudy. This diary from long, long ago, when your daddy was first born, tells how very much she loved him."

Trudy's head bobbed. "She was his mama."

I glanced at Sam. He was watching Trudy, a calm look on his face.

"Who was his daddy?"

"Not supposed to talk about that. Ever. My Liz made me promise." Trudy looked out the window. "Sometimes he'd come to see Jasper in the evenings after dark. They'd sit on Elizabeth's screened-in porch and smoke. I watched the little glows from my bedroom window."

I looked at Sam. "Was it Spencer Wells?"

"Elizabeth never told me. He was the likeliest candidate. Trudy, was Spencer your grandfather?"

Trudy's look darted to the door, and then back and forth between Sam and me. "Spencer Wells is my granddaddy," she whispered.

I shook my head. The Wells family had hidden an illegitimate son for all these years. It was entirely possible that wasn't all they'd hidden.

"Thank you for letting me read this. Now, Sam and I need to put it in a safe place." But my mind whirred on to other things. Somewhere, there was documentation about the transfer of the headright and the guardianship. "Trudy, where else might Elizabeth have hidden something, like papers or old documents?"

Trudy focused on the wall again. She began to hum and then stopped.

"What about the gazebo?" Sam asked. "Was there a secret compartment out there?"

Trudy shrugged.

Sam stood in the doorway for a moment, looking out into the night. I peered over his shoulder. He scanned the surrounding shadows and then stepped outside.

I thought I saw a shadow shift into deeper darkness. "Someone's out there."

He pulled back into Trudy's cottage. "I'll come back tomorrow to check out the gazebo. You keep thinking about where else Elizabeth might have hidden something."

"I'll think about it," Trudy said as she handed me the box with the diary inside. "Don't lose Elizabeth's book. Promise?"

I promised. We waited until we heard the deadbolt click into place before we moved back up the alley to the street where Sam's car was parked.

As we drove, I thought about Elizabeth. I could understand why no one wanted to talk about her early life and what had happened to her parents, but I wished I had known before now. I felt a new appreciation for my aunt, not only for the strong woman she had become but for the optimistic and encouraging attitude she always portrayed.

Sam touched my arm. "You all right?" The truck bounced along the rutted road.

"No," I admitted. He picked up my left hand and squeezed it. "I wish she had talked to me about her life. About what really happened. I don't even know her."

"Do we ever really know anybody—what they're thinking or feeling? Even when they speak to us about things, we can never really know if that's the truth."

I watched his face in the green glow from the dashboard. My heart stuttered.

Chapter 38

Wednesday, April 17—Morning

I woke up drenched in sweat. A pack of coyotes yipped some-where outside, their voices a melodic chorus singing to the moon. For a minute, I lay there, letting the reality of the safe room wash over me and letting the dream of the museum fire fade. Thank God, Vera was alive. I wanted to know how badly Vera had been burned and if the blow that had knocked her unconscious had done any major damage.

Martin's leering face crowded into my thoughts. He had been there so quickly; he could have been waiting outside. He was Jasper's half brother, Trudy's uncle. My heart ached for Elizabeth and the inner shame she had carried all her life.

The living room was empty. In the kitchen, a note was propped up beside the sugar bowl on the table.

Gone to court. Mom and I will both be back for lunch. Rest.

The pot of tea Mrs. Mazie had left on the stove burner was still hot.

I had hoped to go with Sam and to visit Vera. Sam was probably right that I should lay low. I stepped back into the comfortable living room, cupping the mug of hot tea. Pillows of gold, deep red, and brown fabric piled onto the leather sofa invited me to sit and think.

My eyes still burned. I rubbed at my temples and gingerly touched the enormous bump on my forehead. I closed my eyes. The scent of cedar wood from the fireplace permeated the room. I remembered Sam's touch last night, his sweet kisses in the hallway before I slipped away to my bedroom. How was it possible that in the middle of all this, I had fallen in love?

I lay my head against the high back of the sofa. Sam seemed to know everything. He seemed positive the headright had willingly been sold. I didn't want to believe it. James O'Day had surely known what that money would mean to his family in future years.

And then there was Elizabeth and her illegitimate son. Someone else, outside the Wells family, had known about Jasper. The anonymous note writer had tormented Elizabeth ruthlessly.

I had to find out the truth. I couldn't go back to New Mexico wondering if my suspicion about the Wells family and the headright was true. Documents granting guardianship and transferring the headright were on file somewhere. Sam and I had to find them.

The box with all the photographs in Elizabeth's attic contained letters and other papers. Perhaps there were documents with signatures that could eventually be compared to official documents on file.

I pulled myself up from the sofa and went for another cup of Mrs. Mazie's morning tea. Where else could Elizabeth have stored such documents? Mentally, I combed the nooks and crannies of the house.

An image popped into my mind—Elizabeth on that last day, humming "Here We Go 'Round the Mulberry Bush."

The mulberry bush. Sam had pointed out the huge old mulberry tree at the old homestead. When we were children, Elizabeth had used the hole in the trunk for clues to treasure hunts. Could James O'Day have used the deep cavity in the tree as a hiding place for family documents?

From the front window, I watched as the sky spat cold rain, and low clouds hugged the ground. I rummaged in the coat closet for a slicker or jacket to borrow.

Be back by noon. Out for a walk. I jotted the words at the bottom of Sam's note and then stepped outside. Dark clouds pressed against the horizon. I pulled the hood of the sky-blue slicker close around my face and tied the string under my chin.

I wanted the truth. Even if it meant learning O'Day really had sold out his family. I had to know before I went home. The thought of leaving Pawhuska filled me both with relief and a new sense of sadness.

I couldn't remember how far the Mazies' home was from the homestead. The distance had passed quickly when we were in the truck but might have been as much as two or three miles.

As I trudged down the road, I wasn't sure where I was going or even if I was walking in the right direction. Sweat cooled my skin beneath the heavy sweatshirt and slicker. I kept walking. Nothing looked familiar.

Finally, the ancient elm emerged from the low clouds, with the dangling rope strand hanging nearly to the ground. Carefully, I slipped through the barbed-wire fence.

Fog distorted distance and obscured everything toward the rear of the home site. The shape of the mulberry tree loomed just past the stones and charred timbers marking the location of the house.

I picked my way over the ground, stepping over rocks and jagged metal pieces. The lines of the mulberry tree sharpened. Trees limbs arched down to touch the ground, offering shelter to anything that crawled close up against the trunk. I squatted and then duck-walked through dried leaves and matted grass beneath the bowed lower limbs. When I stood next to the trunk, the branches seemed to close around me.

I fingered the rough bark around the tree trunk, feeling for the opening of the old cavity. Some kind of huge woodland spider might have turned it into its lair. I shivered at the thought but kept touching the bark, reaching.

If something had been hidden there long ago, I might not

even be able to get it out; the tree might have closed up around it. And even if I was able to pull something out, it was likely, especially if it was made of paper, that temperature changes and humidity would have made any writing illegible.

My fingers found an opening about four inches across, just above the base of a limb. I shifted my body around the trunk until I could see the hole. Cautiously, I stuck two fingers into it. I felt something. It didn't move, squeak, or bite. I forced my fingers farther in. There was definitely something there.

I pressed my left cheek against the trunk of the tree, extended my reach and stretched my hand as far as I could to get a firm grasp on the object. Slowly, a little at a time, I worked it up and out of the hole until I could grab it and pull it the rest of the way out.

The narrow leather pouch was about eight inches long. When I loosened the rawhide drawstring, I could see the end of a tight roll of papers.

The gusting wind reached me even under the shelter of the tree's limbs. I turned my back to the wind and pulled the papers out of the pouch. My icy hands trembled as I undid the twine bow that held the pages together. Splats of rain hit my back. I held the papers close to my body as I unrolled them.

The tightly curled pages sprang back into a roll when I moved my fingers. But I had seen three words written in elaborate script: "Certificate of Marriage."

I slid the rolled papers back into the leather pouch and reached up under the slicker and black sweatshirt to tuck the pouch under my sports bra.

Using my arms to protect my face from small branches, I backed out of the shelter of the tree. I stumbled on a root and nearly fell but steadied myself and kept moving backwards. Heavy rain began to pelt my back. I drew the hood closer around my face and turned from the tree.

Strong arms clasped my shoulders and jerked me into the driving rain.

Rain needles stung my eyes. The assailant was behind me, holding my arm, out of reach of my kicking legs. My vision blurred as the rain torrents washed into my eyes. I kicked out again. And then, I felt myself being dragged across the ground. The iron grip around me loosened, and in the next instant, a hard shove propelled me forward. I fell into gaping blackness.

The jolt of the landing knocked my breath away. Pain shot up from my left arm and leg, and the nerve endings in my back screamed. Something heavy lay across my body; the weight barely shifted when I moved.

I opened my eyes wide and strained to see in the darkness. Turning my head, I saw a halo of light bobbing a few yards away. A quiver shook my body.

I was in the root cellar. Terror closed off my throat. *Calm down, calm down, and think. You can get out.*

I twisted toward the halo of light. Pain shot from my arm and leg.

Someone coughed.

A black shape crouched in the darkness on the other side of the cellar. The shapeless bulk shifted, dimly illuminated by light from the opening above.

The dank mold smell rose up into my nostrils and regular "pings" sounded around me as water dripped. This cellar had provided storage for canned goods put up in the summer for the family to eat in the winter. I remembered rows and rows of old glass jars on shelves and even on the earthen floor. I reached out and touched a smooth, cold cylinder just a few inches away.

I struggled to get up, and the board on top of me fell away. I rolled to one side and sat up.

The cough came again. The shape stood, looming just feet away in the semi-darkness.

An extreme sense of déjà vu came over me.

I had been trapped down here before.

My mind worked. The only way out was just behind my assailant.

"Did you find what you were looking for in the tree?" the shape hissed.

My stomach clenched. That voice had hissed in my dreams as far back as I could remember. Now it was real.

"You should have minded your own business. You should have gone home, Jamie. Now look where you are and where you're going to stay, forever." The hissing voice gave an odd, strangled cackle.

Was it a man or a woman?

A foggy memory tape played: children darted around the trees, pushed each other in the swing, and dared the rope to break. They took turns jumping out of the swing. Who could land upright, the farthest away? Children played chase, running farther and farther away from the picnic blanket where the adults talked and dozed.

"Talk to me, Jamie. Are you scared? You won't be much longer. It's nearly over," the voice hissed. "Years ago, I lured you down here. I called out for help, and you came. But then when I tried to get near you, you shoved me away. I left you here, alone, hoping the others would forget you and go back to town. Then I could have brought you food and kept you safe, always."

Sam had said something about loving me when we were children. A shiver ran across my back. Surely this wasn't Sam.

My arm and leg prickled. I flexed my fingers and toes, feeling needle-like stabs. I needed a weapon. My fingers curled around an old canning jar, still full of old fruit or tomatoes.

"You didn't like being down here then. How do you like the cellar now?" The blurred shape loomed closer.

I clasped the jar like a baseball. Focused on the shadowy shape, I thought about playing catch with Ben and Matt, and then I jumped to my feet and threw the jar.

The figure crumpled to the ground.

I squinted up toward the halo of light and then stumbled a few feet, hands extended in front of me. The blurred light above took on the partial shape of a rectangular doorway, and just behind the slumped figure was the outline of the steps. I side-stepped the huddled figure and scrambled up, shoving the old metal door away until it fell open.

Rain pelted my face as I reached for the edge of the door and then slammed it shut again. I charged toward a grove of trees to the back of the property.

Behind me, the metal door screeched open and banged down against the earth. I leapt over metal and broken timbers, scampering toward the trees.

The ground opened into a hole in front of me. I bounded over it and ran on. Immediately behind me, someone cried out. I plunged on until I reached the grove of trees, and then I glanced over my shoulder. No one followed.

Panting, I waited. Nothing. Cautiously, I retraced a few steps. The pouring rain had lessened into a light shower. I doubled back. Nothing moved.

The hole gaped a few steps ahead. To one side lay a pile of tumbled bricks, grown over with grass. A dark shape lay motionless several feet down. The person in the black slicker lay still, face hidden.

I ran through the rainy mist to the road and then back toward the Mazies' house. Pain pounded in my back and head with every step. I jogged, then walked, then jogged again, constantly glancing behind and to each side. *Dear God, don't let it have been Sam!*

At the Mazie's house, both Sam's truck and his mother's car were in the yard. Sobs erupted from my chest. By the time I reached the door, the sobbing had become loud, uncontrolled gasps. Would he be in the house, or was he back at the homestead in the bottom of the hole?

Sam jerked the door open and pulled me in. Mrs. Mazie

bustled out of the kitchen, drying her hands on her apron. Queenie barked, tail wagging.

"What's wrong? What happened?" Sam's hands on my shoulders steadied me. He yanked up the blanket that was draped over the back of the recliner and wrapped me in it; then he led me across the room to the sofa. I pulled away when he tried to pull me down with him as he sat. Instead, I stalked across the room, breathing hard. My whole body shook.

"Someone just tried to kill me."

"Shhh. Calm down," Sam urged. "Get your breath."

I paced back and forth across the room, eyes closed. Mrs. Mazie perched on the arm of the recliner.

"He fell in a hole. I left him."

"Who?" Mrs. Mazie asked.

"Could have been anybody. Black hooded slicker. Couldn't see." I pulled in more air.

"Where?" Sam asked.

"The homestead." I still couldn't get my breath. "James O'Day hid something there, in that tree." I stopped moving and bent over, gasping. "Papers. Maybe the proof we need."

Sam crossed the room and grasped me by the shoulders again. "I checked the archives after my hearing this morning. I've got documents, Jamie—the guardianship grant for the Wells family, the transfer of the headright, all with James O'Day's signature." His forehead touched mine, and his damp hair felt cold against my skin.

I reached under my sweatshirt, pulled out the leather pouch, and handed it to Sam.

He slipped out the papers and then spread them on the coffee table: one marriage certificate and two notices of the payment of headrights to Clara O'Day, dated January 1918 and January 1919. He pulled an envelope from his own pocket and laid two folded pages next to the ones I had found.

The truth was obvious. When comparing the original

marriage license from the tree with copies of the guardianship grant from the courthouse, the signatures seemed identical.

I sank down onto the sofa. Mrs. Mazie scooted close, patting my leg. O'Day was guilty after all. He had signed the guardianship papers and the headright transfer. I rocked forward, bracing my head with my hands. Queenie whined from in front of the fireplace.

"It must be true," Sam said. "It's what we've always been told. I'm sorry." He touched my hand.

"We've got to go back. Someone tried to kill me, Sam, and now I'm not even sure why. Call Green."

Sam folded the documents, shoved them back into his pocket, and then reached for the phone.

Chapter 39

Wednesday, April 17—Afternoon

The rain had stopped, but the looming clouds hugged the ground. I led Sam past the old foundation and the mulberry tree, toward the hole where my assailant had fallen.

The body lay face down in the mud. Rain had puddled on a navy-blue windbreaker. I stepped closer, but Sam grabbed my arm and pulled me back. Blood matted the hair on the back of the man's head,"Wait. We shouldn't disturb anything until Toby gets here."

"Something's not right," I said. "The person in the root cellar wore a black slicker with a full hood that covered the head. This isn't the same person."

Wailing sirens abruptly ended. Car doors slammed out on the road. Police Chief Green and three men ducked through the barbed-wire fence and then trotted across the grass.

Green peered into the hole. "Who is it?"

"Whoever this is, he isn't the one who attacked me," I said. "My assailant wore a black jacket."

An officer slipped down into the hole, felt for a pulse on the victim's neck, and then rolled the body over on its side. Even with the bullet hole in his forehead, I recognized Bart Rourke.

"So someone attacked you here, he fell in the hole, and you got away. But it wasn't Bart?" Toby Green squinted at me and shook his head.

"I knocked him out in the root cellar with a canning jar.

Evidence should be there. Blood. Something. Bart wasn't in the cellar," I insisted. "His jacket, his size—they're all wrong." I had seen only the outline of a dark shape, but the figure in the slicker had been much more slender than Bart.

A bolt of lightning zapped the sky, followed close by rolling thunder. Huge drops of rain mixed with icy hail suddenly pelted down from the sky. The three of us raced to take refuge in the squad car.

In the rear seat, Sam slipped his arm around my shoulders and pulled me close. In the front seat, Toby tapped the steering wheel repeatedly with his thumb and peered out the window at the barrage of rain and hail. At his prompting, I told the story again.

"Anything else?" Green asked afterward with an exasperated sigh. "How can you be sure of the size of the figure, what he was wearing, or anything else when it was so dark—and raining to boot?" He blew out his breath and rubbed the back of his neck with one hand.

I turned to look at Sam just as he reached up to push his wet hair off his face. A fresh red-purple bruise colored his left temple.

Sam pulled me closer.

Time seemed to stop as my brain worked. Sam's hair had been wet when I got to the Mazie house. But he said he'd been at the courthouse. And he had the documents.

The hammering of the hail eased. Minutes later, the rain ended too. Sunrays broke through the parting clouds. Green got out of the car and walked back to the root cellar. Sam and I followed. My whole body shivered, but not because I was cold. Sam pulled me close and rubbed my arms.

"It's going to be all right," he murmured.

I wished that were true. Last night, Sam had said something about how one never really knew what a person was thinking or feeling. Had he been speaking of himself?

I waited above ground while Toby and Sam climbed down

into the cellar. I wondered, briefly, if I should have stopped Sam from going with Green. If it had been Sam down there—I didn't want to believe it—he might be contaminating the evidence.

A few minutes later, Toby and Sam climbed back out.

"You played down there as a child?" Toby asked, moving to me.

"I wouldn't call it playing," I said. "Someone trapped me down there once. I've been claustrophobic ever since. Whoever pushed me down there today claimed to have been that same person." My mouth felt like desert sand. I couldn't look at Sam; he had slipped up to stand close beside me.

"Somebody from your childhood." Toby jabbed one hand into his front pants pocket and coins clinked. "That the only time you've been down there? Just that once?"

"Other kids went down there. I never did." In my memory, I could hear the kids, sitting on the mound above the cellar, daring each other to go down. "Sam, you went down there. You said so the other day." My voice shook.

Green gave Sam a hard look. "You've been down there before?"

"As a kid—a few times when someone dared me. We all did it. None of us stayed long. It smelled."

"Either of you remember anything else about what's down there?" Green asked.

Something about the expression on his face made my skin crawl. "It's a root cellar," I said, forcing myself to sound calm. "Shelves, jars, an old chair. Darkness, wet, and spiders. What else?"

A memory flashed. Total darkness. Fear. Panic. In my mind, the child's hand—my hand—reached out and felt for the walls but touched something else instead. Something hard, dry, papery—and hairy.

Police Chief Green's voice sounded distant. "What else? Maybe ... a human skeleton?"

Green radioed for the medical examiner and then pulled

cameras and equipment from the trunk of the car again. A group of men trudged to the root cellar. Sam leaned against the car hood. I sank into the backseat and closed my eyes, willing the full memory to wash over me. If I remembered the other time, maybe I would understand why someone—Sam?—had done this. I concentrated. Forced the sounds of the world away. Focused.

It was dark and quiet, and I couldn't get out.

I crouched at the top of the steps and banged on the metal door. I yelled for help, but no one heard.

I looked for something to pry the door open. Finally, I looked for another way out.

I felt my way around the room, touching the damp stone walls, the shelves, the jars. I brushed away spider webs and choked down fear.

Fresh air spurted out of a small passage. I reached in and felt the dirt walls. The opening was big enough to crawl through. I crawled in on the hard-packed earth, reached out in front with my hands, patted my way forward into the space, and breathed the dry air.

My hand touched something hard and leathery, blocking the passage. I jerked my hand back. I had touched something long and stringy. Something like hair. I touched the leathery surface again and ran my fingertips across it until I felt the surface change into a row of small, smooth squares that edged a hole.

Terror took over.

It was a skull, with hair and teeth. Screaming, I scrambled backwards out of the tunnel, crying in the blackness.

Terrifying darkness turned into sunlight. I was lying on the ground. A ring of faces peered down. Someone offered a sip of water from a paper cup. Muttering adults piled rocks on top of the metal door.

"Don't go down there again. Ever. You hear me!" My mother's

voice and my great-aunt's voice repeated the words over and
over to the children who stood nearby, shocked.

"Yes, ma'am."

"Yes, ma'am."

One after another, the children agreed.

I leaned forward in the backseat and opened my eyes. Thirty years had passed. I looked out at Sam. I saw his noble face and his beautiful hair as he watched the flurry of activity underway at the root cellar. My heart lurched.

They would have the bones dated and determine a cause of death.

My skin felt clammy. The goose egg on my forehead pounded.

"I think they're coming out," Sam called. He hadn't spoken since he came back to the car; he had left me alone with my thoughts and memories.

Was he wondering if I had figured it all out?

The team headed back to the car, led by a somber Toby Green. In one hand, he grasped a small plastic bag. Behind him, four men carried a black zipped body bag.

Toby swung my door closed before he got behind the steering wheel. Sam slipped into the passenger side of the front seat. Toby ran one hand over his chin and then swiveled around in the seat to face me.

"We have a pretty good idea whose skeleton that is. And there's something in this bag you need to see. Can you both come down to the office with me, now?"

I looked at Sam. His face was blank, emotionless.

Chapter 40

Wednesday, April 17—Late Afternoon

Police Chief Green thrust the gearshift into drive and sped away, fishtailing on the washboarded road. Behind us, Sam followed in his truck. Green grabbed the radio handset.

"Get the team ready. It's going down," he said and then replaced the radio.

"What's happening?"

"We've been looking for that skeleton for a long time." He clamped his lips shut.

Behind us, Sam's truck kept pace, avoiding the potholes and shimmying over washboarded sections. If he was guilty, wouldn't he bolt? When we reached the paved highway, I closed my eyes.

"You okay, Jamie?" Green asked.

His somber, stiff professional face had been replaced by the friendly face I had glimpsed once last week. Still, I couldn't tell him what Sam might have done.

"I'll be okay when this is all finally over."

He glanced in the rearview mirror and then back at me. "Sorry about putting you in the holding cell. You were in danger, and there wasn't any place else that seemed safe."

"When did you decide the accidents were not accidents?"

He shook his head. "Our investigation turned up some interesting discrepancies. We've been watching your house. And we've been watching Wells." Toby ran his fingers over his chin and then continued. "Some people have suspected for a long time that his family's fortune was not earned by legitimate means. And recently, he was into some shady deals. We just don't know who he's collaborating with. Finding Bart dead today answers that question and makes a weird kind of sense."

My head ached. There was more to this. I was sure of it.

In the parking lot outside Green's office, Sam slipped his arm around my waist as we entered the station.

Inside, the police chief cleared off his desk, moving pictures and a cluster of trophies to a small table. He laid down a worn, cracked leather pouch. "This pouch was deep in the pocket of the oilskin duster our skeleton was wearing."

Aged yellowed papers crackled as Green pulled them from the pouch and unfolded them. Sam and I leaned close.

Three receipts for headright payments had all been signed by Clara O'Day. The fourth document was Clara O'Day's marriage certificate, signed by both Clara and James.

Sam reached into his pocket, pulled out the documents he'd shown me earlier, and laid them on the desk next to the others. James O'Day's signature on the skeleton's marriage certificate was not the same as the one transferring the headright to Joshua Wells and giving him guardianship of O'Day's daughters.

Toby Green tapped a fingertip on the desk and stared from one document to the other. "Got him." He punched a button on the phone. "Do it now," he said into the desk unit.

"These were with the skeleton?" I asked.

"We won't know for sure until after testing, but it's my guess that the skeleton is your great-grandmother, Clara O'Day," Green said. "Murdered and crammed into that passage off the root cellar, apparently just after collecting her monthly royalty payment." He pointed at the marriage certificate. "She carried this identification with her, since the rolls listed her as Clara Mazie," Green continued. "She's lain down there for decades."

I remembered again the leathery feel of the skull. "Not completely undisturbed," I murmured.

"Are you going to pick up that SOB?" Sam demanded,

leaning forward in his chair. His eyes blazed, and the telltale muscle in his jaw worked in and out. Wasn't he afraid that bringing in Wells would reveal his part in all of this?

"I've sent out an APB to bring Martin Wells in," Toby explained. "Martin was probably the one at the old house site this morning, too, although Bart was in the cellar with you. Maybe Wells intended to frame you for Bart's death."

"But it wasn't Bart in the root cellar!"

"You were scared; it was storming. You couldn't see." Toby tapped his pencil against the desk. "Martin probably planted these pages in the tree." He fingered the papers. "No evidence of aging. Paper looks new, even though the pouch is old. There's no way these documents were in that tree for all those years." He pushed away from the desk. "I'll bet Wells sent Bart out to watch the homestead. Bart alerted him when you arrived. They probably planned to kill you in the cellar. If you somehow survived, the forged papers would convince you that you had been wrong about your suspicions."

"I want to talk to Wells," I said.

"He'll be in custody within the hour."

The phone rang. The police chief picked it up and listened. "I'll be right there." He slammed the phone down and turned to us. "You can consider the case closed. It's safe to go home." He hurried out.

Sam bolted out of his chair and grabbed my hand.

I had to know. I reached up and roughly brushed back his hair, uncovering the bruise on his temple.

"Ow!" He pulled away. "Careful. Still smarts. I hit my head this morning when I was searching the archives for these old documents."

The tension flowed out of my body, and my eyes filled with tears.

He stopped the car in front of Elizabeth's house, and I climbed out.

"I'll pick up a couple of burgers and be right back," Sam called through the open truck window.

I waved him off and then let myself into the house, bolting the door behind me. Mid-afternoon sunlight filtered through the curtained windows beside the front door, catching dust motes floating in silvery light. Only the ticking of the clock in the study broke the silence. I let out a long sigh and crossed the hall to the bench.

Something still didn't feel quite right. It had not been Bart in the root cellar, and I wasn't all that sure it had been Wells. And none of this explained the creepy notes that were tied to Elizabeth's past.

I huddled on the hall bench. I hoped Sam would hurry back. I didn't want to be here in this house, even now.

I thought about Mom. She might be back from the hospital, finally finished with the testing. I picked up the phone.

When there was no dial tone, I punched several times at the disconnect button on the receiver. The phone line was dead. From this morning's storm?

I listened to the silent house.

"Casey would waltz with the strawberry blonde ..." The rasping, toneless whisper slashed through the quiet.

A key scraped in the front-door lock, and then the door creaked open. Two figures, backlit by the full afternoon sun, stepped into the hall—one tall and one stooped.

"Jamie, my girl. Thought I'd find you at home."

"Martin?"

"We've just come from meeting Chief Green. There's been some misunderstanding," Martin Wells said. "It's best if we talk alone. Tie up loose ends, you might say."

He moved toward me, teeth gleaming. The other man

pulled the door closed and waited beside it. I backed toward the kitchen.

"Dear girl, I didn't attack you this morning. What an uncivilized thing to do!" Wells said in a sugary voice. "Wouldn't dream of hurting a single hair on your beautiful body. Gracious no. I've been busy all morning. Gave a program at the Chamber of Commerce for the Ponca City Garden Club. Forty ladies and me with the chamber staff, from nine until nearly noon. Toby can't argue with all those witnesses."

I was nearly at the doorway to the kitchen now. The dining room doorway gaped on my right.

"And I have to take exception with those papers Green mentioned." He shook his head and clucked. "Can't hold me accountable for what my granddaddy did. He's long gone. Oh, I'm forgetting my manners. Have you met my father? Spencer Wells?"

The second man scooted forward into the light. The elderly volunteer from the hospital smiled sheepishly at me. I saw the family resemblance now, the same full head of white hair and the sparkling eyes.

"Guess what we have to do is convince you to settle out of court and out of the media," Spencer said with the same wide smile as his son.

"Is that what you tried to do when you sold this house to Elizabeth?" I asked the old man.

"No," Spencer Wells replied, shaking his head. "My father had just died. Elizabeth's husband had just died. I needed to make things right for her and for my son, Jasper." He pulled something out of his pocket. A round locket dangled from a dainty gold chain. Elizabeth's locket—the locket that had been missing since Elizabeth was nearly suffocated on the day I arrived. "I gave her the house because I love her. I never stopped loving her. She belongs here in this house, paid for by the royalty money. All I've ever wanted is to take care of her and our son, and my granddaughter."

I stared at the locket. He wrapped the chain around his fingers, unwrapped it, and wrapped it around them again. If Spencer had the locket, it had been Spencer who had tried to suffocate Elizabeth.

"Oh, please, Dad," Martin said. "Women like Elizabeth are a dime a dozen. Why do you keep insisting it was love? The beautiful O'Day women inspire *lust*." Martin leered at me as he stepped across the hall. "My daddy has never lost his conscience. Elizabeth never knew the entire reason he was so generous. Thought it was because of Jasper. Anyway, I've got my own way of doing things, and I've got an idea. You ready to hear it?"

I clenched my teeth. I wouldn't let the slime go unpunished for another eighty years, whatever his idea was. *Where is Sam?*

"I'm willing to pay you a tidy sum of money to go back to your family in New Mexico. You have no ties here, no real family. Trudy's nothing to you. What difference does it make now? You don't press charges; you just go away. We'll pay you twice what the house is worth. That's a sizable return on Elizabeth's one-dollar investment."

I sprinted into the kitchen, grabbed a knife from the cutting block, and then turned back toward the hall. Martin watched me from the doorway, his father just behind him.

"Why, honey," Martin drawled. "I'm *not* going to hurt you. There's no reason for that. Not if you do what I ask, and I *know* you're an intelligent, reasonable person."

"You tried to kill Elizabeth to shut her up. She was finally ready to tell everyone about all of it, wasn't she? You can't make things right, not after all this time. Not for any amount of money. Your family stole Clara's headright and killed her and my great-grandfather!"

"Oh, that's all speculation." Martin waved one hand in the air. "You can't prove James O'Day wasn't a willing partner. Even Elizabeth always believed her dad sold her out." He looked over his shoulder at his father and then snickered. "But let's ask my dear daddy about that. He was with her when you arrived in our fair city. Was that it, Dad? Had she finally put two and two together and decided she should hate you? Is that why you tried to kill her?"

"Elizabeth was distraught," the old man whined. "I couldn't get her to quiet down." He rubbed his chin and stared up the backstairs. Tears dribbled down onto his craggy cheeks. His hand had closed into a fist around the locket. "I never would have killed her."

"You've been watching Trudy's house," I said.

"She's my granddaughter." The old man sagged against the kitchen wall. "I tried to watch over her after Jasper died."

"Why did you take the notes from Trudy's house? And why have you been outside watching me?"

"What?" Spencer blinked.

Martin stepped closer. "Jamie, can we agree on a figure? Say a million bucks? I've got a down payment right here, with the rest ready later tonight as you leave town. Ten thousand now." He reached into the inside left pocket of his suit jacket, pulled out a bundle of hundred-dollar bills, and pitched them onto the table. "Yes?"

I stared down at the table. The photograph of the children that I'd left there peeked out from beneath the bills. My childhood playmates smiled their frozen smiles in front of a backstop, with Ellen holding the bat and me clutching the ball.

"Great-Aunt Elizabeth wants the truth to be known," I said, picking up the picture. "I want the truth to be known. Your family murdered Clara. Your family stole the headright. You're not going to buy your way out of that. Not ever. Trudy deserves more than that. And so does the rest of my family."

"Trudy? The rest of your family? You mean all the little bastards in the picture who are connected in assorted ways to your trashy half-breed family?"

A gun blasted. Seconds later, when I glanced up from the floor where I had flung myself, Martin was clutching his chest, eyes wide, and mouth open. A dark red stain spread across the front of his thinly striped white-and-gray silk shirt. "Jamie?" He toppled to the floor.

Spencer Wells ran to his son. The gun blasted again. The old man staggered and then crumpled to the checkered linoleum. Elizabeth's locket flew from his hand and slid across the floor.

A figure in a black hooded slicker glided forward from the shadows of the pantry to pause in the doorway, a gun in one gloved hand, face covered by a ski mask.

"Do you know the muffin man, the muffin man, the muffin man? Do you know the muffin man who lives on Drury Lane?" the raspy, whispery voice recited.

My heart dropped into my stomach.

Expressionless eyes stared out of the mask's eyeholes. "*Yes*, I know the muffin man, the muffin man, the muffin man. Yes, I know the muffin man who lives on Drury Lane," the voice finished.

Every ounce of breath squeezed out of my lungs.

"It's nearly over, Jamie. After all this time."

I pulled myself into a sitting position. My fingers curled tighter around the handle of the kitchen knife. My heart pounded. "Why do you want to kill me? I don't even know you." I forced my voice to sound calm.

"Yesssss, you do!" the figure rasped. Slowly, one hand reached to roll the mask up. "Go next door again. Go see Susan," Drake Goodwin said. "Let her tell you what it was like living next door to our father, begging for scraps." He kicked Martin Wells' body.

"You were Robert Rourke's children."

"Elizabeth refused to let us be part of the family. Elizabeth used people, just like my father did. He used my poor mother and broke her heart. She wasn't good enough for Rourke; she was Osage."

"But Elizabeth was half Osage, too. She never would have intentionally been unkind—"

"She kept him from us!" Drake took a step closer. "Then she let him die in that greenhouse!" Drake's face twisted. His left hand clenched and unclenched in a raised fist.

He spat toward the two men on the kitchen floor. "Wells and his patsy father." He kicked at Martin's body. "They made sure everyone knew what Susan and me were, what my mother was."

"You and Susan wrote the poison-pen letters. You broke the window and had Bart set up the accidents. You stole the notes from Trudy. Drake, I had nothing to do with whatever you think Elizabeth did." I tried not to look at the two bleeding men lying on the kitchen floor. "Drake, let's talk about it," I pleaded as I shifted onto my knees.

"It's too late. Are you *afraid* of me? When we were kids, I wanted to be close to you, wanted you to need *me*, but you screamed for Sam. You were just like Elizabeth, never letting me near! I was never good enough."

"Drake, you're a wonderful doctor. The people in Pawhuska rely on you. I have relied on you." I tightened my grip around the knife.

"I went out there this morning. I knew you'd go back to the homestead. Elizabeth's hidey-hole in the tree, the root cellar. So close to the Mazies' home. My timing was perfect, but Rourke followed me. He wanted to protect you! He was going to tell Green."

"Drake, you'll never get away with this!"

"I've worked it all out. They'll think you shot Martin and Spencer Wells when they broke in and then killed yourself. Poor, paranoid Jamie."

I lunged into him. We crashed against the wall and down to the floor. The gun blasted and blood spurted as the knife cleaved flesh.

Chapter 41

A small group clustered around the table in the parlor as the EMTs rushed Drake Goodwin out of the house to the waiting ambulance. Two other gurneys waited on the porch to be loaded with the black body bags that lay zipped closed on the kitchen floor.

Drake Goodwin would survive. According to the EMT, the stab wound was deep but not life-threatening. Martin and Spencer Wells were both dead.

The old picture of the children by the backstop lay on the parlor table. Queenie lay curled in front of the fireplace. The rosy light of the dropping sun illuminated the room.

"Hatred burned inside him for so long. I should have seen it," Sam said. "And why did we all believe that deceitful story the Wells family spun? Why did no one think better of James O'Day?"

Toby Green peered down at the photo on the table.

I sipped the cup of warm tea Trudy had brought from the cottage. "Drake and Susan were Rourke's children by a mistress. Elizabeth knew they wrote the notes."

Green nodded. "She never even filed a complaint," he said. "Jasper eventually reported it when Elizabeth became distraught."

"You couldn't do anything?"

"You know the law. Threats are one thing; action is another."

"Daddy hid 'em in the greenhouse," Trudy piped in. "Made my Liz sick to see them. Daddy put 'em out where Rourke died."

"Did you know that Jasper was Aunt Elizabeth's son?" I asked Toby.

"Only because Jasper was my mother's half brother," he said. "Another Spencer dalliance."

Trudy smiled shyly at Toby. "Toby, my cousin, taught me how to dance." Trudy touched the face of the freckled boy in the picture. Even though many years had passed, I could see Toby in the boy's eyes and in his stance.

"Yup, that's me, Ballroom Dance King," Toby chuckled.

One by one, I pointed at the other children. "Sam. Trudy?" In the picture, Trudy held the old striped hat she still carried.

"Jasper's cap," Trudy said. "To help me be a good catcher."

"Ellen. Randy. Me. Drake?"

Green nodded at each name. "That little team was as close as he ever let any of us get."

I tapped my finger on another figure. "Bart?"

Sam and Toby nodded.

"But who's this?" I pointed to the freckled child who stood to one side, brown chin-length hair tucked behind ears, hands crammed into overall pockets.

Sam smiled and put his hands on my shoulders. "Vera, your distant cousin. Her grandmother was James O'Day's sister," he explained. "They moved here after Elizabeth married Darcey."

"Would have been nice to have known about all these relatives two weeks ago," I said.

"Is Vera going to be all right?" Trudy asked.

"Skull fracture and second-degree burns, but she's going to make a full recovery," Toby said. "Mostly thanks to Jamie's rescue efforts. No thanks to Martin Wells. I'm confident that the evidence gathered by the arson crew will link him to the fire eventually. He had the means, he had motive, and he had opportunity. Not that it matters now."

Trudy began to hum a familiar melody: "Take Me Out to the Ballgame."

Sam squeezed my shoulders. "You were a pretty good pitcher back then. Good thing Drake didn't remember that before he put you into the root cellar, or he might have thought twice about putting you down there with a cellar full of ammunition."

I reached up and covered his hands with mine. "I've always had horrible dreams about small, dark places. Now I know why."

Toby pulled the rabbit's foot out of his pocket and ran his thumb over the fur. "Glad to finally know for sure what happened to Clara O'Day."

He moved to the doorway. "I never thought you tried to kill Elizabeth, Jamie. Never figured it for Spencer, though. He was my grandfather. Everybody loved him."

"And he loved Elizabeth." I fingered the locket I'd retrieved from the kitchen floor. "I don't believe he really intended to kill her with that pillow, but he did want to keep her quiet."

"He was the one who told me how ill she was." Toby scuffed his shoe against the floor. His cell phone buzzed with a message. A smile lit up his face. "Well, I'll be. It seems Elizabeth is awake. And I've got to get going. You gonna be okay?"

After I nodded, Toby hurried across the parlor. Seconds later, the front door swung shut behind him.

"I need to go see my Liz, too." Trudy slipped an arm into the sleeve of her jacket. Then she frowned and looked toward the front window. "Now there's no one watching over me." She sighed.

I reached out to hug Trudy. She returned the hug as I tucked Elizabeth's locket into her hand. "Elizabeth's still here to watch after you."

Trudy pried the locket open with her fingernail. A young Spencer on one side faced baby Jasper on the other.

"Keep that with you, and remember I'm watching over you now, too," I said. "Whatever you need, you call, okay?"

Trudy kissed me on the cheek and then took Toby's route out of the house.

As the door closed behind her, I turned to Sam. "Did we ruin her face?" I stepped into Sam's open arms and lay my head on his shoulder.

"Trudy *was* accident prone. But her facial deformity was caused by forceps during a difficult delivery. Nancy couldn't have any more kids."

Sam wrapped his arms around me, and we swayed.

"It's over. And Elizabeth's awake," I said. We listened to the silent house. "No creaks. It's quiet."

"And you know, it feels peaceful. The tension in the air is gone," Sam said.

"Elizabeth got what she wanted. The truth is known."

"Yes." His lips nuzzled my neck.

"We should go see Elizabeth."

"Yes." He caressed my cheek with his fingertips.

"I don't want to stay here alone tonight, Sam." My pulse began to race as he held me close. "Half the town has keys to the house."

Sam smiled down into my eyes. "No. That wouldn't be wise. My dog, Ellie—er, your dog, Queenie—and I will stay to protect you."

The dog lifted her head off her paws and whined.

A Real Life Ongoing Cold Case Murder Mystery

Although the characters and the events in this book, *Cobwebs*, are fiction, the historical events recounted as the "Reign of Terror" are true. The name itself can send chills through the bones of those who remember or have been told about those frightening days in the 1920s, when members of the Osage Nation were likely to disappear or be killed, victims of unscrupulous persons seeking to profit from the newfound wealth of Osage Tribal members.

The Osage Nation had become wealthy because of their treaty with the United States government in 1872. In that treaty, they were granted as a tribe joint ownership of all the mineral rights to the land beneath their reservation—what is currently Osage County, Oklahoma. In 1906, a tribal role was created, listing 2,229 tribal members. When the oil boom began, all the royalties from oil and gas production in Osage County belonged to the Osage Tribe as a unit. The tribal role was used to assign one headright to each Osage, and these members received their percentage of the income from the incredibly lucrative Osage County oil and gas fields.

The first full-blood Osage woman murdered during the terror was Anna Kyle Brown, found dead in 1921, shot in the head. The actual number of Osages murdered during the next few years continues to be debated, but without a doubt, the Reign of Terror continued. After a bomb destroyed a house, killing three people, including Anna's sister, the tribal council asked the federal government for help.

Washington responded with the launch of a major investigation and the creation of the Federal Bureau of Investigation (FBI). Using agents and informants, the search for the perpetrators began. Wealthy Osages lived in fear as one by one, Anna's relatives and heirs, died. But theirs was not the only family affected.

As the FBI investigation continued, more Osages died. In all, before they caught and tried the perpetrator, over two dozen people were murdered. However, people who lived during this time claim hundreds of others also died; their deaths were never investigated and instead were listed as accidents. Autopsies were never performed. The missing were often never found.

—Mary Coley

From the Author

Writing has provided an outlet for my busy imagination ever since I learned to write in the second grade. Although I have always worked professionally in jobs requiring extensive writing ability, it is writing fiction that makes my muse dance.

While working as a historic park planner and naturalist for the Oklahoma Tourism and Recreation Department, the pairing of history and mystery solidified in my writing. Then, as a special feature writer for the Ponca City News in the late 80s my love of little known places and ordinary people expanded.

Everyone has a story, every place has a life of its own. The writer's job is to ferret out that story and that life and make it real for the reader.

—*Mary Coley*

About the Author

Mary Coley splits her life between Tulsa, Oklahoma and north central New Mexico. A certified interpretive guide, naturalist and environmental educator as well as a writer, Mary blogs frequently about nature at http://blog.marymcintyrecoley.com. She is a recognized professional both in the environmental education field and as an author. Her book, *Environmentalism: How You Can Make a Difference*, published through Capstone Press, received a first place award for Best Juvenile Book from the Oklahoma Writers Federation, Inc. A frequent winner in annual OWFI contests, Coley has also published two volumes of short stories, including several stories previously published in anthologies.

CPSIA information can be obtained
at www.ICGtesting.com
Printed in the USA
LVHW04s1010121018
593226LV00001B/378/P